Praise for the novels of Kristin Rockaway

"Smart, fun, fast-paced. Rockaway seamlessly blends the trials of modern dating with the challenges of being a woman in a male-dominated workplace."

—Helen Hoang on *How to Hack a Heartbreak*

"For everyone who has been wronged in the world of online dating! Revenge is a dish best served digitally in Kristin Rockaway's book capturing what it's like to pursue ambition and love in New York City. Snappy pacing, a delightful group of best friends, women innovating in tech and a workplace love interest made this a book I really enjoyed."

—Sally Thorne on *How to Hack a Heartbreak*

"Rockaway has masterfully painted the current dating landscape so many are navigating these days."

—Renée Carlino on *How to Hack a Heartbreak*

"Will have readers laughing and celebrating... Perfect for fans of Doree Shafrir's *Startup* and Hannah Orenstein's *Playing with Matches*."

—*Booklist* on *How to Hack a Heartbreak*

"A fun, sexy debut perfect for readers who love exotic settings and a great love story."

—Karma Brown, bestselling author, on
The Wild Woman's Guide to Traveling the World

"Brilliantly navigates one woman's quest to let go of what is practical to pursue her passion and surrender to her inner dreamer."

—Kerry Lonsdale, bestselling author, on
The Wild Woman's Guide to Traveling the World

"Can a novel be smart *and* loads of fun? Kristin Rockaway's debut is proof that it's possible."

—Camille Pagán, bestselling author, on
The Wild Woman's Guide to Traveling the World

Also by Kristin Rockaway

How to Hack a Heartbreak
The Wild Woman's Guide to Traveling the World

SHE'S
FAKING IT

KRISTIN
ROCKAWAY

GRAYDON
HOUSE

**GRAYDON
HOUSE®**

Recycling programs
for this product may
not exist in your area.

ISBN-13: 978-1-525-80456-4

She's Faking It

This edition published by arrangement with Harlequin Books S.A.

Graydon House
22 Adelaide St. West, 40th Floor
Toronto, Ontario M5H 4E3, Canada
www.GraydonHouseBooks.com
www.BookClubbish.com

Printed in U.S.A.

For my big sister, Christine

SHE'S
FAKING IT

CHAPTER 1

As I pressed my fingertip to the doorbell, I realized I'd made a huge mistake.

I forgot the chipotle ranch dressing.

I know it doesn't seem like a big deal, but you had to understand the customers in this neighborhood. They were ruthless. When they ordered ten pieces of gourmet, organic, locally sourced fried chicken, they expected the artisanal dipping sauce to be included with their delivery. If not, they wouldn't hesitate to give you a one-star rating. No excuses.

Though I did have a pretty valid excuse that night, because things were crazy hectic at The Chicken Coop. Between the short-tempered waitstaff and the long lines at the walk-up window, I could barely get Osvaldo's attention when I went to pick up the order. I must've stood at the service entrance for at least five minutes, waving maniacally, before he finally thrust the bag of chicken in my hand, then raced back to the kitchen without so much as a hello.

The frenzy was contagious. So, instead of stopping at the condiment counter like I should have, I skipped past it and hurried to my car, eager to drop off this delivery as quickly as possible so I could come back and pick up another one. I figured if I was lucky and I hustled, I could make a decent amount of money this evening on fried chicken orders alone.

If only I'd remembered the chipotle ranch dressing.

The front door creaked open and a woman appeared at the threshold, wearing a T-shirt that read No Excuses, which wasn't particularly promising. According to the GrubGetters driver app, her name was Andrea T. She looked exactly like someone I'd expect to live in a suburb like this: slender, stylish, stunning even in mesh panel leggings and a messy bun. Perfect from head to toe. Just like my sister.

"Hello." She smiled at me, and for a split second, I thought maybe it was all gonna be okay. Maybe Andrea T. would have mercy on me. After all, from her point of view, I was just a ditzy delivery girl driving a dilapidated rust bucket around town, trying to scrape together some semblance of an income. Meanwhile, she was living the high life in this sprawling Mc-Mansion with two shiny SUVs in the driveway. Surely, she'd give me a five-star rating simply out of pity.

"Hi." I held the chicken bag aloft and forced a smile. "Andrea?"

She nodded and took it out of my hands. "Thanks."

"No problem."

This was my cue to skedaddle, but a pang of uncertainty glued me in place. Should I tell her I forgot the dressing? She was gonna find out sooner or later, and fessing up now could save me from a one-star rating. It would show I was a woman who was ready to own up to my mistakes. A ditzy delivery girl with integrity.

"Is there something else you need?" Andrea's friendly smile was fading fast.

"It's just…" I stammered, knowing it was irrational to worry over something so inconsequential. It was a two-ounce container of ranch dressing, for crying out loud. Andrea probably had a Costco-sized tub of it in her fridge.

What really worried me, though, was that this was so unlike me. I never, ever made mistakes on my orders. And even though I knew there was no prestige in being a GrubGetter, I still took pride in my work. Showing up on time, double-checking orders, maintaining a positive attitude even when suburbanites were chewing me out on their doorsteps. This attention to detail was why I had a perfect five-star average rating. It was what made me a Top Grubber with first dibs on the best shifts in the busiest areas of San Diego.

So it wasn't just a forgotten condiment. It was a blemish on my otherwise flawless delivery record. And since driving for GrubGetter was the only thing I'd ever not failed at, my flawless delivery record meant a lot to me.

"Everything okay?" A man's voice boomed from inside the house. It sounded vaguely familiar, probably because he was a repeat customer. I didn't remember ever coming to this address before, but that didn't mean anything. All the homes in these subdivisions looked the same.

When he popped his head around the doorframe, though, I understood exactly why his voice was so familiar. I'd heard it twice a week for twelve weeks, droning on in a cavernous lecture hall for two hours at a time. I hadn't heard it since I was twenty-one, and I had hoped I'd never hear it again.

The voice belonged to Eddie Trammel, my old physics professor. The guy who'd inspired me to drop out of college.

He looked a little different, slightly older, with a new paunch and some hints of gray around the temples. But he had the same scowl, always glaring like my very existence annoyed him. To see him standing on the threshold of this starter castle with a silk floral wreath hanging on the door was jarring, in more ways than one. I'd always pictured him living alone in some sad, windowless apartment, eating cold beans directly from a can. Not living it up in Encinitas with a hot, yoga-toned wife.

"Hi," I said, because what else was there to say? The last time we'd seen each other, he'd told me I didn't have what it took to succeed in the premed program, and that I'd never get into medical school. He'd called me coddled and entitled and *acutely mediocre*. I'd left his office in tears, then marched off campus and never returned.

At the time, I told myself I just needed to take a semester off to regroup and refocus, to give myself some space so I could find my true passion and pick a new major. I'd planned to return to school in a matter of months, ready to finish my degree with purpose and vigor.

Of course, that never happened. Instead, I holed up in bed and played about two hundred hours of *Trivia Crack* in the hopes of winning big, and when that didn't pan out, I signed up to be a GrubGetter.

It wasn't supposed to be a full-time, long-term gig. But here I was, four years later, still delivering fried chicken for a living. College had now become this distant, fuzzy memory.

Something I'd tried to conquer and failed to finish. I didn't really like to think about it very often. Or at all.

In the moment, however, I couldn't simply brush aside those unwelcome thoughts and pretend the whole thing didn't happen. Because Professor Trammel was right there in front of me, probably wondering how I ended up on his doorstep wearing a stained GrubGetters polo shirt.

Without thinking, I blurted out, "I'm sorry." Not that I owed him an apology—if anything, he owed me one—but the way he was looking at me right now made me feel guilty for merely taking up space.

The line between his brows deepened and he barked, "Is there something you need? I'm starving and this food is getting cold."

"Uh…" I stammered, searching his face. And then I realized he had no idea who I was.

Which made sense, really. He'd probably taught hundreds, if not thousands, of students. In his eyes, I was just another aimless, untalented undergrad. Nobody special. Nobody worth remembering.

A half-dozen sprinkler heads suddenly spurted to life, spraying water all over the lawn and dripping down onto the pavement by my feet. Droplets hit my face like spittle and I was suddenly desperate to flee the suburbs.

"I'm sorry," I repeated. "I forgot your chipotle ranch dressing."

Eddie's scowl remained, but Andrea sighed, as if relieved I wasn't going to try to recruit them into some obscure religion or solicit funds for a questionable charity.

"Don't worry about it," she said. "We never use that stuff, anyway."

"That's not the point," Eddie mumbled, then gave me one last glare before closing the door in my face.

Well, then.

This evening had quickly turned into a parade of my failures, from my unfinished degree to my inability to remember a damn condiment. Moments like these made me wish I had a personal development coach, or a spiritual guru. Someone—anyone—who could just tell me how to live my life.

Of course, coaches and gurus were luxuries I couldn't afford. Not on my meager GrubGetter income, and certainly not if I kept standing here, blinking back tears on Professor Trammel's doorstep. So I took a deep, shaky breath and headed back down the puddle-strewn walkway toward my car. Which looked so out of place on this pristine cul-de-sac.

For over a decade, I'd been driving a little Honda Civic. It was painted an awful shade of teal, except for the passenger-side door, which was black, for some reason. The clear coat was peeling and there was a spiderweb crack in the windshield that had been there ever since my senior year of high school, when I'd bought it off some shady dude on Craigslist with money I'd saved up by tutoring neighborhood kids. It was far from glamorous, but it ran just fine, and it's not like I was in a position to be picky.

Despite my spotty maintenance record, this car had served me well. But as I slipped into the driver's seat, a sudden thought filled me with shame. *Maybe if I'd stuck it out in college, I'd be driving something better by now.*

Whatever. No sense dwelling on the woulda, coulda, shoulda. Natasha always said, *Don't look back, because that's not where you're going.* Or something. She was always spouting off these aphorisms, I couldn't keep them straight. They were annoying. And, usually, annoyingly accurate.

I pulled up the GrubGetter app and tapped the "Available for Pickup" button to find my next assignment. You might think delivering food is a rather brainless endeavor, but believe it or not, there's a strategy involved. Like hanging out in busy areas with lots of restaurants nearby, working peak mealtimes, and choosing the most expensive restaurants to increase the likelihood of bigger tips. That's why I loved working The Chicken Coop. Those forty-dollar ten pieces of fried chicken often yielded nice profits at the end of my shift.

Fortunately, there was a fried chicken order awaiting delivery. Before I could claim it, though, my phone buzzed in my hand and the screen flashed with an incoming call from Natasha. My sister was the only person in my contacts list—possibly, the only person in the entire world—who still made unsolicited phone calls. She probably wanted to talk about her latest professional organizing project, which would undoubtedly lead into some passive-aggressive remark about the cluttered state of my own apartment.

No thanks.

With one swipe, I declined the call. If it was really important, she'd text me, like normal people did.

By the time I returned to the GrubGetter screen, my coveted Chicken Coop job had been claimed by another driver. Dammit. Competition was fierce in this neighborhood during dinnertime. I settled for a delivery from the less desirable Burger Bar, because a job was a job, and the more time I spent parked in Professor Trammel's driveway, the less money I had in my pocket.

After tapping the "Claim" button, I slid my key into the ignition and turned, expecting to hear the satisfying and slightly humiliating rumble of my ancient engine. But there was only a hollow click, followed by a sad staccato whine. And then, nothing.

No.

I cranked it again. Still no juice.

No, no, no, no, no.

Panic swelled beneath my ribs. This could not be happening. Driving for GrubGetter was my only source of income; obviously, I needed a functioning car to get the job done. I turned the key again and again, pumping the gas, then the brake, as if that would make any difference.

It didn't, of course. My car was dead.

The worst part was, I knew this was coming. The check engine light blinked on two weeks ago and never went off. I should've driven it to the mechanic immediately for an inspection, but that would've required cash, which was in eternal short supply. So, I told myself it probably wasn't *that* serious and proceeded to ignore those two angry yellow words screaming at me from the dashboard.

Now I was stuck blocking Professor Trammel's driveway, with the seconds ticking down on a Burger Bar pickup that I was going to have to cancel. I had never canceled a pickup before. My immaculate GrubGetter record was being tarnished in all sorts of new and horrible ways today.

As I considered the ramifications of abandoning my car on this cul-de-sac, my phone buzzed with another call from Natasha. Two calls in five minutes was unheard of, even for her. Maybe there was an actual emergency.

With a racing heart, I answered. "Hey, everything okay?"

"Can you babysit Izzy next Friday?"

"Oh." I exhaled, partly relieved, partly annoyed. "Maybe, I'm not sure."

"Well, I need to know now. If you can't, I have to book a sitter. The last one just canceled on me."

Normally, I'd have jumped at the chance to hang out with my six-year-old niece, but then I glanced down at the keys dangling uselessly from my ignition. "I don't know. You'd have to come pick me up or something. My car just died." My voice caught on the last word, but I swallowed the sob.

Natasha clucked her tongue. "You never started that car maintenance log, did you?"

I clenched my teeth to keep from screaming.

"What's wrong with it?" she asked.

"I have no idea. It literally just died right this second. I'm stalled out in the driveway of some house..." I trailed off, not wanting her to know where I was.

"Have you called AAA?"

As if I could spare the funds for a AAA membership. "I don't have it."

Another cluck of the tongue, followed by a sigh. To Natasha, my whole life was exasperating. "You can use mine."

This was the thing about my sister: even though she often made me feel like the biggest screwup on the planet, she never left me out in the cold.

"Thanks."

"No problem. I'll call for you right now. Where are you?"

"Um..." I looked around the cul-de-sac. A man across the street was rolling a large gray trash can out of his garage. As he plopped it in the gutter with a loud thunk, he paused and narrowed his eyes in my direction. People in this neighborhood didn't appreciate stragglers, especially those in beat-up cars. I quickly looked away. "I can just call myself."

"No, you can't. It's my account, I need to authorize the pickup. You said you're parked in someone's driveway. What's the address?"

I thought about aborting the mission at this point, telling her the car miraculously started all of a sudden. But this guy was still glaring at me from behind his trash can, and I couldn't just linger here forever. There was no other choice than to tell her where I was.

"I'm outside 1846 Blue Bonnet Court."

There was silence on the line. I held my breath, hoping against hope that she wouldn't recognize the street name. But that was me being willfully naive.

"In Encinitas?"

My silence was all the answer she needed.

"You're, like, three blocks away from my house. Why didn't you just say that?"

"I didn't wanna bother you," I said, which was a partial truth. Mostly, I just didn't want her to see me in this state. Or hear the myriad "I told you sos" that were inevitably coming my way.

"Have you eaten dinner?"

"Not yet." My stomach reflexively rumbled. "I've been working since three."

"I've got some leftovers I can bring you. Let me call the tow truck and I'll be right there."

She hung up. I felt a wave of relief, which was swallowed quickly by a larger wave of regret. Natasha had always warned me to have a plan B. To have an alternate stream of income lined up, in case I ever decided to stop being a GrubGetter. I'd dismissed her because up until recently, being a GrubGetter was working out just fine. Plus, it wasn't like I had a burning desire to do anything else, and more to the point, I was too terrified to try anything new. New endeavors introduced the possibility of failure, which I'd already experienced enough of in this lifetime, thank you very much.

But now, the decision had been made for me. I couldn't deliver food if my car wouldn't start. Which reminded me, I had to turn down that Burger Bar order I'd claimed.

I pulled up the GrubGetter app and tapped the "Cancel" button. The screen flashed with a message.

Are you sure? Canceling orders this close to pickup time can result in low GrubGetter performance ratings.

Reluctantly, I tapped "Yes," then tossed my phone into the open hot bag on the passenger seat. Closing my eyes, I tried my hardest not to cry. It didn't work, though, and within seconds, I was full-force sobbing into the steering wheel. Given the facts, it was impossible to hold back the tears.

My rent was due in three days, I was light-years late on my student loans, I had no clue how I was going to pay for whatever repairs my car would need, and my sister was about to save my ass, yet again.

This wasn't how I'd envisioned myself living at age twenty-five. It was way past time for me to get my shit together.

I just wished I knew where to start.

CHAPTER 2

A sharp *rat-tat-tat* on the driver's side window cut in on my crying jag. Natasha stood on the pavement holding a Tupperware container full of something green and cheesy-looking. I swiped the tears from my swollen eyes and opened the door.

"Thanks for coming," I said.

"Don't be silly, I wasn't about to leave you out here all alone. The tow truck should be here in thirty." She jiggled the container in her hands. "I brought something for you to eat while we wait."

Natasha surveyed the interior of my car with an air of disgust. Frankly, I couldn't blame her. While she was a special kind of snob when it came to keeping spaces tidy, I was also a special kind of slob. The floors were littered with burrito wrappers and empty Big Gulp containers. Random papers and forgotten pieces of junk mail crowded the back seat, along with a ripped hoodie and a solitary flip-flop. There were coins and crumbs and errant M&M'S wedged in the center console, and I'm pretty sure I hadn't dusted the dashboard in the nearly ten years I'd owned this thing. Thankfully, Natasha couldn't see the state of my trunk.

"Let's sit in my car," she said, rather diplomatically.

We settled into the buttery leather seats of her Audi Q8, with its gleaming oak dashboard and immaculate floor mats. She tapped one of the three touch screens beside the steering wheel and the panoramic sunroof retracted above our heads.

"Such a gorgeous night." Natasha breathed deeply. "You can almost smell the ocean from here."

All I could smell was her sweet, waxy air freshener and the remnants of fried chicken grease. Even though I never came into direct contact with food, the scent always seeped out through the delivery bags and clung to my clothes. No matter how many times I'd thrown this shirt in the wash, it inevitably came out smelling like a strange combination of French fries and teriyaki sauce. Between the horrible stink and the faded ketchup stains, my GrubGetter polo was beat. I'd been thinking about ordering a new one, but it didn't make any sense to do that now. Seeing as I was temporarily out of a job and everything.

Although, since I couldn't afford to fix my broken car, it was entirely possible that I'd be permanently out of a job.

The thought set me off crying again, which made Natasha sigh. "You've got to get it together, Bree."

"Thanks," I said, my voice thick with tears. "That's such helpful advice, it really makes me feel better."

"Stop. You know I'm only saying this because I love you."

My sister was a firm believer in "tough love." It's not that she didn't sympathize. She just thought there were far more productive ways to handle your problems than wallowing in tears and despair. She was right, of course, but I wasn't in the mood for a lecture right now.

"I've told you before," she continued, "you need to have a plan B."

"Yes, I know, I'm a massive failure. Why don't you go talk to Eddie Trammel about all the ways I've screwed up my life?"

"You're not a failure and you haven't screwed up your life." She pulled a tissue from her purse and thrust it toward me. "You aren't making the best choices, but you can change that. And who's Eddie Trammel?"

"My old physics professor." I snatched the tissue from her hand and nodded to the house beside us. "I just delivered his chicken. He didn't recognize me."

"Hmm." Natasha studied his front lawn, the sprinklers still blaring, the bright green blades of grass completely saturated. "That guy was a jerk to you, wasn't he?"

"Yeah."

To be fair, he was a jerk to everyone. He was one of those academics who was hyperfocused on his research and resentful that he had to teach an undergraduate class, especially one as rudimentary as Physics 1A. I'm not sure if he'd ever insulted anyone quite so thoroughly as he'd insulted me, though.

I blew my nose with a resounding honk as Natasha snapped a photo of his lawn. "What are you doing?"

"It's before sundown," she said. "These sprinklers shouldn't be on right now. This city has very explicit regulations about water usage." She pulled a thick planner from her purse and jotted down a note in the margins of her weekly layout. "My friend Lara is on the Municipal Code Enforcement Board. I'm gonna shoot her an email tomorrow and get this guy ticketed."

"Is that really necessary?"

Natasha stopped writing and met my eyes. This wasn't about improper water usage; this was about getting revenge on someone who'd wronged her little sister.

"Yes. It's really necessary." She slapped her planner closed and tucked it in her bag, then passed me the container of food along with a fork. "Here, eat. It's still warm."

I popped the top and the smell of sulfur and hot feet hit my face. "What is this?"

"Spinach-cauliflower casserole." She shrugged one shoulder apologetically. "It's keto."

"Since when are you doing keto?" Natasha was slender and athletic, an Orangetheory fanatic who did yoga on a stand-up paddleboard to "relax." She liked to eat "clean," whatever that meant, and every so often, she'd try whatever new fad diet was making headlines on the mommy blog circuit. "You know you don't need to lose weight, right?"

"It's not for weight loss. I read that ketosis can spark higher energy levels and improve your mental focus. It's only been a few days, but I'm definitely noticing an upward trend in my mood tracker. Oh! That reminds me." She pulled a small Moleskine labeled FOOD DIARY out of her purse, which was apparently a bottomless pit of storage. "I didn't log my dinner yet."

"How many notebooks do you have in that thing?"

"Just four." She ticked them off on her fingers. "My daily planner, my gratitude journal, my client log, and this."

"Oh. That's all."

Natasha was too busy scribbling in her food diary to pick up on my sarcasm, so I dug my fork into the casserole and took a big, gloppy bite. It tasted exactly as odd as it smelled, but I was hungry, and Natasha was saving my ass, so I swallowed without chewing and lied through my teeth. "It's great!"

"It's gross, but I appreciate the attempt to make me feel better."

I pushed the casserole around the container, searching in vain for something delicious, as if a mound of Tater Tots would magically appear amidst the vegetable slurry. "Is all keto food like this?"

"No, there's some really good stuff. Lots of meat, mostly. This was a new recipe I pinned the other day. Don't think I'll be making it again, though." She wrote "PINTEREST FAIL" in her food diary and returned it to her bag.

"Don't these books make your purse really heavy? There's gotta be some app where you can store all this information."

"Studies show you're more likely to remember things you've written by hand, with physical pen and paper." She reached across my lap and opened the glove compartment, removing a notebook with an antiqued photograph of a vintage luxury car printed on the cover. "For example, this is my auto maintenance log. Maybe if you'd kept one of these, like I told you to, we wouldn't be in this predicament right now."

I loved Natasha, I really did. She was responsible and generous, and without her I'd likely be far worse off than I already was, which was a horrifying thought to consider. But at times like this, I wanted to grab her by the shoulders and shake the shit out of her.

"A maintenance log wouldn't have helped me."

"Yes, it would have. Organization is about more than decluttering your home. It's about decluttering your mind. Making lists, keeping records—these are all ways to help you get your life in order. If you'd had a maintenance log, this problem wouldn't have caught you off guard in the middle of your delivery shift. You'd have seen it coming, and—"

"I saw it coming."

"What?"

"This didn't catch me off guard. The check engine light came on two weeks ago." *Or maybe it was three.*

"Then why didn't you take it to the mechanic?" She blinked, genuinely confused. Everything was so cut-and-dried with her. When a car needed to be serviced, of course you called the mechanic.

That is, if you could afford to pay the repair bill.

Fortunately, she put two and two together without making me say it out loud. "Oh," she murmured, then bit her lip. I could almost hear the squeak and clank of wheels turning in her head as she tried to piece together the solution to this problem. No doubt it included me setting up a journal or logbook of some sort, though we both knew that would be pointless. The last time she'd tried to set me up with a weekly budget planner, I gave up on day two, when I realized I could Grub-Getter around the clock for the rest of my life and still never make enough money to get current on the payments for my student loans. You know, for that degree I'd never finished.

But Natasha was a determined problem solver. It said so in her business bio: "Natasha DeAngelis, Certified Professional Organizer®, is a determined problem solver with a passion for sorting, purging, arranging, and containerizing." My life was a perpetual mess, and though she couldn't seem to be able to clean it up, that didn't stop her from trying. Over and over and over again.

"I'll pay for the repairs," she said.

"No." I shook my head, fending off the very big part of me that wanted to say yes. "I can't take any money from you."

"It's fine," she said. "Business is booming. I've got so much work right now that I've actually had to turn clients away. And ever since Al introduced that new accelerated orthodontic treatment, his office has been raking it in. We can afford to help you."

"I know." Obviously, my sister and her family weren't hurting for cash. Aside from her wildly successful organizing business, her husband, Al, ran his own orthodontics practice. They owned a four-bedroom house, leased luxury cars, and took triannual vacations to warm, sunny places like Maui and Tulum. They had a smart fridge in their kitchen that was undoubtedly worth more than my nonfunctioning car.

But my sister wasn't a safety net, and I needed to stop treating her like one. She'd already done so much for me. More than any big sister should ever have to do.

"I just can't," I said.

"Well, do you really have any other choice?" There was an edge to Natasha's voice now. "If you don't have a car, how are you going to work?"

"I'll figure something out." The words didn't sound very convincing, even to my own ears. For the past four years, all I'd done was deliver food. I had no other marketable skills, no references, no degree.

I was a massive failure.

Tears pooled in my eyes. Natasha sighed again.

"Look," she said, "maybe it's time to admit you need to come up with a solid plan for your life. You've been in a downward spiral ever since Rob left."

She had a point. I'd never been particularly stable, but things got a whole lot worse seven months earlier, when my live-in ex-boyfriend, Rob, had abruptly announced he was ending our three-year relationship, quitting his job, and embarking on an immersive ayahuasca retreat in the depths of the Peruvian Amazon.

"I've lost my way," he'd said, his eyes bloodshot from too many hits on his vape pen. "The Divine Mother Shakti at the Temple of Eternal Light can help me find myself again."

"What?" I'd been incredulous. "Where is this coming from?"

He'd unearthed a book from beneath a pile of dirty clothes on our bed and handed it to me—*Psychedelic Healers: An Exploratory Journey of the Soul*, by Shakti Rebecca Rubinstein.

"What is this?"

"It's the book that changed my life," he'd said. "I'm ready for deep growth. New energy."

Then he'd moved his belongings to a storage unit off the side of the I-8, and left me to pay the full cost of our monthly rent and utilities on my paltry GrubGetter income.

I told myself this situation was only temporary, that Rob would return as soon as he realized that hallucinating in the rainforest wasn't going to lead him to some higher consciousness. But I hadn't heard from him since he took off on that direct flight from LAX to Lima. At this point, it was probably safe to assume he was never coming back.

Which was probably for the best. It's not exactly like Rob was Prince Charming or anything. But being with him was better than being alone. At least I'd had someone to split the bills with.

"Honestly," she continued, "I can't stand to see you so miserable anymore. Happiness is a choice, Bree. Choose happy."

Of all Natasha's pithy sayings, "Choose happy" was the one I hated most. It was printed on the back of her business cards in faux brush lettering, silently accusing each potential client of being complicit in their own misery. If they paid her to clean out their closets, though, they could apparently experience unparalleled joy.

"That's bullshit, and you know it."

She scowled. "It is not."

"It is, actually. Shitty things happen all the time and we have no choice in the matter. I didn't choose to be too broke to fix my car. I work really hard, but this job doesn't pay well. And I didn't choose for Rob to abandon me to go find himself in the Amazon, either. He made that choice for us."

I almost mentioned the shittiest thing that had ever happened to Natasha or to me, a thing neither of us had chosen. But I stopped myself before the words rolled off my lips. This evening was bad enough without rehashing the details of our mother's death.

"Sometimes things happen to us that are beyond our control," Natasha said, her voice infuriatingly calm. "But we *can* control how we react to it. Focus on what you can control. And it does no good to dwell on the past, either. Don't look back, Bree—"

"Because that's not where you're going. Yes, I know. You've said that before." *About a thousand times.*

She took a deep breath, most likely to prepare for a lengthy lecture on why it's important to stay positive and productive in the face of adversity, but then a large tow truck lumbered onto the cul-de-sac and she got out of the car to flag him down.

Grateful for the interruption, I ditched the casserole on her dashboard and walked over to where the driver had double-parked alongside my car.

"What's the problem?" he asked, hopping down from the cab.

"It won't start," I said, to which Natasha quickly followed up with, "The check engine light came on several weeks ago, but the car has not been serviced yet."

He grunted and popped the hood, one thick filthy hand stroking his braided beard as he surveyed the engine. Another grunt, then he asked for the keys and tried to start it, only to hear the same sad click and whine as before.

"It's not the battery." He leaned his head out of the open door. "When was the last time you changed your timing belt?"

"Uh... I don't know."

Natasha shook her head and mouthed, *Maintenance log!* in my direction but I pretended not to see.

The driver got out and slammed the hood shut. "Well, this thing is hosed."

"Hosed?" My heart thrummed in my chest. "What does that mean? It can't be fixed?"

He shrugged, clearly indifferent to my crisis-in-progress. "Can't say for sure. Your mechanic can take a closer look and let you know. Where do you want me to tow it?"

I pulled out my phone to look up the address of the mechanic near my apartment down in Pacific Beach. But Natasha answered before I could google it up. "Just take it to Encinitas Auto Repair," she said. "It's on Second and F."

"You got it," he said, then retreated to his truck to fiddle with some chains.

Natasha avoided my gaze. Instead, she focused on calling a

guy named Jerry, who presumably worked at this repair shop, and told him to expect "a really old Civic that's in rough shape," making sure to specify, "It's not mine, it's my sister's."

I knew she was going to pay for the repairs. It made me feel icky, taking yet another handout from my big sister. But ultimately, she was right. What other choice did I have?

The two of us stayed quiet while the driver finished hooking up my car. After he'd towed it away down the cul-de-sac and out of sight, Natasha turned to me. "Do you want to come over? Izzy's got piano lessons in fifteen minutes, you can hear how good she is now."

Even though I did miss my niece, there was nothing I wanted to do more than go home, tear off these smelly clothes, and cry in solitude. "I'll take a rain check. Thanks again for coming to get me."

"Of course." She started poking at her phone screen. A moment later, she said, "Your Lyft will be here in four minutes. His name is Neil. He drives a black Sentra." A quick kiss on my cheek and she was hustling back to her SUV.

As I watched Natasha drive away, I wished—not for the first time—that I could be more like her: competent, organized, confident enough in my choices to believe I could choose to be happy. Sometimes I felt like she had twenty years on me, instead of only six. So maybe instead of complaining, I should've started taking her advice.

CHAPTER 3

Thanks to rush hour traffic, it took almost forty-five minutes to get down to my neighborhood, Pacific Beach, where Neil deposited me at the curb in front of an adorable blue bungalow on Beryl Street. A white picket fence surrounded a small but tidy front garden blooming with ferns and pygmy palms. The front door was stained mahogany, and there were mustard-colored shutters on each of the two wide windows flanking the entrance. It was so beautiful, it deserved to be featured on one of those Instagram accounts highlighting charming cottages and exterior design.

I didn't live there.

I lived next door, behind a boxy triplex, in a makeshift studio apartment on top of a garage. Technically, I didn't have my own apartment number, which made me think the whole situation was illegal. But it was insanely cheap, and I wasn't exactly in the financial position to go looking for another apartment, anyway. So, I didn't ask too many questions or make too many demands. I just quietly accepted the fact that I couldn't plug my hairdryer and toaster in at the same time without risking an electrical fire.

Pacific Beach—or PB, as the locals called it—was this peculiar mix of picture-perfect houses and unsanctioned hovels. Natasha said the whole town was a shit show, but I liked the vibrancy and variety. Families lived next door to college kids, beach cruisers parked beside baby strollers, lawns were littered with surfboards and beer pong tables, and half the neighbors were only temporary since every other home was a vacation rental.

Like this adorable blue bungalow, for example. Once I'd caught on to the fact that a new car was parked in the driveway each week, I stalked the listing on Airbnb, where it was touted as a "Stylish Retreat, Short Walk to the Beach!" From the photos, the inside was just as cute as the outside, all exposed beams and distressed floors and big fluffy couches that were perfect for napping in after a long day of lazing under the sun. The host was a company called Surf Vacationz LLC and the weekly fee was more than I made in a month.

It was my dream home, and it was completely out of my reach.

Sometimes, when I was feeling particularly low, I liked to stand on the sidewalk in front of the house, my fingers grazing the top of the picket fence, and pretend it was mine. I'd envision myself sitting on the stoop, sipping an herbaceous cocktail out of a mason jar, or wandering aimlessly through the garden and sniffing the flowers. The thought always brought a smile to my face. Even if it was delusional.

After the misery of this afternoon, I desperately needed a pick-me-up. So once the Lyft drove away, I took my usual spot by the picket fence and indulged in a little curbside home-owning fantasy. This time, I closed my eyes and imagined what it would be like to prepare a meal in that immaculate kitchen. Maybe brunch. In real life, I was a terrible cook, but since this was a fantasy, I whipped up my favorite breakfast— perfectly golden coconut-crusted French toast—then sat down at that rustic wood dining nook next to the window and—

"Excuse me?"

Just like that, my daydream was over. When I opened my eyes, though, I saw something even more delectable than that imaginary brunch: a shirtless surfer dude, standing by my side. Droplets of seawater fell from his thick, dark hair, trickling down his chest and pooling in his wet suit, which he'd stripped to the waist. He carried his board effortlessly under one arm, like it weighed nothing.

"Hi." I'd never seen this guy around before. If I had, I definitely would've remembered.

"Hi." He looked confused now. "I didn't order any food."

"What?"

"Aren't you…" His eyes flicked down to my chest, where the GrubGetter logo sat right above my heart.

"Oh, right. No."

"No?"

"No." Humiliating. This was the hottest guy I'd interacted with since Rob left town and I was wearing the filthiest item of clothing in my closet, on one of my worst days in recent memory. Rather than explain that I was off duty, since technically I didn't know if I'd ever be on duty again, I changed the subject and nodded toward the bungalow. "Are you staying here?"

"Yeah."

"I've seen the pictures on Airbnb, it looks really nice inside."

He studied the front door, as if seeing it for the first time. "It's not bad. I mostly just like it for the location."

Pacific Beach was the perfect spot for a surf getaway, and this house was a three-block stroll to the ocean. But if all he was interested in was easy access to the waves, I wondered why he wasn't staying in one of those cheap hostels right on the sand. Maybe he was splitting the rental with some friends. Or a girlfriend.

"Well, you picked a great neighborhood to visit," I said, launching into the usual spiel I gave to tourists who caught me ogling this house. "If you're looking for good Mexican food, you should try Oscar's on Turquoise Street. They make the best fish tacos. PB Shore Club is a fun place to grab a drink and watch the sunset. And at night, there are tons of bars and clubs and stuff on Garnet Street. It can get a little crazy there, though."

The corner of his mouth lifted ever so slightly. "That's not really my scene."

"Me neither. I've lived in PB for four years and I've only been to Garnet, like, three times." It was always a bad time, too. Once, at two in the morning, I puked in a planter in the parking lot of a Jack in the Box. That was the first and last time I'd ever had a Jägerbomb.

"Four years, huh?" He ran a hand over his glistening hair and shook the excess water on the sidewalk at his feet. "That's about when I bought this place."

"What do you mean?"

Tilting his chin toward the bungalow, he said, "I took it down off Airbnb last week."

"Oh." *This* was Surf Vacationz LLC? He didn't look much older than me.

"Where do you live?"

"Next door."

He looked over my shoulder. "In the triplex?"

"Uh...yeah." No need to get into nitty-gritty details at the moment. Instead, I held out my hand. "I'm Bree."

"Trey."

He shook my hand with a firm, respectful grip. It was the handshake of a man who ran an Airbnb business, a gesture that said, *Pleased to meet your acquaintance.* But his eyes said something else. Something a little more mischievous. They were deep set and dancing, and the way they searched my face made me squirm in a not-uncomfortable way.

I really wished I wasn't wearing my stained, smelly Grub-Getter shirt.

Trey released my hand, but kept his eyes on me. "I should probably go dry off now."

"Of course."

But he wasn't making a move to walk away. He rubbed the back of his neck, looking somewhat uncomfortable.

"Is something wrong?" I asked.

He smiled and let out a bubble of nervous laughter.

"Um..." He cleared his throat. "This is kinda awkward."

Nothing seemed awkward to me. What was going on? It almost felt like...

Was he about to ask me out?

Wow. I hadn't been on a proper date in I-didn't-know-how-long. Years. It's not like Rob and I ever went out together. His idea of a rollicking good time was smoking weed on the couch and housing a family-sized bag of Flaming Hot Cheetos before passing out in the middle of an *Adventure Time* marathon. Trey looked far more energetic. And from the cut of his abs, he probably didn't eat a whole lot of Cheetos, either.

"Yes?" I said, trying my best to play it cool.

He glanced down at my hands resting on the gate of the picket fence. "You're kinda blocking my way."

Humiliating.

Heat crept up my neck, spreading across my scalp to the tips of my earlobes. I sidestepped away from the path to the front door. "Sorry."

"No worries." There was that mischievous look again. As he unlatched the gate, he said, "I'll see you around, Bree."

My name sounded good on his lips.

But I was clearly out of my mind to think he might be interested in me, the wacky, unemployed delivery-girl-next-door. With his bronzed body and surfer physique, no doubt he dated Instagram models. This town was crawling with them, taking photos in bikinis as they frolicked on the beach. They tagged themselves drinking in the bars on Garnet or watching the waves at Crystal Pier.

To save myself from further embarrassment, I quickly headed home. Crossing the dying grass in front of the triplex, I stole one quick glance over my shoulder to see Trey, standing in his garden, watching me walk away. He raised his hand to give a little wave. Adorable.

Just as I was about to return the gesture, though, my foot caught on a surf leash someone had carelessly discarded on the lawn. I stumbled forward, arms flailing, and somehow managed to right myself without face-planting onto the desiccated lawn.

Trey yelled out, "You okay?"

"Fine!" I called, too mortified to make eye contact. Instead,

I kept walking with my eyes fixed firmly on the path in front of me, lest I trip over another piece of PB detritus.

After ducking through the narrow alleyway alongside the building where all the legal tenants lived, I crossed the communal courtyard and climbed the flight of rickety wooden steps that led me to my home above the garage. As I pulled my keys from the front pocket of my jeans, my back pocket buzzed. Natasha was calling. She probably saw that my Lyft ride was over and wanted to make sure...what, exactly? That I hadn't been murdered en route? I sent her to voice mail and texted: **I'm fine. Just got home.**

Stop declining my calls, she replied.

Natasha knew I hated talking on the phone, but that didn't stop her from complaining every time I refused to answer. That was typical Natasha, though. Total control freak. One hundred percent type A.

In other words, the exact opposite of me.

Case in point: my apartment, which was a professional organizer's worst nightmare. Every time Natasha stepped foot inside my cluttered little studio, she'd shudder, occasionally throwing in a dramatic dry heave for good measure. She could scoff all she wanted, but according to several psychological studies, disorganization was a sign of genius. Besides, I'd gotten used to the mess by this point. It didn't bother me.

Well, it didn't bother me *that* much.

To be honest, the clutter wore on me sometimes. It was a constant reminder of things I should've been doing or should have already done. Like the towering stack of unpaid student loan bills on my coffee table, or the sad-looking aloe plant withering away on the windowsill, or the brand-new yoga mat jammed in the corner, still in its dust-covered original packaging.

I would never have admitted this to Natasha, though. The one time I had, she'd shown up unannounced on my doorstep bright and early on a Sunday morning, armed with a Swiffer and a box of heavy-duty garbage bags. An impromptu decluttering session, she'd said. It ended fifteen minutes later in an epic, teary fight and we didn't speak to each other for a week.

Now, as I walked through my front door and surveyed the mess, I wished there was a simple way to clean it all up. One that required little to no effort, and definitely no intervention from Natasha. Like a magic spell.

But magic spells were merely a fantasy, much like the idea of living in that cute blue bungalow or hooking up with the hot surfer who owned it. In the real world, I lived in this squalid dump, for which I was two hundred dollars short on the rent that was due in three days. And right now, I needed to find a way to earn some fast cash.

Tossing aside last night's pajamas, I flopped down on my unmade bed, pulled out my phone and googled "how to make money quick in San Diego." There was no shortage of options for last-minute one-off jobs: face painting, sign spinning, housekeeping (though, honestly, was I really qualified to keep anyone's house?). Problem was, these jobs were located all around the county, far from PB and inaccessible by public transportation. Without a car, I'd have to Lyft, which would pretty much cancel out my profits.

So I changed my Google search to "how to make money quick from home" and scrolled through the seemingly endless series of listicles in the search results. The possibilities were interesting. I could charge those dockless electric scooters that were scattered all over the sidewalks or get paid to take online surveys. Apparently, I could self-publish an ebook and make thousands of dollars in passive income, but that would take an upfront investment of time, which I was currently short on. Selling stuff on eBay was a good idea, but unfortunately, I didn't have much that anyone would want to buy. Except for maybe that six-foot bong Rob had left behind. I'd shoved it in the back of my closet, but I bet I could've pulled at least fifty bucks for it. Maybe sixty.

Lots of ideas, but not many that would get me to two hundred dollars in three days. Unless I wanted to become a webcam girl. Those ladies were well paid.

Emotionally exhausted from all that dead-end googling, I decided to take a break from the job hunt and engage in a quick, mindless scroll through Instagram. I never posted any photos of my own—it's not like I ever did anything worth Instagramming—but there was nothing more deliciously distracting from the difficulties of real life than an endless stream of beautifully filtered photographs.

While I followed a few friends, I mostly paid attention to strangers and faceless brands: random celebrities, luxury cosmetics companies, artsy Etsy shops, animal shelters that shared daily pics of their fluffiest adoptable cats. I followed influencers, travelgrammers, fashion bloggers, lifestyle models, and hashtags like #goals, #glamour, and #instastyle. There was something deeply satisfying about looking at all those pretty pictures of pretty people, perfectly posed in pretty places.

It was also much easier to lose myself in the aspirational imagery of someone else's flawless feed than it was to plan out a life of my own.

I swiped up slowly, studying each snapshot. A woman in a bikini doing yoga in a field of flowers. A close-up of an expertly executed smoky eye. A plate of food. A city skyline. A disembodied pair of legs artfully positioned beside a romance novel and a steaming cup of tea.

Then, gold words stamped on a plain pink background: *No Excuses.*

Instantly, I thought of Andrea T. and her T-shirt, Professor Trammel and his total lack of recognition when he saw my face. The worst parts of my day came flooding back to me at the sight of these two little words.

The image belonged to an account by the name of @demidipalma. It was a sponsored post, probably targeting me because of my most recent, desperate Google search, because the caption was eerily relevant.

Have you been struggling to make ends meet? Do you need to make a change in your life, but don't know where to start? Are you convinced everyone else has it all figured out except for you?

Well, I've got news for you, sweetie: if you're broke, lost, and miserable, THAT'S ON YOU.

You are not a victim of circumstance. The power to succeed is in your hands. And you are UTTERLY and ENTIRELY in control of the trajectory of your life. All you have to do is STOP MAKING EXCUSES for your failures.

It's time to start #SLAYING your days, #DOMINATING your desires, and #MANIFESTING your dreams into a reality.

Demi DiPalma can help you #EVOLVE.

#noexcuses

#aspirationalactionplan

Intrigued, I tapped **Learn More** and was directed to Demi DiPalma's website. The home page featured a photo of her smiling beatifically, her smooth, pale skin practically glowing.

From her appearance, you'd have thought she lived a completely stress-free, blissed-out life, but she was clearly an extremely busy woman—and kind of a big deal. Not only was she a "lifestyle guru" and bestselling author, but she had her own YouTube channel called *Aspire Higher*. According to her "Praise" page, she'd been described by the *Huffington Post* as "Goop meets *The Secret*, for the Instagram generation," and had been a featured guest on Oprah's podcast, *SuperSoul Conversations*.

She also offered a whole slew of products and services listed under her "Shop" link: online courses, immersive retreats, books and planners, and one-on-one coaching sessions. She even had her own apparel line, including Andrea T.'s No Excuses T-shirt, and a rose gold bar necklace that said Choose Happy.

So that's where my sister got that saying from.

Look, I wasn't completely cynical. There was a big part of me that wanted to believe happiness was a choice. But a bigger, more rational part of me knew bad feelings weren't optional. Sadness, disappointment, anger—they showed up unannounced, barged their way in, and often overstayed their welcome.

Still, it was a tempting idea, wasn't it? That you could create a happy life simply by wishing it into existence.

Whatever. The only thing I needed to wish into existence right about now was an extra two hundred dollars. So I shut down Instagram and pulled up a website called SurveyAllDay. According to one listicle, I could earn up to twelve bucks an hour on this site answering simple questions about movies and politicians. If I buckled down, I figured maybe I could make enough to cover both my rent *and* the cost of my car repairs.

Unfortunately, I thought wrong.

CHAPTER 4

Fourteen dollars and sixty-three cents.

That's how much I made after five continuous hours of completing online surveys.

It certainly wasn't rocket science. All I had to do was tap and swipe through a series of straightforward questions.

Are you over eighteen? Yes.
What's your marital status? Single.
What's the highest level of education you've completed? Some college.
What's your annual salary? Prefer not to answer.

Each question was a reminder of how little I'd accomplished in my twenty-five years, but I tried not to think about that. I simply focused on my endgame of tapping and swiping for dollars. I didn't pay any attention to how much I was earning, either. All I did was tap, tap, tap, swipe. For five hours straight.

At around one in the morning, my wrist cramped up and my fingertips started to go numb, so I figured it was time to call it a night. My plan was to catch a few z's, then wake up bright and early to tap, tap, swipe all day.

Just before I turned off my phone, though, I opened my SurveyAllDay Earnings Report to see that paltry dollar amount, and suddenly realized no amount of tapping and swiping would help me pay my rent on time. To add insult to injury, I couldn't even transfer that fourteen dollars and sixty-three cents to my PayPal account for a full seven days. So I'd just wasted five hours of my life. Which, I supposed, was par for the course, but it didn't make it any less infuriating.

I closed my eyes, resolving that tomorrow I'd find something of value to sell on eBay. Or better yet on Craigslist, since in-person sales would get me cash in hand right away. In the meantime, I'd start brainstorming ideas for a lucrative ebook. Maybe an inverse self-help guide on how not to live your life titled, *From Dropout to Delivery Girl: A Cautionary Tale.*

With my mind racing, I fired up a nature sounds app to help drown out the chatter in my brain. Scrolling right past the Exotic Rainforest track (too reminiscent of Rob), I settled on the Stream of Serenity and pressed Play. I closed my eyes, willing myself to envision a tranquil woodland, with soft beams of sunlight shining through the branches of lush, green trees and tiny, adorable creatures scampering underfoot. It took some effort, but eventually, I replaced my frantic thoughts with soothing fantasies and fell asleep to the gentle burble of water gliding over smooth stones.

Eight hours later, I awoke to the grinding screech of rusty

gears echoing through the floor. This was nothing to be concerned about; it was merely the garage door opening beneath my apartment. One of the legal tenants stored their car in there, so I was acutely aware of their comings and goings. Some grease on the hinges of the door would probably make it a lot less noisy, but again, I didn't like to complain.

I was glad to be up, anyway. I needed time to concoct a fund-raising plan.

But first, coffee.

With bleary eyes, I rolled out of bed and crossed the room to my kitchenette, which was sparse, but serviceable. There was a small sink, a microwave, a minifridge, and a narrow countertop on which I'd placed a toaster and a single-cup coffee maker. From the cabinet above my head, I grabbed a canister of Folgers, but when I popped off the top, I discovered it was tragically empty. I'd meant to pick some up on my way home from work last night. Obviously, that plan got derailed.

The grocery store was a twenty-minute walk from home, but I needed caffeine immediately, if not sooner. Fortunately, my BFF Mari was the head barista at The Bean House, a cozy little coffee shop just two blocks away. They served all sorts of costly, frothy espresso drinks, but their drip coffee was reasonably priced, and Mari usually hooked me up with a free cup, anyway. So I threw on my least dirty pair of joggers and an oversize T-shirt, then grabbed a protein bar from the cabinet for a quick breakfast to go.

Outside, the weather was predictably pleasant. San Diego came through with its usual balmy breezes, rustling the palm trees against the clear blue sky. I took a deep breath, letting the salt air fill my lungs. Dumpy apartment notwithstanding,

I was extraordinarily lucky to live here, a stone's throw from the ocean, in a city where the sun always shined.

I hustled past the blue bungalow, relieved Trey was nowhere in sight, then turned left onto Cass Street, where a homeless man was digging through a trash can on the corner. With the ever-growing homeless population in PB, this was a pretty common sight. Normally, I'd avert my eyes and keep walking, but when he unearthed a half-eaten, rancid burrito and thoughtfully sniffed it, as if contemplating his breakfast, I found it hard to turn away.

"Excuse me." I approached him cautiously, the unopened protein bar in my outstretched hand. "If you're hungry, you can have this."

There was a glint of suspicion in his watery eyes. I shifted my weight onto my back foot, just in case things took a turn for the worse. Fortunately, he dropped the burrito and grabbed the protein bar, grunting something that sounded vaguely like "Thanks," before trudging away.

Well, that put some stuff in perspective. I may have been jobless, carless, and in danger of imminent eviction, but at least I didn't have to go digging through the trash for my breakfast. Though now that I'd given my own breakfast away, coffee would have to sustain me this morning. Thankfully, I was lucky enough to have a friend who'd provide it for free.

The Bean House was located two blocks south, in a bright yellow, 1920s-era cottage. Considered a PB institution, it had been run by the same owner for almost twenty years. Mari had worked there for ten of them, and I'd been hanging out on the patio during her shifts ever since.

I'd met Mari in seventh grade, when she and her family moved into our apartment complex on the side of the freeway. My mom, Natasha, and I were in unit 209; Mari and her mother were down the hall in 202. I distinctly remember the first time I saw her, hauling a massive milk crate full of books up the stairs. When I offered to help, she accepted with a grateful smile. We quickly bonded over our shared love of *The Hunger Games* (way better than the *Twilight* series) and the tweenage frustrations of being raised by strict single moms.

Twelve years later, we were still inseparable. We both still lived in PB, too—though I was alone in my tiny apartment, while she split a bigger, nicer space with two roommates on the other side of town.

The Bean House wasn't very busy right now, but that was to be expected. According to Mari, their weekday morning rush hours were between five o'clock, before the surfers hit the waves for dawn patrol, and eight o'clock, after all the commuters hit the highway for a long day at work. I was neither a surfer nor a commuter, so I often took advantage of the subsequent lull to say hi.

When I walked in, I spotted Mari at the register, tending to a customer with an extremely specific request for his latte.

"Half-caf, nonfat, two-shot, extra hot, with absolutely no foam."

There was murder in her big brown eyes. When she caught sight of me in the doorway, though, her face lit up. She called over to a guy standing at the condiment bar, stuffing napkins into a dispenser. "Hey, Logan, can you take care of this gentleman's order, please? I'm going on break."

Logan complied, and as the man repeated his lengthy instructions, Mari filled two cups with dark roast, then stepped out from behind the counter. "Let's sit outside," she said.

We settled down at a bistro table on the back patio, right

beside the rose-filled garden and beneath the shade of a crape myrtle tree.

"What's going on?" I asked, then took a luxurious sip of the hot brown life elixir.

She shrugged. "Nothing new. Things have been kind of slow around here, which is good because it gives me extra time to write."

Although Mari worked at The Bean House to pay the bills, her true passion was comedy. Her ultimate goal was to be a Hollywood screenwriter; she had a whole drawer full of original rom-com scripts she'd been pitching to agents with no luck. In the meantime, she'd set herself up with a moderately successful YouTube channel, *Marisol Vega Hates Everything*, in which she complained about the world in a way that was both hilarious and endearing. In my opinion, she should've been famous by now, but it was hard to gain traction in the overcrowded web series world.

"How are you doing?" she asked.

"Fine." I swallowed hard. "But my car broke down."

"Oh, no."

"Oh, yeah. Right in the middle of a shift. And you'll never guess who I was delivering to. Remember that physics professor I had? The one who accused me of grade grubbing?"

"Of course I remember. What a dick."

I'd spent hours crying on this patio after that happened, Mari consoling me with a bottomless cup of joe.

But the truth is, I *had* been grade grubbing, just a little. My GPA had been on a downward slide for the past two semesters, and I was desperate to bring it back up. Five extra points on my physics final would've brought me from a D+ to a C- in that class, saving me from academic probation. With grades like that, Professor Trammel was right that I didn't have what it took to succeed in the premed program.

Honestly, I wasn't sure I wanted to pursue a career in medicine, anyway. At that point, I'd switched majors five times in three years. Six months before I dropped out, I'd been sure my calling in life was urban planning. The semester before that, it was philosophy. No accredited med school would've admitted me.

So Trammel was probably also right about me being mediocre.

I wouldn't have considered myself coddled, though. Mostly, I was just confused.

When I'd dropped out of school, Mari had told me I was making the right decision. That college was a scam fueled by the "education industrial complex" and I was lucky to escape before I'd accrued any more debt.

Natasha, on the other hand, had told me I'd live to regret it. And as I sat here, sipping my coffee, recounting the tale of how I delivered fried chicken to my old physics professor before my car died in his driveway, I had to admit my sister was right.

"Where's your car now?" Mari asked.

"At some mechanic in Encinitas. I don't know if they'll be able to fix it, though."

"Geez, I'm sorry." She fidgeted with her earring, a look of genuine concern clouding her face. "What're you gonna do now?"

"Well, I'm gonna try to find some stuff to sell on Craigslist."

Her fidgeting stopped abruptly. "What, as, like, your job?"

"No." Though I hadn't exactly ruled it out. "I just have to score enough cash to pay my rent on Sunday. I'm short two hundred bucks. Rob left his bong in my closet, I'm thinking of selling that off."

"Forget the bong," she said. "You should go swipe some shit from his storage unit."

Rob did have some good stuff in there. Video game systems, barely used surfboards, collectible sports memorabilia, a camera drone. All courtesy of his parents, who gave their son a monthly "stipend" to subsidize the income he made from his part-time job as a marijuana dispensary clerk.

Now, *that* was a guy who'd been coddled. What a waste of three years of my life.

Still, it would be wrong to steal from him. "I can't do that."

"Why not? He owes you!" Mari's brown eyes got wide and fiery, the tiny stud in her nose shimmering as her nostrils flared. "If he hadn't ditched out and stuck you with all the bills, you wouldn't even be in this situation."

She had a valid point. But getting revenge didn't seem cathartic. On the contrary, it felt like I'd be tethering myself to Rob through spite and resentment, when at this point, I should be cutting myself free.

A thought popped into my head, unbidden and kind of annoying. *Don't look back, because that's not where you're going.*

"The past is in the past," I said, channeling Natasha and her aphorisms. "I need to focus on moving forward. Right now, that means coming up with rent money. But my eventual goal is to figure out some other career path. Something I can pursue in the long term."

"That's great." Mari's voice was stilted, like she was trying not to sound surprised, though it was obvious in the way her eyebrows shot up. She never pushed the issue like Natasha did, but every so often she'd ask if I'd ever given thought to pursuing a more meaningful line of work, something I had a passion for. Usually, I'd respond with a shrug, and that would be the end of the conversation. "Have you come up with any ideas?"

"Not yet, no." I sipped my coffee and thought back to last night's Google search. "I heard you can make a lot of money by writing an ebook."

She blinked. "An ebook about what?"

"I hadn't thought that far ahead yet."

"Okay." The word came out slowly, and I knew what she was thinking, because I was thinking it, too. *You've lost your mind, Bree Bozeman.*

"Yo, Marisol!"

A guy was standing on the threshold to the patio, decked out in typical surfer bro attire: board shorts, tank top, bare feet. He waved to Mari and held up a stack of flyers. "Can I put one of these in the window?"

"Sure, Cam. You can hang it with the others, right next to the front door." She turned to me and said, "He's the new sign spinner for SurfRack."

SurfRack was another PB institution, the oldest family-run surf shop in all of San Diego. It was located right on the boardwalk, just a few feet from the ocean. They mostly catered to tourists, offering surf lessons and rentals out of their unpretentious wooden shack, but they also held surf camps and birthday parties for kids. I'd attended one of those birthday parties when I was in fifth grade, and nearly drowned while trying to paddle out. It was my first—and last—encounter with a surfboard, and I hadn't dipped more than a toe in the Pacific since then. While I loved living by the beach, I much preferred the stillness of the sand to the tumult of the sea.

Cam nodded thanks and retreated into the store, leaving

Mari to pick up where she'd left off. "So, where exactly did you hear about this ebook idea?"

"Some website," I said, wishing I'd never mentioned it in the first place. "I know it's not realistic. I was just brainstorming."

"Well, maybe start by finding what you're passionate about."

Everyone always talked about finding your passion as if it was this evasive creature you had to smoke out of a burrow. They also seemed to operate under the assumption that everyone had a passion to find. But I had long since accepted the sad reality that I was born passionless.

"Nothing," I said.

"Come on, that's bullshit. First of all, I know how much you love to read. That most definitely counts as a passion."

I shrugged and sipped, not wanting to admit out loud how long it had been since I'd finished reading a book.

"And you're a really hard worker," she said. "In high school, you were a rock star. You used to get As in every subject."

"Yeah, well, that changed when I got to college, didn't it? I couldn't get an A to save my life."

"That's because college is a scam." She tapped her chin. "Let's try something else. Complete the following sentence. 'My life is thriving when...'"

"When I have money to pay the rent."

"That's not thriving. That's surviving."

"Isn't surviving enough?"

Mari took a deep breath. "I don't think it is. Not for me, at least. I survive by pouring coffee, but it doesn't feed my soul. That's what comedy is for. It's what makes me thrive."

A loud voice emerged from inside the shop. "I said, *six* pumps of syrup! Not five!"

We glanced through the window and spotted an angry woman standing at the pickup counter, yelling at a terrified Logan.

"Goddammit," Mari muttered. "I'll be happy when I don't need this job anymore."

"At least it gives you good material for your videos," I said.

"Yeah, but a decade behind the espresso machine is a long time. And the clientele just seems to get ruder and more entitled with every passing year." She stood up and straightened her apron. "I've gotta go squash this situation. Text and let me know what happens with your car, okay?"

I nodded and gave her a quick hug before she ran off to save Logan from the lady with the undersweetened latte.

Despite my enduring cynicism, the idea of thriving really did appeal to me. It sounded lovely to be able to craft a life that was purposeful and fulfilling, to leave an imprint on the world. To strive for something greater than the ability to barely coast by.

Unfortunately, I had no idea what that something was.

I polished off my coffee and stepped down off the patio, taking the long way around through the rose garden to the exit. As I passed by the front window, I caught a glimpse of the SurfRack flyer Cam had just posted. White text on a blue background advertised a new instructor giving lessons by appointment only. Apparently, he was a big-name surfer who'd just come off a pro championship tour.

There was a photo of him on the bottom, standing onshore in his wet suit, which he'd stripped to the waist. His board was tucked under one arm, his dark hair glistened with seawater. According to the poster, his name was Trey Cantu. The same Trey who lived in the blue bungalow next door.

Great. I'd humiliated myself in front of a famous surfer.

No point in dwelling on it, though. *Don't look back yada yada.* Instead, I walked home with purpose, mentally crafting some descriptive text for the first Craigslist ad I was going to place. "Six-foot bong, gently used. Resin included at no extra charge!"

My phone began to buzz in my pocket. From the continuous drone, it was clearly an incoming call. Which meant it could only be one person.

"Hi, Natasha," I said.

"Hi." She sounded tightly wound, like a slingshot pulled taut and ready to launch. "What are you doing today?"

The question felt like a personal attack. "Figuring out how to make rent money by Sunday. Why?"

"Well, I have an appointment in Bird Rock this afternoon and I was wondering if I could drop by your place beforehand."

Strange. Natasha hadn't been to my apartment since that failed attempt to help me reorganize, and that was months ago. She also never "dropped by" without a Swiffer in her hand.

"You're not planning another guerrilla decluttering session, are you?" I asked. "Because I'm really not in the headspace for it right now."

"No, it's not that. I...just have something I want to give you."

"Promise me this has nothing to do with cleaning my apartment."

"Promise. I'll be by around noon, okay?"

"Okay. By the way, when do you think you might hear back about my car?"

Natasha paused, as if contemplating her response. Then,

in one hasty breath, she said, "Listen, I've gotta shower and get my stuff together before I head out, I'll see you in a few, love you."

"Love you, too," I said, but she'd already hung up.

So that's what this was about.

Natasha didn't come out and say it, but she didn't have to. I knew the truth, deep in my bones: my car was hosed, and it was never coming back.

CHAPTER 5

Normally, I would've tried to straighten up a little before Natasha came over. Despite her promise, I knew she wouldn't be able to stop herself from making helpful "suggestions" about how to get my apartment in order, and it was in a particularly horrific state right now. Jamming some of these dirty clothes into the closet and cleaning off my coffee table would've made me appear slightly less slovenly.

But at the moment, I had bigger fish to fry. Like coming up with two hundred dollars in the next forty-eight hours and finding a new job that didn't require a car.

I have no car.

I have no job.

I can't pay my rent.

As the reality of my situation sank in, I fought the desire

to curl up on my futon in a sniveling, shivering ball. There was no time for that.

After posting the bong for sale on Craigslist, I applied for accounts at half a dozen websites that catered to gig economy workers like myself. Opportunities within walking distance were seemingly limitless. I could do odd jobs with Handy-Minion or walk dogs with BarkBuddy. The odds of me getting approved and hired in time to make rent on Sunday were slim, but in the meantime, maybe I could search the neighborhood for some of those electric scooters in need of a charge.

I was reviewing a list of paid medical research studies seeking participants when I heard the distinct sound of footsteps climbing the stairs leading to my apartment. It was 11:59. Natasha was one minute early.

As soon as I opened the door, she thrust a Tupperware container into my hands. "I brought you lunch. Enchiladas. Don't worry, they're not keto."

"Thanks," I said, trying not to notice her eyes bulging at the sight of my mess. To her credit, she didn't comment. She just stepped inside and flashed an uncomfortable smile.

"How are you?" she asked, but I was eager to cut to the chase.

"My car can't be fixed, can it?"

She winced. "I'm sorry. I wanted to tell you in person, but I should've known you'd have figured it out."

A queasy feeling socked me right in the gut, and for a moment I was sure I would puke. But the nausea quickly passed, replaced by a burning sensation deep in the pit of my stomach. Like I was having an internal core meltdown.

As I collapsed on the futon with my head in my hands, Natasha said helpfully, "It will be fine."

"Natasha, I have no car. Which means I have no job." My voice was craggy and I sounded slightly unhinged.

"Well, there's a silver lining in all this." She sat down beside me and plucked a white envelope from her purse. "A thin one, but still."

With shaky fingers, I tore open the flap and pulled out the contents: a single check, made out to me, in the amount of $467. It was signed by Jerry, the owner and proprietor of Encinitas Auto Repair.

"I don't understand. What is this?"

Natasha breathed deeply, held it for a second, then said, too brightly, "It's the scrap value of your car."

"Oh."

At least I no longer had to worry about coming up with two hundred dollars by Sunday. This check from the mechanic covered my rent and then some.

It did make me a little sad to think about my car getting torn apart at a junkyard, though. Sure, it was hideous and long past its prime, but we'd been through some good times together, and now my trusty Honda Civic was nothing more than a shredded pile of rusty metal. The image made me whimper.

"It'll be fine," Natasha repeated, more firmly this time, because whenever I threatened to fall to pieces, she was the glue determined to hold me together. "I have a book I want you to read. I think it'll help you a lot."

There was a time in my life when I believed a book might have solved all my problems. Sadly, that time had long passed. "A book."

"Yes, a book. And don't say it like that." She scowled.

"Unless this book has four wheels and gets forty-two high-way miles to the gallon, it's not gonna help me."

"I'm serious. It changed my life and I think it could change yours, too."

This was all too reminiscent of the conversation I had with Rob on this very futon seven months ago, in which he told me all about the Divine Mother Shakti and the book that changed his life.

"You're not gonna suggest I run off to an ayahuasca lodge in the Amazon, are you?"

"I'm not your loser ex-boyfriend, Bree." Her tone was sharp. "I'm your big sister, and I'm trying to give you some important advice. It would be nice if you listened to me for once."

Ouch.

"Sorry," I said. "Go on."

"For a long time, I felt very unsatisfied with the way my life was going. Yes, I had Al and Izzy—and I love them more than anything, don't get me wrong—but taking care of a home and a family…it wasn't enough for me. I felt lost. Stagnant. Some-times, it was a struggle just to get out of bed in the morning."

No way. Natasha was so focused, so put-together, so ex-traordinarily satisfied with the direction of her life. It was nearly impossible to imagine her struggling to get out of bed, especially since I knew she liked to arrive early for her 5 a.m. Orangetheory classes.

I must've looked skeptical, because she said, "I hid it well. I didn't want you worrying about me. You had enough on your plate. Anyway, one day, I was googling around for in-spirational advice, and I happened across a YouTube channel called, *Aspire Higher*. Have you ever heard of Demi DiPalma?"

A bell chimed in my brain. "I saw her on Instagram last night, actually. She's a lifestyle guru, right?"

"A lifestyle guru, a wellness vlogger, a bestselling author. An all-around genius. Her advice is so spot-on and the way she shares her experiences and emotions is so raw and electrifying. I binge-watched her entire collection of videos in a weekend, and then I bought this."

She pulled a slender book out of her purse, a glossy white hardcover with the title embossed in shimmery gold block letters: *The Aspirational Action Plan*, by Demi DiPalma.

I took it in my hands and flipped through the pages. "What's it about?"

"It's a self-help guide that teaches you how to dig deep to discover your most authentic self and then manifest your dreams into existence. I know it sounds crazy, but it works. Her 'fake it till you make it' philosophy was the catalyst for getting my business off the ground."

"Really?"

"Really. I never considered becoming a professional organizer until I went through Demi's four-step manifesting process. Once I defined my aspiration and created my vision board, I suddenly discovered I had this passion for organizing. And when I decided to monetize that, I didn't even have to advertise, people started contacting *me* to streamline their homes. Then, one thing led to another, and now I have a really successful small business. The advice in this book is like a magic spell."

"A magic spell?"

If these words had been coming from anyone else, I'd be nodding politely while internally rolling my eyes at how preposterous the whole thing sounded. But this was Natasha speaking. She was the most pulled-together and down-to-earth person I knew. My big sister, my rock, my role model. Whatever she said had to be true.

"I'm telling you, Bree, reading this book lit a fire under me that I thought had been completely extinguished a long time ago. Back when...you know."

I nodded, a silent acknowledgment that I knew what she meant even if she couldn't actually say it.

Natasha didn't like to talk about our mom's death. She always referred to it as "that time" or "you know" or "when it all went down." I couldn't blame her for not wanting to discuss it at length; it was a painful experience fraught with trauma and grief. But she avoided the topic so thoroughly, sometimes it felt like she preferred to pretend Mom had never existed at all.

I never called her out on it, though, because when it came to the whole experience of "that time," between the two of us, Natasha had drawn the shorter straw. I'd only been fourteen. Too young to lose my mom, sure, but for the most part, after she died, most aspects of my life remained unchanged. I still lived in the same apartment, I still went to the same high school, I still had the same friends and the same general goals of doing my homework and getting good grades. Natasha, on the other hand, watched her whole world get blown to bits.

Technically, it was all my fault because I needed a guardian, and Natasha was my only option. Last we'd heard of our dad, he was off in Vegas doing god-knows-what with god-knows-who, and we had no grandparents to speak of. So during the very start of her sophomore year at UCLA, my extremely bright and ambitious big sister dropped out of school, moved back to our apartment in Pacific Beach, and started waiting tables to pay the rent.

To say I felt guilty was an understatement. It was self-imposed, though. Natasha never laid a guilt trip on me, not once. She simply cared for me, with all her heart and all her strength, picking up where Mom had left off. If it hadn't been for her, I never would've graduated high school, never would've been accepted to UCSD. She'd sacrificed her chance at a college degree so I could have one.

Then I'd squandered it.

Initially, I figured she'd reenroll after I turned eighteen. But then she met Al, and her life took a sharp turn in a completely different direction. One that I thought made her happy, but apparently there was some deep dissatisfaction simmering beneath the surface.

Or there had been, before she discovered Demi DiPalma.

"I love you, Bree." She squeezed my arm and fixed me with her big-sister stare. One of care and concern, tinged with exasperation. I took in her perfectly blended foundation, her neatly manicured fingernails, her crisp, white button-down shirt. She always presented herself so impeccably.

"I love you, too."

"Then listen to me. Take my advice and read this book. And then take control of your life."

I turned the book over in my hands. The back cover featured a photo of Demi DiPalma, decked out in a gauzy white robe, looking as ethereal as ever. Hadn't I just been wishing for a spiritual guru to point me in the right direction? Maybe *The Aspirational Action Plan* was exactly what I needed to help me find my passion and start to thrive.

"I'll start reading it right away," I said.

"Great." She looked relieved, like she'd been afraid I was going to put up a fight. Then she let out a big breath and said,

"I'd better get going. My appointment's at one, I don't want to be late." As she stood up, her eyes scanned the room. "While I'm here, though, I could take a quick look around, maybe offer some suggestions about how you could make better use of this space."

See? She couldn't help herself.

"No, thanks. This has been a pleasant visit, and I'd like to keep it that way."

"Fair enough. Will you walk me to my car, though? I've got something else for you."

That something else was a big heavy box filled with the contents of my now-scrapped Civic. Mercifully, it looked like the mechanic had discarded all the empty Big Gulp containers and burrito wrappers, but there was still a bunch of random stuff in there. The hoodie, the flip-flop, some long-forgotten paperwork. It was too much to process at the moment, so I dropped it in the middle of my floor and told myself I'd deal with it later.

Besides, right now, I had other priorities. Like wolfing down these enchiladas and digging into *The Aspirational Action Plan*.

THE ASPIRATIONAL ACTION PLAN
INTRODUCTION
Get Ready to Evolve

Psst.

Hey, you.

Yeah, I'm talking to you. The woman reading this book.

I see you, sweetie.

I see right straight into your heart. There's hurt there, and disappointment. Hidden longing and dormant ambition. Echoes of your past struggles and shadows of your unmanifested dreams.

I see how desperately you want to make a change, and how utterly impossible you think it is to do so.

I know you want to be better. I know you *can* be better.

Because—and here's where I'll let you in on a little secret—I used to be you.

I used to be the woman who wanted greatness, but never achieved it. I watched everyone around me move onward and upward, yet I stayed still as a stone. I allowed my past to weigh me down and my negative thoughts to hold me back. I made excuses for my multitudinous failures.

Then one morning, I woke up, drew back the curtains, let great golden beams of sunshine stream into my bedroom, and declared, NO MORE.

I would stop making excuses.

I would move forward.

I would achieve greatness.

In that moment, I resolved to manifest my aspirations into being.

And it worked.

Now I'm ready to share the secrets of my success with you. Contained within these pages is a system for recalibrating your entire existence. You'll learn all about my four-step manifesting process, including:

1. DEFINING YOUR ASPIRATION

Use creative visualization to meander through your subconscious mind and decide what you want your new life to look like.

2. SENDING YOUR DESIRES OUT INTO THE UNIVERSE

Construct a tangible representation of your aspiration with a vision board and cement it with positive affirmations.

3. CLEARING AWAY NEGATIVE ENERGY

Explore rituals such as sage burning and fire ceremonies to banish destructive thought patterns and cleanse your physical spaces.

4. RECEIVING YOUR ABUNDANCE

Open your heart, mind, and spirit to the wonders that are coming your way.

The Aspirational Action Plan will help you put your past in the past and guide you toward an extraordinary future that's brimming with possibility and abundance. By reading this book, you're choosing to walk the path toward happy.

But first, a warning: you've got to want this more than anything you've ever wanted in your life. You've got to believe this will be yours. And you've got to know you deserve this, deep down in your soft, spongy marrow. Because energy follows thought. And if you tell the universe, "Hey, I want this, and I know it will be mine!" then it'll obey.

You may be thinking, *This is too hard, Demi, my dreams are too big for this one small woman.* But the truth is, sweetie, no dream is too big for you. And if you're having trouble believing it, then fake it.

Fake it until you make it your reality.

Your life doesn't manifest out of nothingness. It is born of thought, energy, desire, craving. Tune your emotions and attentions to the frequency of success, and the universe will dial right in. The universe will listen and the universe will deliver.

In other words, pretend you already have what you want, and eventually it will be yours.

So...are you ready?

Then buckle up, sweetie. It's going to be a wild ride.

You're about to #EVOLVE.

CHAPTER 6

There was a funny sort of swirling in my brain. Thoughts came at me fast, spinning in circles and generating sparks. A jolt shot down my spine and out toward my fingers and toes, making my entire body vibrate with a rare and welcome feeling: validation.

Call me crazy, but it kind of felt like Demi DiPalma was speaking directly to me. Like she really could see right straight into my heart. All those struggles she'd described sounded achingly familiar. Especially the feeling that everyone else was moving forward, while I was standing still, mired in the quicksand of past failures, old boyfriends, dead and deadbeat parents.

It was a short book, more of a glorified pamphlet, so I devoured it in under an hour. True, there were certain parts that made me raise an eyebrow, like the chart detailing the essential oil and crystal combinations that would assuredly help me "manifest abundance," whatever that meant. Perhaps I would have been less skeptical had she not included a discount code for ordering the sets, dubbed "Prosperity Packages," on demi-dipalma.com.

For the most part, though, I was into her whole spiel. The focused ritual of creating a vision board, the confidence-boosting power of positive affirmations, the cathartic symbolism of throwing all your negative experiences and energies into a fire and watching them burn. It sounded inspiring. Though I wasn't exactly sure how it was going to change my life.

Because I kept getting tripped up on the first step: defining my aspiration. That was the crux of my whole problem, right? I had no idea what would lead me on the path to happy, no clue where it started or which direction to walk in to get there. No passion I was aching to pursue.

I tried using that whole "creative visualization" technique, but when I closed my eyes, all I saw was an Instagram feed scrolling through my brain. Pictures of kittens and beaches and enviable thigh gaps flew by on an infinite loop. Apparently, social media had zapped me of my ability to generate an original thought.

Then again, maybe I was—as Demi would put it— "meandering through my subconscious mind." Even though I had no interest in being an Instagram influencer, I certainly wouldn't have minded if my life *looked like* one of those perfectly curated feeds. And according to Demi, aspirations were all about what you wanted your life to *look like*, not about what you actually did.

Which somehow didn't seem right. Shouldn't an "action plan" be about taking action?

The more time I spent on this, the more ridiculous it seemed. The universe wasn't going to dial into my desires, no matter what frequency I tuned them to. That didn't even make sense! Besides, right now my only desire was to chuck this book across the room and take a leisurely scroll through Instagram.

But if I gave in to that desire, I'd be letting Natasha down. She'd asked me to follow her advice. To read this book and to take control of my life. There was no way I could ignore her, not after everything she'd done for me. And honestly, it's not like I had any other solid plan to turn my life around.

Obviously, there was no other choice. Even though I didn't believe in Demi DiPalma's four-step manifesting process, I was just going to have to fake it.

Rather than staying hung up on step one forever, I decided to push forward and get started on step two: sending my desires out into the universe. My aspiration wasn't clearly defined, but I could still put together a vision board based on the Instagram feed in my mind. The instructions were outlined in the following chapter.

Now it's time to get those visualizations out of your brain and into the atmosphere, providing a beacon toward which the universe can guide its energy.

Your vision board will be a physical representation of everything you want to manifest into your life. Include photos of anything you wish to acquire: money, cars, homes, opportunities for luxury travel. You can also incorporate words and phrases that describe your new life and affirm how worthy you are of the abundance you're about to receive.

Use vivid, clear imagery. Let there be no room for ambiguity in your quest for greatness.

And don't limit yourself, either. Remember: no dream is too big for you, sweetie.

To create a vision board, Demi suggested lighting a candle, turning on some soft music, and sitting down with a stack of old magazines to search for pictures that inspired you. For me, that wasn't very practical. I may have had a lot of garbage hanging around this apartment, but old magazines were in short supply. I could search the internet for photos, but I didn't have a printer. Or scissors or glue, for that matter.

So I decided to assemble a virtual vision board. And what better platform for an Instagram-inspired vision board than Instagram itself?

I fired up the app and looked at my long-neglected profile. My bio was empty, my photo was taken who-knows-how-many years ago, and my feed hadn't been updated since before I'd dropped out of school. There were still pictures of my old dorm room in there, for crying out loud. Talk about negative energy.

If this was going to be a representation of everything extraordinary I wanted my future to hold, I couldn't allow my mediocre past anywhere near it.

With a few quick taps, I deleted my old profile and created a brand-new one, @breebythesea. And this time I filled in the bio.

Bree
25 | San Diego, CA | 🌴 ☀
I manifest my dreams and dominate my desires.
#noexcuses #choosehappy #aspirationalactionplan

I took a quick selfie, applied the most flattering filter I could find, and uploaded it as my profile photo. Then I started searching for my dreams.

Hashtags made it easy. #instaglam led me to photos of

women posed with perfect outfits, perfect haircuts, perfect makeup. #luxurylifestyle delivered gorgeous interior design and scenic travel destinations. #goals turned up graphics with inspirational quotes like, "Remain open to possibility," and "You are stronger than your fears." I reposted them all to my feed, only using hashtags in the captions: #noexcuses and #choosehappy. No need to muddy the manifesting waters with descriptive text. Surely, photographs alone were enough to convey my message to the universe.

I even threw in a photo of an orange tabby I found on #catstagram, simply because I loved cats, and I thought it was cute. My landlord had a strict no-pets policy, but according to Demi, no dream was too big for me!

While browsing the hashtag #goodvibesonly, I paused on a photo of a woman in a bright red bikini wading into the waves on an empty beach. She turned away from the camera, so her face wasn't visible. All you could see was her long dark hair cascading down the center of her tanned, toned back. Her fingertips grazed the surface of the water as she stared out on an epic orange sunset.

No doubt the photo was aspirational content at its very finest, but I was hesitant to repost it to my feed. This dream definitely seemed too big for me. Frankly, I'd be more likely to harbor an illegal cat in my illegal apartment than to wander out into the ocean.

Ever since that horrible experience in the fifth grade, that surf lesson gone awry, I'd been too afraid to go back in. The waves were unpredictable, they could eat me alive. And with the water churning, you couldn't see very far beneath the surface. Who knew what dangerous creatures lurked in the darkness below? There could be sharks or jellyfish or swarms of pinchy crabs.

It looked so fun, though. Especially on hot summer days, when the beaches reached maximum capacity, and there were throngs of people swimming and splashing around. While everyone else cooled off in the ocean, I'd cower onshore in a full sweat, trying and failing to work up the courage to charge into the waves.

Rob had always teased me mercilessly about my fear. Whenever we went to the beach, he'd point out little children body-surfing with confidence, and my cheeks would burn with shame. It's not like I enjoyed being a scaredy-cat. There's nothing more I would've loved than to dive in without a care. I just couldn't.

I knew what Demi DiPalma would say to this line of thinking, though. She'd tell me I was allowing my past to weigh me down and my negative thoughts to hold me back. That I was making excuses for my failures. That the power to change was in my hands.

And though I wasn't sure I believed her, I was struck by the sudden urge to post the photo of the woman in the water to my virtual vision board. It looked so perfect positioned right next to the assertion that I was stronger than my fears. In fact, seeing those two images beside each other made me wonder: If I could conquer my fear of the ocean, what other hurdles in life could I clear?

Sunset was fast approaching. If I hustled, I could make it to Law Street Beach with plenty of time to catch it—and re-create this photo in real life.

As I wriggled into my bikini, I told myself there was no pressure. Maybe once I got there, I'd be too scared to get my feet wet. Or maybe I'd be brave enough to wade all the way in. Either way, I pledged to remain open to possibility.

After throwing on a maxidress, I grabbed my phone and headed out the door. The beach was four blocks west, which meant I had to pass by the blue bungalow. Inside, the lights were off, with no sign of Trey. I thought of all the times I'd stood beside that picket fence, daydreaming about what it would be like to live there. Demi DiPalma would probably call this fantasizing habit of mine "creative visualization," a way to home in on my deepest desires.

Which meant this house probably belonged on my vision board.

So I snapped a photo, uploaded it to Instagram, and continued on my way.

By the time I arrived at the beach, the sun was hanging low over the water. Crowds gathered to watch the big event; sunsets were a nightly celebration on the San Diego coastline. Lovers held hands, children ran in circles, friends toasted with a contraband bottle of wine. Dozens of phones were aimed toward the sky. I wondered how many of these photos would end up on Instagram in a matter of minutes.

I pulled my dress over my head and set it on a boulder, hiding my phone in the folds of the fabric, then walked unsteadily toward the shoreline, where I let my toes sink into the cool, wet sand. This was as far out as I usually ventured; the boundary of my comfort zone ended here.

The thinnest ripple of water washed over the tops of my feet, sending chills up the backs of my legs. Reflexively, I recoiled, hopping back toward dry land.

This was a stupid idea. Supremely, extraordinarily stupid. Although the dozens of other people playing around in the ocean at the moment would've likely disagreed with me. They were all happy and relaxed, free from irrational fear.

Meanwhile, I was terrified. Not only of the ocean, but of other things, too: failure, judgment, rejection. But if I was ever going to make any progress in this life, I would have to pretend those fears didn't exist.

In other words, I would have to fake it.

So I kept putting one foot in front of the other. They were small steps, but they brought me forward into the shallows. I continued on, passing a mom dipping her baby's toes in the water, an elderly couple holding hands as the waves lapped their ankles, some teenagers tossing a football and diving to catch it before it hit the surface.

Always looking ahead of me, never looking back. Progress was happening, right before my eyes.

The positive affirmations, the vision board, the "fake it till you make it" philosophy. I'd scoffed at them, but maybe there was value in this whole process. Because now, I was standing thigh-deep in the Pacific Ocean for the first time in years. And it was incredible.

I felt strong, capable, fearless. Like I had finally found the trailhead of the path to happy.

I was proving Rob wrong. I was making Natasha proud.

Then suddenly I was face down in the water.

After some panicked flailing, I managed to right myself. One of those teenagers had knocked me off my feet during a dive to catch the football. With an apology, he grabbed my arm to steady me. Freaked out, I wiggled away from his grip and stumbled backward, only to fall again, this time on my bottom.

This was a stupid idea. Supremely, extraordinarily stupid.

Scrambling to my feet again, I stepped to the right, down into an unseen hole. Water sloshed against my stomach and I scrambled out of the pit before the next wave rolled in, crashing against my thighs, threatening my already precarious center of balance.

Telling myself not to panic was futile—my heart was already threatening to bust through my ribs—so instead I focused on getting out of the water as quickly as possible. There was a lull in the waves now and the water rippled around my shins. Just a few big steps and I'd be back on dry land.

I took great long strides, digging my toes into the sand for traction. At one point, I stepped on a shell or a rock, something sharp that cut the bottom of my foot, but I kept on walking, eager to reach the shore. When I did, I collapsed in a heap, my hair soaked, my chest heaving.

What the hell had I been thinking? As if some aspirational Instagram photo and a dime-a-dozen aphorism would've miraculously cured me of my very real, very deep-seated fear.

Salt water dripped from my skin, and I realized I'd forgotten to bring a towel. As I wrung out my hair with my sand-covered hands, I cursed myself for being so foolish as to believe in aspirations and abundance and energy following thought. If the universe really was delivering a message, then it was telling me to stay the hell home. Which is where I wanted to go, immediately.

But as I tried to stand up, my left foot began to burn. I sat back down and inspected the cut on the bottom. It was small, like a narrow shard of glass had lodged itself in there. The pain was enormous, though, spreading outward and upward. Then, it was all I could feel or hear or see.

Pain. Deep, throbbing, excruciating pain.

My scream ripped across the beach, echoing off the dunes.

CHAPTER 7

"We need to get you to the lifeguard tower. Can you stand up?"

There was a crowd around me now. Helpful, concerned citizens were rubbing my back and holding my hand. A few teenagers hung back and gawked. I'd have been humiliated if I wasn't in agony.

"I think so." I pushed myself up, leaning forward and putting all my weight on my right foot. The movement caused my left leg to throb fiercely. Shaking from the pain, I faltered and fell sideways, but a woman wrapped her arm around my back and steadied me.

"We'll support you, okay?" A man was on my opposite side, his hand hooked under my armpit. "We're just gonna walk over there."

He pointed across the infinite expanse of sand, toward the lifeguard tower back by the entrance to the beach.

"Okay," I said, though I felt far from okay, and I was pretty sure I wasn't gonna make it. Still, I forged on, hopping over uneven mounds of sand, crying out each time my body made contact with the earth. At any moment, I expected my left foot to spontaneously combust.

My eyes were focused on the ground, making sure the path in front of me was clear. The last thing I needed was to trip on a tangle of kelp and twist my remaining good ankle. After sweating and hopping for what seemed like an eternity, I raised my eyes, only to see the lifeguard station still an impossible distance away. Unwittingly, I moaned.

"You're almost there," said the helpful, concerned woman with her arm around my back. But I wasn't almost there, not by a long shot, and my foot and leg were getting worse by the second.

There was a commotion behind me, some kind of chipper chatter. Surfer bros commenting on waves or something. I couldn't focus well enough to make out exactly what they were saying, but there was a lot of "dude" and "sweet" and "stoked" getting thrown around. Then, a shadow appeared on the sand in front of me, and the people supporting me stopped in their tracks.

"What happened? Is she okay?"

The voice sounded vaguely familiar. I looked up, and there was Trey Cantu, famous pro surfer, sopping wet and hot as ever. As my saviors explained how I'd stumbled from the water and screamed uncontrollably, he glanced at my rapidly swelling foot and said, "I'll take her the rest of the way."

In one swift movement, he grabbed me around the waist

and hoisted me over his shoulder. Instinctively, I shrieked, but quickly settled down when I felt his firm grip on the backs of my thighs. I was safe here, nestled up against him, his strong legs carrying us capably over the uneven terrain. My ass was dangerously close to his face, but I was surprisingly indifferent about that. It was hard to worry about anything aside from the pain.

Moments later, Trey sat me down gently in a blue plastic chair outside the lifeguard tower, placed my dress and phone in my lap (how had he found them?), then stuck his head inside the doorway, yelling, "Stingray wound out here!" He came back and knelt at my feet, inspecting the cut on my sole. "Looks pretty clean."

"It hurts!" I screamed like an animal.

A lifeguard rushed out of the tower with a white five-gallon bucket in her hands. It was lined with a clear plastic bag and filled with water. "Put your foot in here," she said, and I complied.

The water was scalding, so hot I thought for sure blisters must be forming on my skin. But the deep, throbbing pain disappeared instantaneously. In that moment, I'd have gladly suffered third-degree burns for this blissful sensation of relief.

Steam billowed from the bucket. I leaned back into the chair, closing my eyes and sighing out all the tension in my body. When I opened them again, Trey was crouched down in front of me, silently studying my face. So I took the opportunity to study his.

The first thing I noticed were his eyes, deep set and angular. They were far lighter than I'd originally thought, more hazel than brown. His skin was smooth, almost buttery, like he'd never had a blemish in his entire life. And his lips were positively pillowy. I bet they felt so soft.

"Bree, are you okay?" His brow furrowed with concern.

"I think so."

"Oh, good." He relaxed his features and breathed out. "You looked a little spacey for a second, I was worried you might be going into shock."

No, just fantasizing about the texture of your lips.

"Stingray injuries can sometimes cause larger systemic issues, especially if you're panicked."

"I'm not panicked."

"You were screaming pretty loudly. I heard you from clear across the beach."

"I was in pain." *And also, a little panicked.* "It feels a lot better now, though. What's in this bucket besides boiling water?"

"Nothing. Hot water's the usual treatment in this situation. The heat neutralizes the toxin in the venom. You'll need to soak it for another half hour or so."

He disappeared back into the lifeguard tower and returned a few seconds later with a bottle of water and two red pills. "Advil helps, too," he said, and handed them over before plopping down in the chair beside me.

"Thanks." I swallowed the pills and took a long swig of cold water. "I've heard of stingray attacks happening around here, but I didn't realize how painful they were."

"Yeah, they can be pretty rough, but the pain passes quickly once you start soaking it. You'll be fine." Trey smiled, and the corners of his eyes crinkled. "You need to learn the Stingray Shuffle."

"What's that?"

"When you're walking in the shallows, never take big,

heavy steps. Instead of lifting your feet up, just shuffle them along." He demonstrated by sliding his feet back and forth along the ground. "The movement sends vibrations through the water that scare the stingrays away."

"Good to know, but I won't be going back in the ocean anytime soon." *Or ever.*

"You're just saying that because you're in pain right now. You'll be ready to dive back in tomorrow."

I shook my head. "No, I'm afraid that's not gonna happen."

"Come on, don't let one bad experience in the water scare you off."

"This was actually my second bad experience, and I'm not interested in seeing what the Pacific has planned for my third."

"What was the first one?"

I briefly considered concocting a dramatic lie, like a shark attack or an encounter with pirates. Something that made me sound like less of a wuss than "a scary surf lesson about a half-mile south of here." As a pro surfer, Trey had undoubtedly experienced far more life-threatening situations in far more dangerous waters. Did I really want to embarrass myself by telling the truth?

Fortunately, I didn't have to, because the lifeguard came back with a kettle full of hot water. She poured it in the bucket and a fresh wave of intense heat washed over my throbbing foot, dissolving the pain even further.

"Thanks," I said, and when she left, I swiftly executed a change of subject. "So, this morning I went to The Bean House and saw the SurfRack poster."

"What SurfRack poster?"

"The one advertising lessons with pro surfer Trey Cantu."

He audibly gulped. "They made posters?"

"Apparently so." Weird that he didn't know about it. "Anyway, I didn't realize my next-door neighbor was famous."

"I'm not famous."

"You're telling me that if I googled your name right now, there wouldn't be millions of search results?"

"Did you google me?" He looked horrified, as if I'd admitted to hacking his email or rifling through his underwear drawer.

"No." Though his response made me think that I should. "Not yet, anyway."

"But you would?"

"Of course I would." As his eyes widened with disbelief, I said, "Don't act like I'm some sort of stalker. Everyone googles people."

"I don't google people."

"Well, you should. It's a totally normal part of twenty-first century human interaction." I pulled my phone out from the wrinkled dress and thrust it toward him. "Here, google me."

He breathed out a nervous laugh. "Are you serious?"

"Dead serious." I shook the phone. "We've all gotta start somewhere."

One of his dark eyebrows shot skyward and the hint of a smile touched his lips. "Okay, fine." As he took my phone, he said, "I don't know your last name, though."

"It's Bozeman. *B-o-z-e-m-a-n.*" I looked over his shoulder as his thumbs tapped out the words. "My first name is *e-e,* not *i-e.*"

As suspected, there were only six pages of results, most of which confused me with the three other Bree Bozemans in the United States. I leaned back and let him scroll and tap, knowing he'd find nothing of any interest. That was one of the perks of living an acutely mediocre life: no internet scandals to worry about.

Then he asked, "Who's Rob McCrory?"

My heart tumbled into my stomach. Hearing Rob's name spoken out loud—by Trey Cantu, of all people—was jarring in itself. But that the internet had linked Rob and I together was perhaps more troublesome.

"What?" I snatched the phone from his hand. "Let me see."

It was a photo of the two of us during last year's neighborhood Halloween Pub Crawl, posted on an Instagram account for Bob's Bar & Grill. Rob was wasted out of his mind, but you couldn't tell because he was wearing a gorilla suit. I was stone-cold sober and staring daggers at the camera, my banana costume covered in freshly spilled beer. The caption read: **PB locals Rob McCrory and Bree Bozeman having a little too much fun. #sloppybanana.**

Lovely.

"He's my horrible ex." I dimmed the phone screen, disgusted. "He's long gone, but I've still got that stupid gorilla suit in my closet."

"I've got one of those."

"A gorilla suit?"

"No, a horrible ex."

"Did she work in a marijuana dispensary, too?"

He chuckled. "Nah. She's an Instagram model."

Of course.

Trey looked past me, his gaze stretching down the beach toward the water. Then his hand was on my forearm and the heat of his unexpected touch made me shiver.

"Check it out." His voice was a throaty whisper as he nodded toward the ocean. I turned and took in the glorious view:

the sun kissing the horizon, painting the cloudless blue sky with broad pink strokes.

No matter how many times you've seen it, a sunset over the Pacific Ocean would always blow you away. We sat in awe-struck silence, watching the sun slip from view, inch by inch, until it was nothing but a single speck of bright yellow light, and then, nothing.

"Did you see the green flash?" Trey asked.

"I'm pretty sure that's a myth." Despite witnessing count-less sunsets in my twenty-five years, I'd never once seen the green flash, the fleeting display of green light that supposedly shows up during the last moment of a sunset.

He laughed, his eyes crinkling again. "It's a scientifically proven phenomenon."

"In theory, sure. But conditions have to be just right for it to happen, so it's rare. People probably *think* they see it a whole lot more than they *actually* see it."

"So you think all those people are lying?"

"I think they're fooling themselves because they want to say they've seen it."

He leaned over the arm of his chair, a glint of mischief in his hazel eyes. "Do you think I'm fooling myself?"

My mouth hung open, unable to form a response. I'd been staring at that sunset, too, and I didn't see anything but pink and yellow and blue. Not a single flash of green. But I wasn't about to tell the man who'd carried me across the beach when I was blinded by pain that he was a fool.

Finally, I said, "I think you're an optimist. And I think that's refreshing."

His lip quirked, like he was about to say something else, but the lifeguard returned with yet another kettle of hot water.

"We'll be closing down at dusk," she said. "That's in another twenty minutes or so. You should be good to go by then."

"Great, thanks again."

Trey nodded at the lifeguard, then stared out at the sand and the water, the waves as they rolled gently onto the shore. He looked bored.

"You don't have to wait here with me," I said. "I'll be fine."

"I know." He flicked his gaze toward me, then back again at the water. "You're really never going back in the ocean, huh?"

"Afraid not."

"But you live so close to it."

"Well, I love going to the beach. I just prefer to stay on the sand."

"Why?" His eyes were on me again. "What was the first bad experience you had in the water?"

There was no escaping him, and I wasn't about to make up a lie. So I took a deep breath, and told him my truth.

"When I was ten, I went to a birthday party. At SurfRack, actually. They had some instructors show us the basics of paddling out, popping up, riding a wave. They kept us together in a small group and didn't take us out very far, but I wasn't very coordinated, so I had a hard time with the whole thing. At some point, I started drifting and couldn't get back to the group. Then a big wave came, and I lost my footing and fell over. Before I could stand up, another one came, then another one. I was tumbling head over heels, I couldn't breathe, I couldn't see. For a second, I thought I was going to die.

"Eventually, a lifeguard came and pulled me back to shore. Turns out, I hadn't even been in deep water, I just panicked and couldn't get my bearings."

My cheeks started to burn, a reflexive response from all

those times Rob had teased me about this. Admittedly, now that I said the whole story out loud again, it seemed completely ridiculous. I was a grown-ass woman, still holding on to a childhood fear. My life probably hadn't even been in danger that day. I'd simply surrendered to anxiety, convincing myself the ocean was a perilous place.

I steeled myself for the mockery that would inevitably ensue. But Trey only looked at me, his eyes soft and kind. "That's awful. Your surf instructor never should've let you out of their sight. I can see why you were traumatized."

It felt as though I'd melted into the chair, my skin melding with the plastic beneath me. Here was a man who lived his life in the ocean yet understood my irrational fear. Unlike Rob, who rarely left the couch, and regularly used my weakness as an opportunity to ridicule me. The difference between them was staggering. Just the thought of it caused my stomach to lurch.

And rumble. Loudly.

On second thought, maybe that was hunger.

Trey bit back a smile. "Hungry, huh?"

Humiliating.

"I guess so," I said, right as my stomach rumbled again.

He kneeled at my feet and slowly lifted my left foot out of the water. With a delicate grip, he turned it over in his hands, examining it from all angles. The pain had mostly subsided. It was hard to believe that mere minutes ago, I'd been totally anguished, shrieking like I'd lost my mind.

"How's it feeling?" he asked.

"Better," I said. "Still not a hundred percent, but compared to before, it's nothing."

"Great." He set my foot back in the water, then went into

the lifeguard tower and returned with a towel. As he tenderly dried my foot, I felt a pang of despair. Because this evening, though fraught with panic and pain, had also been magical, and I didn't want it to end. Not yet, anyway.

So, I took a cue from Trey and faked a little optimism. "Wanna get something to eat?"

Oh, boy. That was a mistake. I could tell from the lines creasing his forehead. They spoke volumes, saying things like, *Who does this girl think she is? I only date Instagram models.*

I fumbled with my dress, pulling it over my head to cover my shame. No matter what positive energy I put out there, the universe wasn't going to perform some miracle and convince Trey Cantu to sit down to dinner with an ex-GrubGetter who couldn't stick a toe in the ocean without spiraling into uncontrolled hysteria.

But then, something kind of miraculous did happen. The lines in Trey's forehead disappeared, and he smiled, and said, "Sure."

Thanks, Universe.

CHAPTER 8

Trey slipped my flip-flop back on my foot, and when I went to stand, I stumbled. The pain was still there in hiding. Putting pressure on the wound brought it screaming back to the surface. With my hand on his shoulder for balance, I propped myself up on one foot and slapped a fake smile on my face. "Where to?"

"I'm not sure you can walk yet."

"Pssh." Eager to get on with our dinner date, I waved away his very valid concern. "I can hobble. Probably."

Another laugh, another crinkle of his eyes. "Do you want me to carry you?"

"As grateful as I am for your beach rescue, I'm not sure I'd be comfortable parading down Mission Boulevard like a cavewoman thrown over your shoulder."

"Then I can carry you piggyback." At once, he crouched

down in front of me, his bare back at my hips, his arms spread and ready to take hold. "Get on."

This was too much. Wasn't this too much?

"Are you sure?" I said. "Won't I hurt your back?"

He side-eyed me over his shoulder. "Are you saying I'm not strong?"

"No, of course not."

"Then get on."

At this point, it would've been rude to turn him down, so I complied, hugging his shoulders close to my chest as he threaded his arms around my legs.

"You good?" he asked.

"I'm good."

We took off, and I quickly realized how silly I was to think I'd hurt his back. He carried me the same way he carried his surfboard, like I weighed nothing. His arms were massive, and now that I got a closer look, they were much bigger than I'd originally thought. Firm and muscular, just like his hands, which grasped the backs of my knees with a touch that was strong yet soft. And his skin felt as buttery as it looked, smooth against mine as I squeezed my thighs tightly around his hips and—

"Bree?"

"Huh?"

"You okay?"

"Yeah." *Just fantasizing about my thighs on your hips.* "Why?"

"You didn't answer me. I asked if you were down with Roberto's."

"Oh, yeah, definitely."

Pacific Beach—and San Diego, in general—was blessed with a proliferation of casual taco shops, one more delicious than the next. Many of them were open 24/7, like Roberto's, meaning you could get your Mexican food fix whenever you needed it. The way my stomach was still growling, I could have easily housed an entire tray of taquitos, but when Trey set me down on a bench outside the restaurant, I kept my gluttony in check and told him I'd have "one California burrito, please, and a *horchata*."

As I sat alone waiting for him to bring back our dinner, I scrolled through my Instagram notifications, of which there were a surprising number. Considering I'd posted next to no original content, I had an awful lot of engagement. Over one hundred likes and a few dozen followers—my very first followers!—in only a matter of hours. Must have been the #choosehappy and #noexcuses hashtags. Demi DiPalma clearly had a significant presence on this platform.

When Trey returned, we unwrapped our respective burritos and dove in. The first bite was sheer heaven. Whoever had the bright idea to stuff meat, cheese, *and* French fries into an oversize flour tortilla was a culinary genius.

Wiping a glob of guacamole from my chin, I smiled at Trey. "Thanks for this."

"The pleasure's all mine. I'm glad you're feeling better."

"I never should've gone in the water."

"That's the trauma speaking."

"Right." I took a long creamy sip of *horchata* and watched Trey bite into his burrito. This guy could be anywhere he wanted right now: surfing waves in Indonesia or partying in Hollywood or making out with an Instagram model. Yet he appeared totally content to be here, outside an ordinary taco shop, eating an ordinary burrito, with me, an ordinary girl.

What was his deal?

"I feel like there's an imbalance of power between us," I said.

Trey stopped chewing and shot me a hesitant look. His mouth full, he mumbled, "What does that mean?"

"It means I've told you about one of my most formative traumatic experiences, yet I feel like I know nothing about you. Tell me something."

He swallowed. "What do you wanna know?"

"Anything. Let's start with the basics. How did you get into surfing?"

"I was raised in Hawaii and grew up on the beach."

Rather than elaborate, he polished off his burrito and crumpled the wrapper in one hand. Clearly, he was uninterested in sharing his origin story.

I tried a different tack. "Where are you off to next?"

"What makes you think I'm going somewhere?"

"According to that poster, you just came off a championship tour. And since I've never seen you around in the four years I've lived next door to your house, I kind of assumed you'd be taking off again at some point. Aren't you?"

He shrugged. "I'm not sure." Then he clammed up again.

"You're not giving me much to go on here." Holding up my phone, I said, "If you prefer, I could just google you."

That got a laugh, albeit a weak one. "Okay. I'm not sure where I'm going next, or if I'm going anywhere at all." He paused, weighing his next words carefully, almost as if he was afraid to speak them. "I'm thinking I might be done with the whole pro thing."

Trey's eyes went dull and droopy, and his lips became a fine line. I felt bad for pushing him this far, so I backed off and muttered a feeble, "I'm sorry."

"There's nothing to be sorry about. I just realized it's not the life I want to live."

"What kind of life do you want to live, then?"

He lifted the corner of his mouth in a sad little half smile. "One that's real. One where people are honest and like you for who you are and not what you can do for them. One where surfing is about the love of the sport and not about corporate sponsorships or media coverage. That's not why I do it."

"So why do you do it?"

The sad smile turned happy. "When I'm out there, it's nothing else but me, my board, and the ocean. It's a spiritual experience. You learn to read the waves, you commune with the water. You develop a connection with the earth, the sky, the whole universe."

This was venturing into dangerous Divine Mother Shakti territory, but I smiled back, because his love for surfing was obviously so pure.

"That's why I decided to take a break from touring for a while," he continued. "To get back to my roots, to surf for the sheer joy of it. And to teach other people to love it, too. There's so much beauty in the ocean. It's a shame you've had such bad experiences."

Popping the last of the burrito into my mouth, I threw up a hand as if to say, *Oh, well.*

Then Trey's eyes went from dull to twinkly and danced across my face. "Let me help you. I can take you out on the water and show you there's no reason to be afraid."

As tempting as it was to spend more time around Trey, wearing nothing but skimpy swimsuits, my fear outweighed my desire. "Thank you, but no."

He opened his mouth to protest, but I loudly slurped back the rest of my *horchata* and shook my head.

"Okay. I guess it's probably asking too much of you to say yes when you've still got stingray venom in your foot."

I glanced down, taking in the swollen pink skin. "It feels a lot better. I wonder if I can walk on it now." Standing up, I wobbled and quickly sat back down. "That would be a no."

"No worries. I got you." Trey kneeled at my feet and I hopped on his back. Without a word, he carried me home through the calm, cool San Diego evening. Laughter and music trickled from the open doors of restaurants and bars. The post–happy hour Friday night crowds were ramping up, but I was more than ready to hunker down in the quiet and comfort of my own bed.

Though snuggled up here against Trey's back was a pretty pleasant place to be, too.

When we got to the triplex, he stopped. "Which unit is yours?"

"I actually live in the back," I said. "On top of the garage."

"Oh. I didn't realize it was legal to rent those out."

"It might not be, but I don't ask too many questions."

We walked through the passageway leading to the back of the building and passed through the courtyard. When Trey approached the rickety wooden steps, I panicked. There was no way I wanted him to see my apartment, not in its current state of chaos.

"You can leave me here!" The words came out too loud, too anxious. I cleared my throat and tried again. "This is good, thanks. I can make it upstairs by myself."

"You sure?"

"Absolutely."

He set me down at the base of the staircase, where I held on to the banister for support and gave him an awkward thumbs-up.

"Listen," he said, "my offer to help you feel comfortable in the water is always on the table. Give it some thought, okay? You might feel differently after you've had a chance to recover."

"Yeah, maybe I will." *No, I definitely won't.* "Thanks again for everything."

"It was really my pleasure."

Trey stared at me now, his eyes laser-focused directly on my lips, which started tingling under his gaze. There was nothing more I wanted than to kiss him good-night, burrito breath be damned.

But that wasn't gonna happen, because he was already backing away across the courtyard. With a casual wave, he said, "See ya around."

"See ya."

As soon as he was gone, I clasped my hand over my mouth to muffle the squeals of delight. It had been so long since I'd felt this way in the company of a man—desired, interesting, dare I say special?—that I wanted to bottle up this moment and keep it forever.

And maybe even send it out into the universe.

I whipped out my phone and set the camera to selfie mode. The soft lighting in the backyard cast a warm amber glow around my face. I swear, you could actually see my lips tingle. I curved them into a smile, snapped a photo, and uploaded it to my vision board.

This time, I added a caption: a single kiss emoji.

Hopefully, the universe would know exactly what that meant.

CHAPTER 9

The next day I woke to the screeching of the garage door, but oddly, I didn't mind. Because the pain in my foot was gone, my lips were still tingling, and I was consumed with the overwhelming feeling that good things were about to come my way.

A scroll through my phone confirmed that feeling. I'd received preliminary approval for a HandyMinion account. My virtual onboarding session was scheduled for Monday morning, and after that I could start taking on paid work for random odd jobs around the neighborhood.

Furthermore, my Instagram account had garnered over a hundred more likes overnight as well as a gaggle of new followers. They left encouraging comments like, "You're a warrior, sweetie!" and "Get it, girl!" Someone named @dipalmatribe had even featured my profile in one of their stories, overlayed with an animated GIF of a little girl twerking in a pageant dress and the message: **@breebythesea bringing the #aspirationalactionplan vibes and #manifesting her dreams!**

This vision board was getting me noticed, and I had to admit, it felt kind of cool to have random strangers cheering me on. Maybe this is what Demi DiPalma meant by "energy follows thought." I'd put my positive thoughts out there, and people sent their positive thoughts back, which energized me in a most welcome and unexpected way.

If that was the case, *The Aspirational Action Plan* was doing its job. So it was probably time to get started on step three: clearing away negative energy.

A quick glance around my apartment revealed no shortage of bad vibes. Reminders of my debt and my failures, and of course, reminders of Rob. Even seemingly innocuous things were tied to memories of our doomed, pointless relationship. Like those coasters we'd bought after we toured the Stone brewery together. Or that hideous faux-fur papasan chair, the first and only item of furniture we'd ever picked out and purchased together.

There was also the yoga mat, the one I hadn't taken out of its original packaging. Rob had given it to me for my last birthday, even though I'd never expressed an interest in taking up yoga. After I unwrapped it, he must've seen the perplexed look on my face, because he'd said, "You're always saying how you wish you had a hobby."

"Yeah, but I meant something crafty, like scrapbooking or origami." I'd turned the box over and saw a Target clearance sticker on the back. He hadn't even bothered to scrape it off.

"This is better," he'd said. "Yoga'll help you get in shape."

"Oh." I hadn't realized I needed to get in shape, but apparently Rob thought otherwise.

Suddenly, I wanted everything he'd ever touched out of this apartment, immediately and forever. It was time for him to GTFO of my life.

For the next hour, I scoured my home for remnants of Rob, checking every crevice and cranny for stuff he'd left behind. In the closet, I found that old gorilla suit, the one from the #sloppybanana photo. In the folds of the futon, I found some old rolling papers. All of it went in a pile in the center of the room, and when I was done, I stood back and admired my work, feeling like I'd just performed a ritual cleansing without the sage or the healing crystals.

I texted Mari.

> What time do you get off of work today?

> In a half hour, why?

> Any interest in driving me down to Rob's storage unit?

> HELL YES.

I asked her to swing by as soon as she was done. If we hurried, I could unload Rob's crap at the StoreSmart in Mission Valley and get back here before lunch.

After throwing on some clothes, I crammed everything into a garbage bag—the coasters, the gorilla suit, the yoga mat, everything—and when it was filled to the brim, I tied it shut. Then I grabbed the six-foot bong, the one I'd unsuccessfully tried to sell on Craigslist, and put it and the bag on top of the papasan chair, before dragging the whole mess out to the curb.

Now all I had to do was find the key to the storage unit. I knew it was in here somewhere; Rob had left it behind, though I wasn't sure he realized that. The night before he left for Peru, we had an abbreviated session of disappointing goodbye sex. When I woke the next morning, he was already gone, but a bright orange key tag labeled #252 was poking out from beneath a pile of my dirty clothes.

There had been no sense in texting him about it. Earlier that week, he'd made a big point of disconnecting his cell phone because *the Divine Mother Shakti says technology is a trap.* Anyway, I'd figured he would be back soon, begging for forgiveness, and in the meantime, I'd keep the key safe. Which meant chucking it in my junk drawer and never looking at it again.

Built-in storage was at a minimum in this apartment, but I did have a single sliding drawer in my kitchenette. Rather than use it to store cutlery (as Natasha had suggested that one time before she stormed out in tears), it became a catchall for little items that didn't have an assigned home. And considering the disorganized state of my apartment, there were a *lot* of things that didn't have an assigned home.

Needless to say, the drawer was overstuffed, so when I tried to open it, it got stuck. Something way in the back had wedged itself between the slide and the cabinet. Every time I yanked on the door, I heard it grinding against the particleboard. I grabbed a wooden spoon from the cabinet above my head and jammed the handle inside, trying to dislodge whatever was caught up, but then the spoon got stuck, too. Cursing myself for being such a slob, I pulled on the handle with both hands, hard. There was a sharp crack before the drawer flew out of the cabinet and onto the floor, the contents flying everywhere.

The orange key tag stood out among the detritus. I picked it up and put it in my pocket, then surveyed the disaster at my feet. Crumpled papers, dried-out glue sticks, a roll of electrical tape, chargers for devices I'd long since discarded, a beer koozie from Belmont Park, a stress ball stamped with the GrubGetter logo.

So. Much. Junk.

And in the middle of it all was my face staring back at me.

It was a younger version of myself: hair a little shorter, eyes a little brighter, skin radiating hope. Beneath my smiling photo, in black block letters, was the word STUDENT. I picked up the old ID card, now covered in dirt and crumbs, and saw it had expired two years ago.

This ID wasn't the only obsolete vestige of my college years hanging around the apartment. Behind the futon, I had a Bankers Box crammed full of papers, notebooks, transcripts, and even some textbooks that were so old and used I couldn't sell them back. I knew I'd never need *Fundamentals of Philosophy* again, yet I'd clung to it, allowing it to take up precious limited space in my home.

Why was I keeping this stuff? I'd long since accepted the fact that, for me, college was a failed experiment. I had no illusions of ever going back to UCSD. And if I did—though at this point, it was highly unlikely—it's not like I could reuse this expired ID card or this outdated, ratty textbook.

To throw it all away, though, seemed so permanent. So final. Like I was closing the door forever on a rare and privileged opportunity. An opportunity my sister would've killed for.

Still, it was my past, and I didn't need it here cluttering up my present. Even if I couldn't bring myself to trash it all, I could at least get it out of my sight.

I hefted the box of college memories out from behind the futon and tossed my ID card inside. Just to be thorough, I grabbed the stack of past-due student loan bills off my coffee table and added them, too. Let's get real: they weren't getting paid anytime soon. Plus, if I didn't see them, maybe I could convince myself they didn't exist, and then the universe would send some positive energy to scrub away my debt.

When I returned to the curb, Mari was already there, her royal blue hatchback idling in the driveway. She spotted me approaching and popped the rear door.

"What've you got there?" she called, watching me in the rearview mirror.

"Some stuff I need to get out of the house." I set the box down and examined the cargo area. "Do you think we could fold down the back seats?"

"Why?"

"We need to fit this in there," I said, gesturing toward the papasan chair and the trash bag and the…wait, what happened to the bong? Apparently, in the ten minutes I'd left it unattended on the sidewalk, some marijuana enthusiast had sniffed it out and swiped it. Whatever. Rob could always buy another one.

Mari got out of the car, frowning. "I thought we were going to this storage unit to raid it for shit you can sell."

"No. I told you, I'm not gonna steal from him."

"You're too nice."

After lowering the seat backs, we crammed everything in and took off down the highway. StoreSmart was about fifteen minutes south of PB, which meant a picturesque drive past Mission Bay. On a sunny Saturday morning like this, the bay was packed with people taking advantage of the great San Diego outdoors. Bicyclists sprinted down winding paths, friends played volleyball in the sand, and kayaks bobbed on top of the calm, shimmery water.

I always wished I could be the kind of person who enjoyed outdoor activity like that. A fitness junkie or adventure seeker or whatever you called it. There was a sense of fearlessness about them, that no matter what pain or strain or challenge they faced, they could overcome it through sheer endurance and a burning desire to be better.

Instead, I'd allowed one bad experience to scare me away from the ocean forever. Okay, two bad experiences, but still. Maybe it was time to stop letting my past weigh me down. Maybe I'd take Trey up on his offer, after all.

"What inspired you to declutter?" Mari asked. "Did Natasha have another heart-to-heart with you about the state of your apartment?"

"No. I finally realized that I need to put my relationship with Rob behind me, and it's hard to do that when I keep finding remnants of him all over the place."

She nodded. "Makes sense. I'm glad you're coming to terms with the whole situation."

"What other choice do I have? It's been seven months. He's obviously not coming back. I was so stupid for believing he would."

"Go easy on yourself. He pulled that shit out of nowhere."

"I'm mad at myself for wasting so much time with him, though."

Mari heaved a great sigh. "Yeah, but we've all been there."

She was obviously referring to the two years she'd spent

with her on-again, off-again boyfriend, Zach. They'd met during some comedy festival, where he was a headliner and she was volunteering in the hospitality room, fetching drinks for the comics. He never took her screenwriting aspirations seriously, always cutting her down with cruel, almost microscopic insults, then gaslighting her into believing she was talentless.

On one of their many "breaks," she started her YouTube channel. That's when she discovered she wasn't talentless, because people actually found her funny—lots of people. After that, she decided to tell Zach to fuck off once and for all. Via YouTube, of course. "Fuck Off, Zach" was an instant classic, and one of Mari's most viewed videos.

"We stay with people who aren't good for us," she continued, "because it's a convenient excuse to stagnate."

"That doesn't even make sense. No one wants an excuse to stagnate."

"No one wants to *admit* it, but they do. It's easier than the alternative, which is to face your fears and forge ahead. Look, Zach was a manipulative douche, right? He always told me I'd never make it in comedy, that I wasn't funny and that I didn't have what it takes. I chose to believe him, because if I convinced myself I had no talent, then it gave me an excuse not to try. And if I didn't try, I couldn't fail. It's the same reason you stayed with Rob."

"It's not the same. Rob never said I was talentless." *Just out of shape. And cowardly.*

"No, but he treated you that way."

Mari was starting to annoy me with this unsolicited psychoanalysis. "What are you talking about?"

"I'm talking about the fact that you're brilliant, capable, and multifaceted. You could've been doing a thousand different interesting things, yet you spent your entire relationship delivering food and then coming home and sitting on the couch to watch him get stoned. He didn't challenge you to be better or encourage you to aim high. He didn't appreciate how extraordinary you are."

"Oh." My voice wavered and my eyes burned. It was overwhelming to hear my life laid out like that so plainly. While I didn't feel particularly brilliant or capable or multifaceted, Mari mostly had the right of it. I purposely kept my expectations low so I'd never be disappointed. I didn't believe I could succeed, so nothing ever happened. I never tried so I'd never have to fail.

In other words, I put negative thoughts out into the world, and negative energy had followed closely behind.

"I'm sorry." Mari reached over the center console and squeezed my knee, her eyes still on the road. "I shouldn't have said that, I got carried away. I'm just mad at him for being such a shithead to you."

"You have nothing to apologize for. You're absolutely right." I swiped at my eyes with the back of my hand and took a deep, cleansing breath. "That's why I'm moving on now. Putting the past in the past."

"Awesome."

"Better late than never, right?"

"Absolutely!"

"I'm cleaning out my apartment, I got a new job—"

"Oh, did you?" Mari interrupted, a note of surprise in her tone. "That was fast. Congratulations! What're you doing now?"

"Well, I still have to complete the onboarding process, but I got approved for HandyMinion. In the long term, though, I'm hoping to work toward something bigger."

A few seconds of silence ensued, and when I didn't elaborate on what that bigger something was, Mari said, "Like what?"

I hesitated, embarrassed to admit the truth. Mari was a committed skeptic of even the most widely accepted customs and institutions—college, marriage, democracy—so I could only imagine how she'd react if I said the words *vision board* and *manifesting*. I'd probably be laughed right out of the car. "I don't wanna tell you."

"You're freaking me out here." Her eyes went wide with panic. "Please don't tell me you're becoming a webcam girl. I know they make a lot of money, but it's not worth it, Bree."

"Of course not!" Since the truth was far less scandalous than stripping for strangers on the internet, I decided to suck it up and confess. "I'm working through a self-help book right now. *The Aspirational Action Plan* by Demi DiPalma."

To my surprise, Mari nodded approvingly. "That's great. Introspection is always a good thing."

"Yeah. I was dubious at first because the philosophy's a little out there, but Natasha gave it to me and I trust her advice. She said this book changed her life, and honestly, I feel like it's already starting to change mine. Between the HandyMinion gig and my date last night—"

"Wait a minute, hold up. Why didn't you tell me you were going on a date?"

"It was kind of impromptu. Maybe it wasn't actually a date. See, I got stung by a stingray and he—"

"What?" Mari shrieked out a laugh. "This story is getting crazier by the second. Since when do you go in the ocean?"

"I know. It was a failed experiment brought on by the self-help book. Anyway, he brought me to the lifeguard tower, then stayed with me while I soaked my foot. Afterward, he bought me a burrito and gave me a piggyback ride home."

"That sounds like a date. Who is this guy?"

"My new next-door neighbor, Trey. He's a pro surfer."

"He must have a superhot body, then."

"Super superhot." An image flashed through my mind: his bare, brown chest covered in beads of sea water, glistening in the sun.

"Well, good for you. No wonder you're ready to banish Rob from your life." Mari slowed the car to a crawl as we approached a bright orange warehouse. "Is this it?"

I glanced up at the sign. StoreSmart, just like it said on the key ring. "This is it."

We parked by the entrance and carried everything into the lobby, Mari holding the Bankers Box while I finagled the garbage bag and papasan chair sideways through the front door. I flashed my orange key ring at the receptionist, and he waved us into the storage area. Then we meandered around the narrow gray hallways for a while, scanning the numbers painted above each steel roll-up door, until we finally found unit 252.

Dropping the chair at my feet, I slid the key in the lock and popped the latch, then tugged on the door. It retracted easily into the ceiling, revealing a ten-by-ten room packed from wall to wall with stuff. In typical Rob fashion, he hadn't properly boxed anything. It was all thrown in haphazardly. Designer clothes were strewn on top of stacks of video games and old comic books, surfboards jammed in at an angle amidst it all. It was like my junk drawer, except on a much larger scale, and with far more expensive contents.

"I don't think there's room for anything else in here," Mari said.

"We'll make room."

I refused to return home with this chair or this gorilla suit or this box full of old college memories. There was plenty of unused vertical space, so I started condensing things, piling them on top of each other. I'd cleared about two square feet of space before the bottom split on a Target shopping bag and a high-tech helicopter-looking contraption clattered to the concrete.

Mari picked it up. "Holy shit, is this a drone?"

"Yep. Rob used it exactly once. It got stuck in a palm tree and we had to ask the gardener to help us get it down."

"I'm taking it."

"No, you're not." I grabbed it from her hands. "We're not stealing."

"Who said anything about stealing? I'm borrowing it. It's not like he needs it right now. I've had this great idea for an aerial video for my channel, but I haven't been able to get my hands on a drone. I'll bring it back when I'm done." Smirking, she mimed crossing her heart. "Promise."

I couldn't think of a convincing reason to tell her no. Especially after seeing the state in which he kept his supposedly prized possessions. That drone must've cost at least $750, and he stored it in a ripped plastic bag on the floor, next to a precariously balanced bicycle that looked like it could topple over at any moment.

Hmm. I'd forgotten about that bicycle.

Handing the drone back to Mari, I said, "Here, take it. I might borrow something, too."

I had to pry the back wheel out from between a guitar case (he only ever learned to play two chords) and a taxidermy mount of a deer head (don't ask) before I could roll the bike into the hallway to take a closer look. It appeared to be in good condition. Both tires were still mostly full of air, and the brakes were springy. This seemed like the perfect way to help me get around the neighborhood. There was even a U-lock dangling from the frame, which was odd, because it's not like Rob had ever ridden this anywhere.

By now, there was enough space in the unit to fit the box, the bag, and the papasan chair, so we shoved it all in and took one last look around. This room held a mishmash of stupid choices and abandoned goals, which was really the perfect metaphor for my relationship with Rob. What we had wasn't love. It was inertia. An excuse to never move forward. In a way, I couldn't blame him for following the Divine Mother Shakti into the Amazon. At least he was making a change.

But that was the past. And I was riding this bicycle into the future.

I lowered the gate and slammed the lock shut, closing the door on this messy chapter of my life forever.

CHAPTER 10

Natasha always told me she got a physical rush from tidying up. Every trash bag she tied off and tossed in the dumpster made her heart pound and her breath deepen. After an intense decluttering session, she said she felt giddy, often collapsing in a fit of giggles.

To me, this sounded completely bananas—who gets high off reorganizing a closet?—but when I returned home from the storage unit, it suddenly all made sense. Without Rob's crap everywhere, my apartment looked a whole lot...*neater* wasn't the right word, because it was still a mess. But the mess finally seemed somewhat manageable, and it actually *did* make me feel sort of giddy—and raring to clean this place up.

The first item of business would be to deal with my busted junk drawer, the contents of which still lay scattered all over the floor. After giving it all a cursory glance, I realized I didn't need most of this stuff, so I grabbed the trash can and began the process of purging.

Natasha had this saying she used whenever she coached a client to dispose of their clutter: *get rid of anything that BUGS you*. BUGS was an acronym—professional organizers loved acronyms—to help you remember to throw away things that were broken, unused, garbage, or sentimental.

The first three were no-brainers. Those crumpled papers and mystery chargers had been sitting in that drawer untouched for months, if not years. The stress ball had a rip in it, and the glue sticks had dried out a long time ago. I picked them all up and tossed them in the bin without a second thought.

The electrical tape could come in handy, so I set it aside, then kept on sorting through the junk. A nonfunctioning flashlight, a single playing card, an expired packet of Emergen-C. All of it, into the trash. By the time I'd gone through everything, all I had left was the electrical tape and the beer koozie.

I didn't need this beer koozie. I rarely drank beer—or anything out of a bottle or can, really—and when I did, I was out with friends, never home alone. I'd only kept it because it reminded me of a special time I'd had with Mari.

It was right after Rob left, when I'd been having trouble completing whole sentences without bursting into tears. Early one Saturday morning, Mari had come over, forced me out of bed, and took me to Belmont Park, an amusement park on the water in Mission Beach. We spent the whole day riding the rickety roller coaster, going crazy in the bumper cars, and eating deep-fried everything. It was the first time I'd laughed since the breakup, the first time I'd spent several consecutive hours without Rob's face popping into my thoughts.

We stayed until well after sundown, and just before we left, we spun prize wheels to try to win return tickets. Mari came up empty, but I scored the koozie. Though I knew I'd never use it, I squealed with joy when the attendant handed it over. Winning a prize, no matter how small, was the perfect way to end that perfect day.

As I knelt on the floor with the koozie in my hand, I heard Natasha's voice in my head, *They're just things, Bree.* Natasha would've told me this was sentimental clutter and should therefore be disposed of at once. So I chucked it in the trash.

And then I panicked and picked it back out.

Look, I respected my sister's opinions. She was extremely talented and hardworking, with a long list of satisfied customers whose lives she'd successfully organized from top to bottom. However, I disagreed with her hard-line stance on sentimental clutter.

Filling entire rooms with nostalgic bric-a-brac? That was a problem. But what was wrong with keeping a few key items as reminders of experiences you enjoyed or moments you cherished or people you missed? As far as I could see, nothing. Natasha would disagree.

That's why her one attempt to get my apartment in order ended in tears. When she'd showed up on my doorstep holding the garbage bags and the Swiffer, I was initially glad to see her. With her organizing expertise and knack for making the best use of small spaces, I figured she could do wonders for my cluttered little studio.

As soon as we got down to business, though, I started having second thoughts. First, she set up a system to tackle the apartment in quadrants, scouring every nook and cranny for clutter. Then she told me all about BUGS, explaining how sentimental items were always the hardest to get rid of—but *they're just things, Bree.* Suddenly, I had a vision of her finding the box under my bed and forcing me to toss the whole thing in the trash. That's when I flipped out and told her to leave.

I was not willing to part with that box.

My sister didn't know the box existed. If she did, she'd have been horrified. Because it was filled with things she thought we'd disposed of a long time ago.

When our mom died, Natasha had been adamant about clearing out her stuff as soon as possible. *They're just things, Bree*, she'd said, after tossing out what seemed like the hundredth garbage bag full of Mom's belongings. *The sooner we get this process over with, the sooner our healing can begin.*

I trusted Natasha implicitly. Plus, she was my new caretaker now that Mom was gone, so I had no choice but to follow her orders.

She was right, though. We didn't need these things anymore.

But these things had touched our mom's skin. They still held traces of her fingerprints. I couldn't haul them to the dump, when it was all I had left of her to hold.

So when Natasha took a bathroom break, I snuck a few things out of one of the garbage bags. Nothing special, just a few random items to remind me of her. A dog-eared copy of her favorite Danielle Steel novel. The flour-stained cookbook with the recipe for those delicious cupcakes she always baked on our birthdays. A ratty red T-shirt that smelled of soap and food and sweat, the toil of unconditional love that was now gone forever.

I crammed it all into a bag and hid it under my bed, way in the back toward the wall. When I moved out of the apartment, I took it with me and transferred the items to one of those flat plastic bins.

I didn't need these things. I never used them, barely even looked at them anymore. But I wanted them all the same.

Secure in my decision to keep selective sentimental clutter, I placed the now-empty junk drawer back onto its track, put the electrical tape and koozie inside, and pushed it closed. It slid forward easily, effortlessly.

Energized, I practically dove into the cabinet under the sink, reorganizing cleaning products and purging old rags. When that was done, I went to the shelving above it, filling my trash can with stale crackers and that empty canister of Folgers and a bag full of skunky weed Rob had shoved in a sugar bowl.

I unearthed a long-forgotten bottle of Fantastik, and sprayed down each surface, wiping them until they shined. I arranged my favorite pink mug artfully next to my single-cup coffee maker. I watered the withering aloe plant on my windowsill. Then I stepped back and took in the scene.

It looked positively Instagram-worthy.

Inspired to make the rest of my apartment look just as fabulous as this tiny corner, I searched the #organize hashtag for some ideas of how to spruce things up. Most of the results didn't apply to a space as small as mine, though they did provide some highly satisfying eye candy. Pantries, walk-in closets, laundry rooms, all of them monochromatic and neat as a pin.

Then there was a sponsored post, another one from Demi DiPalma. Considering my bio contained the #aspirationalactionplan hashtag, I wasn't surprised. It was a photo of wildflowers in a valley surrounded by brown mountains and blue sky. Black text in the foreground read **SYNERGIZE**.

If you're looking to get more out of your Aspirational Action Plan—more #DRIVE, more #HAPPY, more #PASSION—sign up to attend my next Semiannual Synergy Summit in Palm Desert.

Featuring some of the greatest thought leaders and wellness experts of our time, the Summit is an intense inspirational experience that will help you #SYNERGIZE your dreams, #ORGANIZE your purpose, and #REALIZE your deepest desires.

During this immersive, restorative, and educational three-day gathering, you'll exchange positive vibrations with other members of the DiPalma Tribe, release negative energies into our ceremonial firepit, and make crucial connections that will elevate your mind, body, and spirit.

Space is extremely limited and tickets are selling out fast. To dwell in possibility with me and the rest of your Tribe, follow the link and sign up now!

#choosehappy

#synergysummit

#aspirationalactionplan

The targeted ad worked, because I followed the link to check out the details. Apparently, these Synergy Summits took place twice a year, not far from where the Coachella Music Festival was usually held. The agenda seemed interesting, albeit slightly unfocused, with a variety of interactive chat sessions, wellness workshops, product demonstrations, and chanting circles.

Accommodations were provided on-site in the form of glamping tents, replete with beds and carpets and places to plug in your phone. Every morning there were sunrise yoga classes, and every evening there were farm-to-table dinners. It sounded kind of wonderful.

Unfortunately, the cheapest ticket was twenty-five hundred dollars, so it also sounded totally out of my reach.

I scrolled on, through the endless feed of organization porn, until I reached a photo of a tidy little kitchen. It wasn't much bigger than my own, but everything in it looked so clean and chic. Chrome drawer pulls, color-coordinated dinnerware. There was even a huge vase of round, pink peonies on the windowsill. It put my single-cup coffee maker and half-dead aloe plant to shame.

So I reposted it to my vision board. Even if my kitchen wasn't currently Instagram-worthy, maybe one day it would be.

The original photo belonged to @nomessnostress, one of those official Instagram accounts with the coveted blue checkmark next to their name. The profile read,

Ellie B. | Certified Professional Organizer®
Helping you reach your #organizing #goals.
Preorder my book, NO-STRESS DECLUTTERING, today!
For collaborations, email EllieB@nomessnostress.com.

Her photos reminded me of the kinds of projects Natasha told me she took on, organizing playrooms and cleaning out closets. But Ellie B. had over ninety-one thousand followers, and a quick scan of her feed showed numerous partnerships with furniture stores and cleaning products. On top of that, she had a book coming out.

I texted Natasha: **You need to get an Instagram account.**

Not ten seconds later, my phone rang.

"I already have an Instagram account," she said. "But I

haven't used it since Izzy turned five and asked me to stop putting her pictures online. What kind of paranoid kindergarten teacher warns their students about the dangers of a digital footprint?"

"Well, you should be worried about *your* digital footprint. Or your lack thereof. Have you ever heard of Ellie B.?"

"Yeah, I love that song she does with Adam Levine. Why?"

Suppressing a giggle, I said, "Not Cardi B. I'm talking about the professional organizer, Ellie B."

"Oh. I have no idea who that is."

"A professional organizer with over ninety-one thousand Instagram followers. Why don't you have an Instagram for your business?"

"I don't really need another method of advertising. I already have a website, and word of mouth has been getting me plenty of work. I told you, I've had to turn customers away."

"Yeah, but have you been offered a book deal?"

A moment of silence, then she said, "Ellie B. got a book deal?"

"*No-Stress Decluttering* comes out in June."

I heard the distinct tap of fingertips on a computer keyboard and envisioned her sitting at her desk in her immaculate home office, scrolling through what I'm sure were tens of thousands of Google search results for Ellie B.

She grunted. "Her work is good."

"It's nothing you're not already doing and can't do better. You could totally become an Instagram-famous organizer."

She grunted again. "How did she even get that many followers?"

"Maybe she manifested them into existence."

"Oh, you read the book?" Her voice was suddenly chipper.

"From cover to cover."

"Isn't Demi DiPalma a genius?"

Genius was a strong word, but I went with it anyway. "Totally. I'm following the action plan, just like you asked. This vision board thing—"

"Wait, Bree, hold on a sec." A ruckus had broken out on Natasha's end. Izzy's giggles echoed in the background, then seemed to multiply, followed by a resonant crash. "I gotta go. Izzy's got a couple of friends over. They're decorating cookies and it's becoming more of a mess than I can handle."

"Go, I'll talk to you later," I said. "Love you."

"Love you. Isabella! I leave you alone for thirty seconds and this is what—" The call ended, cutting her off midscold.

My screen reverted to Instagram, where a little pink dot in the corner alerted me to a new comment. It was on my selfie, the one I'd taken last night while I was dreaming about kissing Trey, from an account called @kissyfacelips.

Love the smile, girl. DM us if you'd like to collab. 😙

I had to read it a few times before it made sense. "DM us if you'd like to collab." That sounded like something a business would ask an influencer. I pulled up the profile for @kissyfacelips.

Kissy Face 💋
The lip gloss everyone's talking about.
Soft, sexy, shiny. 24 shades.
http://kissy-face-lips.co

There was no blue checkmark, but they did have over a

thousand followers. Plus, the website was professionally done and seemed completely aboveboard.

Surely, though, this comment was a mistake. With my sixty-four followers, Kissy Face couldn't deem me worthy of professional collaboration.

Could they?

There was only one way to find out. I DM'd them.

> Hi!
> Your lip gloss looks amazing.
> I'd love to collab.
> What did you have in mind?

> Hi Bree!
> We're about to kick off a campaign featuring nano-influencers with unique profiles, and we'd love to have you participate. All you'd have to do is post a pic of you wearing our brand-new shade, Burgundy Wine, while prominently displaying the tube—and don't forget to hashtag it #kissyfacelipgloss.
> If interested, please DM us your preferred address and we'll ship it to you—free of charge!
> xo Kissy Face

Nano-influencer.

I'd never heard that word before, but apparently, I was one. It sounded completely ridiculous.

Or did it?

Either way, I sent Kissy Face my address. Who was I to say no to free lip gloss?

My stomach growled, obnoxious and insistent, like it had last night in front of Trey. Time to start thinking about dinner. Since all that was left in my kitchenette after The Great Purge were condiments and ice cream, a trip to the grocery store was in order. This would be the perfect opportunity to try out my new bike.

Outside, I extricated it from its home under the stairs, then pedaled off toward Foodmart. It had been years since I rode a bicycle, but the old saying proved to be true: you never forget. In a matter of minutes, I was zooming down Cass Street with the wind in my hair.

Whenever I shopped for groceries, I only bought the bare necessities: ramen, coffee, protein bars, whatever brand of ice cream happened to be on sale. But today, I was feeling slightly more indulgent. I don't know if it was all the purging I'd done, or the fact that I had an extra $267 in my bank account thanks to that scrap-yard check, but I was in the mood to treat myself.

Instead of ramen, I splurged on organic pasta bowls. Not only did I get the extra-large canister of Folgers, but I also selected a delectable French Vanilla creamer to go with it. I even passed through the produce section and picked up a few Asian pears, which were criminally expensive but insanely delicious.

On my way to check out, I passed the flower buckets. Right in front of me, there was a huge bouquet of round, pink peonies, exactly like the ones in the photo I'd posted to my vision board.

It felt like a sign from the universe.

The blooms looked so pretty sticking out of the top of my grocery bag as it dangled from the handlebars of the bicycle. I smiled the whole ride home, thinking again how lucky I was to live in this neighborhood, to breathe this fresh salty air.

Sure, my life was far from ideal, but it could definitely be worse, and it was getting better every day. I made this month's rent money, I was about to start a new job, and I'd manifested a free lip gloss into my life. Not too shabby, if you asked me.

Turning onto Beryl Street, I passed by the blue bungalow, where Trey was outside hanging his wet suit from the eaves.

The click of the bike gears caught his attention, and I slowed to a stop in front of his fence. "Sweet ride," he said.

"Thanks." I tucked my hair behind my ear as he approached, his hazel eyes scanning me from head to toe.

"I guess your foot's feeling better."

"A lot better. It's still a little sore to the touch, but compared to last night, it's nothing. Thanks again for everything."

He waved away the gratitude. "Like I said, it was my pleasure."

We stood in silence, on opposite sides of the white picket fence, but close enough to touch. There were words trapped in the base of my throat, pinned in place by fear. Fear of failure, fear of judgment, fear of rejection.

But if I was ever going to make any progress in this life, I would have to pretend those fears didn't exist.

"I'd like to take you up on your offer," I said. "To help me get more comfortable in the water."

A smile spread across his face, eyes crinkling. "Awesome! Let's do it. I'm booked with lessons pretty much all day tomorrow, but what about Monday?"

I was about to say yes, until I remembered my virtual onboarding session with HandyMinion. "I have a meeting on Monday morning. It's a new job, so I'm not sure how long it'll take or what my schedule's gonna be like."

"Okay, no worries." He pulled his phone from the pocket

of his board shorts. "What's your number? I'll text you later this week and we can figure something out."

He tapped my number into his phone, then I walked my bike back home with what felt like a million fairy wings fluttering in my chest.

Inside, I put my groceries away, then trimmed the stems off the peonies and arranged them in a vase I'd found while I was cleaning out my cabinets. I removed the aloe plant from the windowsill, and replaced it with the flowers, adjusting the petals against the backdrop of the darkening sky. Then I stepped back and took in the scene.

It wasn't quite like the photo on my vision board—not quite Instagram-worthy—but it was a pretty good start.

CHAPTER 11

Monday morning marked the beginning of a brand-new phase of my life: the HandyMinion phase.

The onboarding process began at 9 a.m. and was easily completed from the comfort of my futon. All I had to do was attend a webinar explaining the ground rules of HandyMinion life—Don't harass your clients! No swearing on the job! Keep your PayPal account active to ensure timely compensation!—and then take a few multiple-choice quizzes with glaringly obvious answers.

Only sociopaths would've failed this test, but I still took pride in my perfect score, doing a little happy dance when the words **Welcome Aboard, Minion BREE!** splashed across my screen.

I started out where every other newbie Minion does, on level one. I'd be competing for jobs with more experienced Minions, many of whom had extensive work histories and lots of customer reviews. Needless to say, I was at a disadvantage.

Oh, how I missed my five-star GrubGetter rating! I'd worked so hard to maintain that Top Grubber badge, rolling through countless stop signs to make sure deliveries were on time and smiling through countless doorstep diatribes.

Ultimately, it had gotten me nowhere, since my GrubGetter account was now officially "on hiatus." But there'd been something so satisfying about being Top Grubber. It meant hundreds of people had cast their votes, and the decision was unanimous: Bree Bozeman was *not* mediocre.

Determined to achieve Level Ten Minion status quickly, I planned to accept as many jobs as I could and kick ass at every single one. Those bottom-of-the-barrel assignments no one else wanted? I'd revel in them.

For the next few days, I was up to my eyeballs in busywork. I packed boxes for an impending office move. I pulled weeds in an overgrown garden. I deep-cleaned a Winnebago. I waited for three hours in someone's home to sign for a furniture delivery.

No task was too small or too tedious. I completed them all on time and with a smile, and by Thursday, I'd already achieved Level Six Minion status, with a perfect five-star rating. In my humble opinion, that was quite an un-mediocre accomplishment.

When I arrived home after my final assignment that night, there was a small padded envelope on my doormat, addressed to "Bree Bozeman c/o @breebythesea." The lip gloss!

I raced inside and tore it open. Out fell a tube of Burgundy Wine and a note card with the handwritten message, "Thanks for supporting Kissy Face!" Smiling, I unscrewed the top to examine the glob of gloss dripping from the applicator wand.

Yick.

This color was...not my favorite. It was more puce than

burgundy, and had this weird iridescent sheen. Plus, it seemed kind of thick. More like a nail polish than a lip gloss.

Maybe it would look better once I put it on.

First, I'd have to make myself selfie ready. I grabbed my makeup bag from the bathroom and put on a thick coat of foundation, then eyeliner, and a wispy coat of mascara. I blew my hair out so it had kind of a windswept look, too. Far from perfect, but if I angled the photo right, I'd look okay. Plus, I could always retouch it.

Finally, the lip gloss. I spread a rich layer of Burgundy Wine on my lower lip, then my upper lip, and pressed them together ever so gently before checking my reflection in the mirror.

Man. This color was really ugly.

Nothing a filter couldn't fix, though.

I snapped about two dozen selfies from varying angles, then selected the best one for fine-tuning in my photo editing app. After applying a filter called "Breezy," I made some minor adjustments to the saturation, warmth, and contrast of the image.

Fortunately, once I muted the colors, my lips didn't appear quite so hideous. Other parts of my face could've used a few tweaks, though. So while I was at it, I added virtual contours to my cheekbones and smoothed out some wrinkles under my eyes. I whitened my teeth and brightened my eyes. I deepened my suntan.

Satisfied with the final result, I uploaded it to Instagram with a caption.

. . . .

Feeling fine in Burgundy Wine.
(#collab with #kissyfacelipgloss)

. . . .

Tapping the "Share" button sent a little thrill through me.

I was officially collaborating with a brand on Instagram. Me!
A week ago, I'd been daydreaming about crafting a life that
resembled the carefully curated feed of an Instagram influencer. And now, I actually *was* one.

Sort of.

The point is, change was happening. Slowly, but surely,
I was moving forward. Maybe I'd been wrong to doubt the
power of Demi DiPalma's four-step manifesting process.

With the photo session now complete, I washed off all my
makeup. The lip gloss didn't budge, though. I scrubbed it hard
with a washcloth, and when that didn't work, I smeared it in
Vaseline, but neither method removed the color. Instead, it
left the skin around my lips all red and raw.

Maybe Kissy Face was one of those long-lasting lip glosses,
although I didn't remember reading anything about that on
their website. Either way, I figured I'd give it some time, hoping it would wear off while I ate my dinner—a sumptuous
organic pasta bowl.

As I popped it in the microwave, my phone pinged with a
text from Trey. *Squee!*

Hey. Hope your new job is going well.
Things have been crazy here but tomorrow
morning looks free. Up for a swim around 10?

Absolutely! What should I bring?

Just your swimsuit and yourself.
Meet you at the lifeguard tower.

Don't get me wrong, I was excited. But there was an undercurrent of fear, the nagging feeling that I was about to walk into something dangerous. Possibly even deadly.

On top of that, I was also nervous about making a fool of myself in front of Trey, which would quite possibly be worse than a swift, watery death.

The very thought gave me stress hives.

In fact, I couldn't stop scratching the lower half of my face. My lips and chin felt like they were on fire. I walked into the bathroom and flipped on the light, then shrieked at my reflection in the mirror.

Everything south of my nostrils was red and raw and swollen. As though I'd been attacked by a swarm of bees. You could barely tell where my skin began and the Burgundy Wine ended.

Oh, no. The lip gloss.

Obviously, I was having an allergic reaction of epic proportions.

Panicked, I reached for the Kissy Face tube, searching for any sort of ingredient list or warning label, but there was nothing printed on it anywhere. Actually, now that I took a closer look, it seemed like this lip gloss may have been homemade. Was Kissy Face even a legitimate brand or was this some sort of amateur experiment?

What the hell did I just put on my face?

I riffled through my medicine cabinet for anything that might've brought relief, but found only expired Tylenol and empty boxes of Band-Aids. Meanwhile, my lips continued to swell and itch, like a couple of puce-colored balloons. I needed to do something, fast.

There was no way I could be seen in public like this, so I yanked a towel off the back of the bathroom door and wrapped it around my face like an oversize scarf. With my mouth concealed, I ran outside, hopped on my bike, and pedaled to CVS as fast as my legs could carry me.

Once there, I realized I had no idea what I came for. Some sort of ointment, maybe, or an antihistamine? I wandered aimlessly up and down the aisles, reading labels, resisting the urge to claw at my lips.

Soon, the whispers and wide-eyed stares from fellow shoppers made it clear the girl with the bath towel around her face was not to be trusted. Before security could be summoned to my side, I approached the pharmacy counter to ask for some expert advice.

The woman in the white lab coat eyed me suspiciously until I lowered the towel beneath my chin. She grimaced and said, "What happened?"

"I think I'm having an allergic reaction to some lip gloss."

"Did you buy it here?"

"No. I got it online."

She clucked her tongue, as if she saw this kind of thing all the time. "You can never trust the stuff you buy off the internet."

I didn't actually buy it, but that was neither here nor there.

The pharmacist pointed me toward a bottle of Claritin and a tube of hydrocortisone cream—as well as makeup remover to get all the gloss off—then sent me on my way with instructions to see a doctor if the swelling didn't go down by morning.

After plonking down an exorbitant amount of money, I biked home feeling like a fool. The life of a nano-influencer wasn't exactly the glamorous one I had dreamed of. I'm sure Trey's ex-girlfriend, the legit Instagram model, never found herself wandering the aisles of a CVS with a towel wrapped around her face.

She probably didn't have to add fake contours to her cheeks or artificially brighten her eyes, either. She was probably naturally perfect.

Eager to slather my face in anti-itch cream, I turned onto Beryl Street and headed for home. As I passed by the blue bungalow, I spotted Trey standing outside, wearing board shorts, hanging his wet suit from the eaves. Since he was fully engrossed in the task at hand, I hoped he wouldn't see me.

Except he did.

And then he waved.

And then I panicked.

Instead of waving back, I gripped the handlebars even harder and kept right on pedaling, faster, straight across the lawn of the triplex. I'd almost made it to the alleyway, where I could duck behind the building and pretend I'd never seen him. But my front tire hitched on something—that damn surf leash again!—and the bike wobbled precariously before toppling over on its side.

Humiliating.

"You okay?" Trey was walking down his front path toward the white picket fence. "Do you need help?"

"No!" I screamed so forcefully, he paused with his hand on the gate. "I'm totally fine, really! No need to come over!" Hustling to my feet, I pushed the towel back over my face and yelled a muffled, "See you tomorrow!" before running out of sight, dragging my bike behind me.

What a nightmare.

I chucked the bike under the stairs, defeated. Arguably, it would've been less embarrassing to have let Trey see me in all my swollen, hive-ridden shame. Now he just thought I was a weirdo who liked to ride around the neighborhood at dusk with a towel for a scarf.

To make matters worse, once I got inside, he texted me.

> You sure you ok?

>> Yeah. Thanks. All good! 👍

> Cool.
> Um...not to pry or anything,
> but what was up with the towel?

>> I have a thing.
>> On my face.

After a moment of uncomfortable text silence, I clarified.

>> It's fine, though.
>> No biggie.

> Ok.
> See you tomorrow.

How was I going to face him tomorrow? I'd made a fool of myself before we even got in the water.

A big part of me wanted to cancel this whole endeavor. But a bigger, more rational part of me knew I'd regret it.

The only reason I wanted to quit was because I was afraid. Afraid of failure, afraid of judgment, afraid of rejection. I was just going to have to pretend those fears didn't exist.

But I needed some reinforcements. So I pulled out my copy

of *The Aspirational Action Plan* and flipped to the appendix in search of some appropriate positive affirmations. When I found some, I spoke them out loud.

"I am fierce."

"I am fearless."

"I am a warrior."

They sounded totally wrong coming out of my mouth, but I spent the rest of the night periodically repeating them, anyway. Because if I said them again and again, until they were burned into the skin of my eardrums and fused to the folds of my brain, I might actually believe them to be true.

CHAPTER 12

Swollen face aside, the Kissy Face collab was a hit, with hundreds of likes and dozens of comments. Plus, thanks to a repost from the official Kissy Face account, I surpassed the hundred-follower mark on Instagram. By the next morning, I was well on my way to two hundred followers. Things were looking up.

I also got a request for another collaboration, this time from a luxury footwear brand called FRANGELICO. The name seemed totally made-up, but a quick scan of the website confirmed that the shoes were indeed very real—and very cute.

And very free!

Sure, my first foray into nano-influencing was a bit of a debacle, but everyone hit a few bumps along the path to happy. Besides, the odds of having an allergic reaction to a shoe were extremely small. I DM'd FRANGELICO my address and hoped that by the time they arrived in my mailbox, my face would be back to normal.

Because right now, things were looking iffy. The pills and the ointment provided great relief, but my skin was still pink and angry from the residual irritation.

A little redness wasn't going to stop me from diving into my first oceanic adventure with Trey Cantu, though. After all, I was a fierce, fearless warrior! So I piled an ungodly amount of powder on my chin, then strapped on my bikini and maxidress before heading out the door. I was ready to conquer the waves!

But first, coffee.

Since the morning rush was already over, I decided to drop by The Bean House to grab some good luck vibes from Mari, and also to congratulate her on her latest video: a comedy short in which drones replaced human GrubGetters with hilarious results. She'd only released it the day before, so there hadn't been too many views yet. I knew they were coming, though. Mari was too talented not to succeed.

The Bean House was mostly empty, with one patron sitting in the far corner, typing away on his laptop, while Logan mopped the floors. Mari was fiddling with an espresso machine when I approached the register and said, "Hey!"

"Hey!" She turned around and immediately recoiled. "What happened to your face?"

"Oh." I touched my chin, my lips, my cheeks, making sure everything was intact. "Does it still look gnarly?"

"Um…" Mari moved closer, inspecting the damage. "It's pink. Really pink."

"Shit." Apparently, the powder hadn't done much.

"What happened?" she asked.

"I had an allergic reaction to this new lip gloss."

"Geez. Did you contact the manufacturer?"

"Yeah." If by "contact" she meant tagging them in an effusive Instagram advertisement.

Mari grabbed two coffees and led us to our usual seat on the patio. "How's the new HandyMinion gig going?"

"Great. I'm at level six now with a five-star average rating."

"I would expect no less from you."

"How are things on your end? I saw the video you posted yesterday, it was amazing."

She shrugged one shoulder and rolled her eyes. "It's all right."

Oh, no. When Mari got all defeatist about her work, that could only mean one thing. "The trolls aren't back, are they?"

A heavy sigh was all the answer I needed.

"Look," I said, "it's easier to criticize than it is—"

"—to create," she said, finishing the sentence I always repeated whenever some anonymous asshole left a nasty comment on her video. "I know, I know. But I've been at this for a while now, and I haven't gained any traction. My YouTube views are in the toilet, my subscribers are stagnant. I'm starting to wonder if it makes sense to keep going or if I should give up this whole endeavor and get an office job somewhere. Something reliable with good health insurance benefits."

"You would be miserable." Though, frankly, that sounded pretty good to me. "What happened to all that 'thrive, don't survive' stuff you were talking about last week? This is your dream, you can't give up on it." When she opened her mouth to protest, I grabbed both of her hands in mine. "Marisol Vega, you are a fierce, fearless warrior. You can make your dream into a reality. You've just got to believe that you deserve it."

She scowled and shook her head. "What's that supposed to mean? Of course I believe I deserve it. But I can't invent subscribers out of thin air and I can't force a video to go viral. I can only bust my ass to do my best work and then put it out there. If I'm not seeing any progress, though, how much longer am I supposed to keep it up?"

"What if you tried a different approach?"

"You think I haven't already read every single YouTube marketing strategy article that's out there?"

"I'm not talking about marketing. I'm talking about mindset."

"That doesn't make any sense." She extracted her hands from my grip and took a sip of coffee.

"Remember that self-help book I was telling you about the other day, *The Aspirational Action Plan* by Demi DiPalma? It lays out this four-step process to help you shape your future and achieve whatever you want to achieve, and so much of it has to do with your thoughts and your attitude."

The way Mari glared at me, I hoped she wasn't hiding a knife in her apron. "So, you're telling me I'm not a successful YouTube star because I don't have the right attitude?"

"No. Not exactly. The thing I'm learning is that energy follows thought, and if you envision the success that you want in your life, then success will come to you."

"You sound completely insane, you know that, right?"

"I know. But what if I told you that by following this process, I was able to launch a career as an Instagram influencer in under a week?"

"I'd say you sounded completely insane. Also, the Instagram economy is a scam."

"No, it isn't!" Although, it kind of was. I mean, I'd just posted a heavily filtered photo talking about how much I loved an ugly lip gloss that gave me a rash. Coming from Mari, though, the word *scam* was beginning to lose all meaning. She wouldn't even sign up for an Instagram account, which was frankly ridiculous for someone who was trying to make it as a YouTube star. "It's not any more dishonest than any other form of advertising."

Mari sat forward in her chair, elbows on the table. "Wait, I thought you were joking. Are you seriously an Instagram influencer now?"

"Kind of. I'm a nano-influencer."

"What the hell is that?"

"According to *The New York Times*, nanos are the most powerful of all the influencer groups. They don't have a ton of followers, but they work with Instagram brands by posting ads in their feeds in exchange for free products."

"So, you haven't actually made any money off of this?"

"No." She grunted, smug, and I quickly added, "But I get paid in free stuff."

"What brands are you advertising for?"

"A luxury shoe designer just contacted me this morning. And I already did a campaign for a cosmetics company."

"You mean the lip gloss that made you break out in hives?"

I didn't have to answer that.

"I'm just saying, this process works. I was skeptical at first, too, but it's worth giving it a shot. Especially if you're considering giving up. You're so talented, Mari, and the world needs your videos."

She smiled. "Thanks."

Her smile didn't last long because there was suddenly an angry customer at the register, screaming at Logan.

"What do you mean you can't break a hundred-dollar bill?"

he bellowed. "What kind of coffee shop doesn't stock small bills in their register?"

"Goddammit," Mari whispered under her breath. "These fucking people. You know, if I worked in an office, I would be the one making the coffee orders, not the one taking them."

"I'm sure you'd treat the baristas with the utmost respect."

"And I'd always leave a dollar in the tip jar."

"Where is your manager?" The man was in full disgruntled consumer mode. "I'd like to speak to whomever's in charge here."

"That's you," I said, with a smirk.

We stood up and exchanged a quick hug. "Keep your phone handy, I might need someone to bail me out if I lose it on this guy."

"I'm actually headed to the beach right now to go swimming with Trey, so if you get arrested just text me the deets."

"Swimming? Who are you and what have you done with Bree Bozeman?"

I tapped my temple. "I told you, I'm shifting my mindset."

"Well, good luck," she said. "And don't step on any stingrays this time."

While Mari went inside to pacify the man with the hundred-dollar bill, I walked around the patio and down the path to Cass Street, then made my way a few blocks west to the beach. It was the perfect day for a dip in the water, with warm, gentle breezes and not a cloud in the sky. But as the ocean came into view, the waves rolling forward and crashing against the sand with echoing cracks, my nerves started to fire on all cylinders.

Maybe this was a mistake. Not everyone was meant to be a water dweller, and I'd already proven myself to be clumsy in the surf. Besides, there were too many potential dangers. Last time, the stingray got me in the foot, but next time it could be my heart.

Worse, I could have a close encounter with a shark, which wasn't as far-fetched an idea as you might think. Two years ago, a little boy was bitten by a great white while diving for lobsters in Encinitas. By some miracle, he survived, but knowing me, I wouldn't be so lucky.

I was so close now, though, I couldn't turn around and leave. Odds were, I'd be fine. This was merely my fear talking. To make progress, I had to push those fears aside, stop making excuses, and start moving forward.

With every step I took toward the lifeguard tower, I muttered an affirmation under my breath.

"I am fierce."

"I am fearless."

"I am a warrior."

And then I saw Trey standing where the sand met the sidewalk, wearing nothing but patterned, blue board shorts. He stared off into the ocean with this intense, brooding look, probably reading the waves or communing with the water or whatever it was he did.

As I approached, he turned toward me with his perfect smile, his eyes all crinkly. "Hey."

"Hey, yourself." Man, he was hot.

His smile faded to a concerned frown. "I see what you mean about your face. Are you okay?"

Goddammit.

"I had an allergic reaction. I'm fine now, it's just…residual."

"Oh, good." The smile returned. "You ready?"

"Ready!" I said, with possibly a little too much enthusiasm.

Because I wasn't feeling ready; I was feeling terrified, and now that I was mere steps from the shoreline, I regretted this stupid decision. When I'd said yes, I'd been thinking with my loins instead of my brains, imagining how nice it would be to get up close and personal with Trey, pressing our bodies together in the salty swell of the Pacific as his strong arms supported me and my legs wrapped around his hips and...

Okay, this was a good idea, after all.

"You can leave your bag and stuff in here." He pointed through the glass doors into the lifeguard station. "They know me, it's okay."

"Great." I pulled my dress over my head and stuffed it in my bag, then set it inside on the floor next to my flip-flops. "Let's do this."

He met my eyes, beaming. "Let's do this." Then he grabbed me by the hand and led me toward the water.

When his fingers threaded through mine, every last iota of doubt and fear dissolved into nothing. Whatever happened out there, he was my spotter. If I got scared, I could simply cling to him in a completely platonic and not-at-all amorous way.

We paused at the water's edge, where I took a deep, centering breath. The briny air was sharp and cool.

"How are you feeling?" he asked.

"Surprisingly good." And I meant it. Sure, there was that low-level fear lingering in the background, but mostly, I was excited to tackle this new challenge. To be the girl who swims fearlessly in the ocean.

"Before we go in," he said, "I want you to know that you can tell me to stop at any time. We can go at your pace, however fast or slow you want, okay? It's important to me that you're comfortable."

I couldn't help but smirk. "Exactly what are we getting into here?"

His cheeks flushed when he realized the unintentional double entendre. "I just mean, I don't want you to get into another situation where you're panicking. This should be a positive experience, without any fear."

The fear must've been written all over my face, because Trey squeezed my hand. "The ocean is powerful, but there's no need to fear it. You just need to respect it. To understand it."

A light ripple washed over my toes as he gave a brief overview of how to read the ocean. He said the direction of the wind could shift the currents, turning them from relatively safe to potentially dangerous within seconds. Then he taught me how to identify a riptide by looking for gaps between the waves and told me that if I got knocked off my feet, the best way to deal with it wasn't to fight it, but to curl up in a ball and go with the flow.

I couldn't imagine being able to calmly surrender to a wave that was pulling me under. But when Trey asked me if I felt prepared, I nodded confidently because there was no way I was going to let on that I was still afraid.

He squeezed my hand again. "You take the lead."

Okay, this was happening.

One foot in front of the other, one step at a time, we walked into the water. "Remember to shuffle your feet," he said, and I became hyperaware of the movement between my toes, the sand shifting beneath me. When something cold and slimy grazed my ankle, I screeched.

"I think it's a stingray!"

Trey crouched down and pulled a green clump of leaves

from the water. "It's kelp." He held it aloft, watching it drip, before throwing it aside with a splash.

"Oh. I guess I'm a little jumpy."

"Are you sure you're okay? We can go back anytime you want."

I shook my head, determined to overcome this irrational fear. "No, I want to do this."

We kept walking, shuffling our feet, until we were knee-deep, thigh-deep, waist-deep. When the waves rolled in, we braced ourselves for impact.

Keep moving forward.

The water was at my breasts, then my shoulders. Waves continued coming, only now they lifted us up and set us down before crashing behind us on shore.

Keep moving forward.

My toes barely touched the ground. And then suddenly, there was no ground anymore.

Adrenaline coursed through my veins as my body reflexively slipped into old patterns of panic. My legs kicked of their own volition, and Trey slipped his arm around my midsection, whispering so close I could feel his breath in my ear, "You're totally safe. The water's calm."

His touch took the edge off my anxiety. The longer I stayed here, treading water, eye level with the horizon, the less anxious I felt. The bob and sway of the water was suddenly soothing, the cool prickle comforting against my skin. Though anything could be lurking down there by my feet—a shark, a stingray, a massive wad of kelp—I stopped thinking about all of that.

I was floating in the unknown, and I loved it.

"This is amazing," I practically screamed. Then I turned to

face Trey, grasping his biceps, high on sea water. "Why did I wait so long to do this?"

He looked as happy as I felt. "I told you, there's no reason to be afraid."

"I want to do this every day."

"Good thing you live so close to the beach, then."

Maybe it was the motion of the ocean, or the firmness of his biceps, or the feel of his fingertips caressing the small of my back. Or it could've been the exhilaration of overcoming one of my most fundamental fears. Whatever it was, in that moment, looking at Trey's beautiful face, his pillowy lips and deep-set eyes and buttery skin, all I could think was that I wanted him more than I'd wanted anyone in my entire life.

So I flung my arms around his neck and I kissed him.

And he kissed me back.

And my lips exploded in pain.

"Ow!" I jerked back.

"What happened? Are you okay?"

"I'm fine, it's just this stupid...my lips are still swollen from this cheap lip gloss."

He grimaced. "Sorry."

No, I was the sorry one. This ugly Kissy Face lip gloss had ruined my first kiss with Trey.

Fortunately, he salvaged the moment, wrapping his arms around me and pulling me close, my back against his chest so we were both facing the horizon. "See? It's beautiful out here. Nothing but us and the waves."

"Yeah. Now I understand what you meant when you said this is a spiritual experience."

There was nothing to see but shades of blue, nothing to hear but the splash of the water and the faint whisper of Trey's breath behind me. It felt like I'd slipped into an alternate universe, one without fear or doubt, where it was normal to spend a Friday floating in the ocean, wrapped in the arms of a handsome pro surfer.

It wasn't an alternate universe, though. It was *this* universe, the same one I'd inhabited my entire life. Except now, the universe was listening to me, delivering my deepest desires. I had changed my thoughts, and the energy around me changed, as well.

Faking it was really starting to pay off.

CHAPTER 13

Trey and I swam around until early afternoon. It felt like an eternity and a split second all at the same time. I even worked up the courage to let go of him and float independently for a while. Though honestly, it felt much better when we were in contact, not so much for safety reasons as for the pure intimacy of his touch.

His strong hands supported me in a way that was both gentle and sturdy, and each time his fingers grazed my skin, I felt it all the way through to my bones. It had been so long since I'd been touched like that. Toward the end of our relationship, Rob was barely touching me at all. Our sex life was pathetic, and we never cuddled or held hands or exchanged any sort of intimate physical contact, either. We slept in the same bed, inches apart, facing opposite walls. It was awful.

Thinking back on it now, I couldn't believe we'd stayed to-gether as long as we had.

Every time Rob invaded my thoughts, I shoved them away as quickly as possible, hearing Natasha's voice in my head. *Don't look back, because that's not where you're going.* Instead, I chose to focus fully on the here and now, on the sensation of the water surrounding my body and the presence of a guy who actually cheered on my victories, as opposed to laugh-ing at my failures.

When our fingertips shriveled like raisins, we decided it was as good a time as any to swim to shore. Trey taught me how to catch a wave and ride it on my belly. I fumbled the first few, but quickly adjusted, and felt like Supergirl flying back to dry land.

As we toweled off, my stomach grumbled again. Wasn't there some way to shut this thing off?

Trey smiled. "Should we hit up our spot for lunch?"

I loved that we already had a spot that was ours. "You bet."

We walked over to Roberto's and claimed the same bench we had the week before—I liked to think of it as *our* bench. While Trey went inside to order burritos, I sat down and pulled my phone from my bag, scrolling through my Insta-gram notifications to see what I'd missed. There'd only been a few new likes since this morning, so I scrolled back further to the notifications I'd already seen.

Sometimes (okay, a lot of the time) I liked to reread older comments that were particularly positive. Even though I didn't know any of the people—or in some cases, brands—that left these notes of encouragement, I found them satisfying, none-theless. Getting validation from complete strangers on the in-ternet was like taking a hit of some wonderful drug.

The most recent positive comments were on my Kissy Face post. People wrote things like, "**You are so gorgeous! xo 🐬**" and "**Totally obsessed with this look on you, girl.**" They were instant self-esteem boosters. I couldn't get enough.

Trey returned with our burritos, individually wrapped in paper, along with two Cokes (the good kind from Mexico with real sugar) and a huge stack of napkins. I thanked him, then split mine open to reveal the meaty, cheesy, guacamole-covered goodness within. It looked so beautiful, so delectable, only one thought sprang to mind. *This is totally Instagrammable.*

Maybe if I posted a photo of it to my feed, I could score some free meals at Roberto's. I *was* a local nano-influencer, after all.

As I arranged the burrito artfully on a napkin, Trey bit into his and said, "You did so great today. You were a natural out there."

"Thanks," I said, my eyes on the burrito, trying to figure out the best way to angle it for the photo. I could shoot it head-on or stack the two halves crosswise. Maybe I could hold it with one hand and take a picture with the other.

"Next time we'll need to get you on a board."

"I doubt I'll be able to stand, but I'll definitely give it a shot." I held up the burrito, trying to frame it so the Roberto's storefront appeared in the background. This was good. Original, A+ content.

As soon as I picked up my phone and aimed the camera at my hand, Trey squinted. "Please don't tell me you're taking a photo of your burrito to post on Instagram."

My cheeks burned. Part of me was embarrassed for being called out. Another part of me was furious, also for being called out. What did it matter to him if I was posting my burrito on Instagram? This was my personal social media narrative.

"Yes, I was planning on it," I said, almost defiantly. I'd spent enough time with a man who mocked me in subtle yet cutting ways. I wasn't about to deal with that again.

He wiped his lips with a napkin and cleared his throat. "If you don't mind, I'd like to be left out of it."

"Okay. I wasn't planning on tagging you in it or anything. So, you know..." The second half of that sentence remained unspoken, but clearly would've been something along the lines of, *it's none of your business.*

"You couldn't tag me in it, anyway. I deleted all my social once I left the tour."

Giant red warning flags fluttered inside my head. There was really only one reason a quasi-famous person would delete all their social media accounts: a scandal. No wonder he looked panic-stricken when he thought I'd googled him.

I was totally going to google him when I got home.

"Why?" I asked, expecting some rehearsed, self-important answer about the inauthenticity of Instagram and the dearth of meaningful, in-person connection.

"There were a bunch of reasons," he said. "But the biggest one was because my ex-girlfriend and her new boyfriend kept popping up in my feed, and every time I saw them together it was like ripping open a wound, over and over again."

"Oh." That was not the answer I was expecting. "Bad breakup?"

"You could say that. Her new boyfriend is the guy she cheated on me with for the last six months of our relationship."

Yikes. "I'm sorry."

"It was for the best. We were wrong for each other." He

chewed thoughtfully with a sad droop to his eyes, then swallowed. "Anyway, I unfollowed them both, but we have a bunch of mutual friends, so it was impossible to escape them. It seemed like they were in the background of every picture. Of course, I'm sure it wasn't a coincidence, Shayla knows how to make sure she's seen. Her entire life revolves around how many Instagram followers she has."

There was a bitter edge to his voice. At least now I understood where his Instagram issues stemmed from.

"You said she was a model, right?"

"Model, influencer, shill, whatever you wanna call it. Anyway, I needed a clean break from her—from that whole group of people, honestly—so I deleted my accounts. Instagram, Twitter, Facebook—it's all gone. It's been nice, actually. I haven't thought much about her...or him...until now."

He stared off into the distance, his lower lip jutting out ever so slightly. I recognized the hurt in his eyes, the pain of betrayal and the grief of getting over someone who may have never really loved you in the first place. It was all so familiar to me.

"But that has nothing to do with you," he said. "You do you. Instagram your burrito, if that's what makes you happy."

"It's not some private matter. It's just a burrito," I said, and to make him feel more at ease, I added, "I'm not some famous influencer or anything."

He nodded. "Right. Like I said, I just want to keep my name and my face off social media. If you don't mind."

"Of course I don't mind. And honestly, this doesn't need to happen now." I darkened my phone screen and tossed it into my purse, then finally dug into my lunch, taking delicate bites to avoid irritating the sensitive skin around my mouth. "So, you really think I'm ready for a surf lesson?"

"I think you're ready, but the question is, do *you* think you're ready? As far as I saw today, you were confident and—"

"Yo, are you Trey Cantu?"

Out of nowhere, a gaggle of teenage boys descended on Trey. Under his breath, he murmured, "Ah, fuck," then plastered on a painfully insincere smile and said, "Hey, guys."

"So cool that you're here, man," one kid said, clapping him on the shoulder as if they were old friends. "I saw the posters at SurfRack and was hoping to run into you."

"Yep. Here I am." He looked like he wanted to crawl under the table and hide until these kids were gone. I silently ate my burrito while they prattled on.

"Dude, what happened with Zander in Sydney was bullshit."

"Yeah, man, you were robbed."

"You think you'll be back in for Pipe Masters?"

Trey turned bright pink as his eyes darted from the kids to the ground to me and back. "Uh...not sure."

An awkward silence ensued, then the guys looked at each other and said, "Well, it was awesome meeting you."

"And we're pulling for you, man."

One guy whipped out his phone and switched on the camera. "Do you think we could get a pic?"

The table trembled as Trey's knee bounced up and down. He didn't respond at first, and I could tell he was thinking about which social media outlet this selfie would end up on. Finally, he said, "You know what, guys? I really appreciate your support, but I'm not comfortable taking a photo right now."

All three of their mouths fell open in unison, totally shocked that anyone would turn down a photo op. It would've been hilarious if the vibe wasn't so tense.

"Cool, yeah." The guy put his phone back in his pocket. "Well, good luck with everything."

They took off down Mission Boulevard with their heads huddled together, most likely whispering about what the hell Trey Cantu's problem was. For his part, Trey regarded the remainder of his burrito with disgust before carelessly tossing it onto a napkin.

The whole thing was so uncomfortable, I didn't know what to say. So I said nothing and tucked into my food with renewed zeal, while a thousand questions ran through my head: *What happened in Sydney? Who was Zander? And why was Trey robbed?*

"That was awkward," Trey said, scrubbing a hand through his salty hair. "Sorry."

I waved away his apology. "You have nothing to be sorry for. They were just excited to see you. I told you, you're famous."

He grunted. "I can't believe SurfRack made those stupid posters. I mean, I get it, the advertising brings in business. But I told them I wanted to be low-key about it."

"You can't really blame them for using your celebrity status to attract customers, though."

"No, I guess not." He took a long swig from his Coke. "I think I'm just still feeling burned by Shayla. She always used her relationship with me to score brand partnerships and stuff. Now that she's with Zander, though, I'm sure she's getting twice as much work out of it."

Oh, boy. We were deep in the ex-files. If Trey was still pining over Shayla, perhaps it was a bad idea to keep spending time with him. I wasn't interested in being his rebound. "When did you guys break up?"

"Five months ago." He shook his head. "I'm over her completely, I'm just mad at myself for staying with her for so long. We were wrong for each other from the start."

"I know what you mean. I wasted three years of my life with a part-time dispensary clerk who spent most of his waking hours baked out of his mind. Then, seven months ago, he dumped me out of the blue to go trip his face off with some psychedelic healer in the Amazon rainforest."

Trey gave a great chuckle of disbelief but abruptly stopped himself. "I'm sorry to laugh, it's just…who does that?"

"It's okay to laugh. I'm finally at the point where I can laugh about it, too." As soon as I said that, I felt it was true. Rob was no longer a negative force in my life. He was completely irrelevant, and I was completely over him. Now he was nothing more than an extended anecdote from my past. A joke.

We bused our table and walked back home, talking about things other than our exes. Positive, happy things, like our mutual love of Jordan Peele movies and the upcoming Pacific Beach Street Fair. As we turned onto Beryl Street, I shifted my purse from one arm to the other and felt my phone buzzing inside. When I pulled it out, Natasha's name flashed on the screen, so I sent it to voice mail, as usual.

While debating who served the best fish taco in town—I said PB Shore Club, Trey said PB Fish Shop—Natasha called again. Assuming this was another one of her nonemergencies, I declined it, and almost immediately, she sent me a text.

> Please call me, Bree. Super urgent.

If Natasha was sending texts, there was definitely something wrong. I interrupted Trey in the middle of his comparative taco analysis to say, "I'm really sorry, but I think my sister has some sort of emergency. I need to call her."

"Of course. I hope everything's okay."

I shrugged and hit the call button, silently hoping everything was okay, too.

Natasha answered before the first ring completed its chime, sounding breathless. "Thank God you called. Are you free tonight?"

"Yes, why, what's wrong?"

"Tonight's the San Diego Orthodontists Gala in La Jolla, but our replacement sitter just canceled at the last minute."

"Oh, I can watch Izzy, no problem."

She sighed with intense relief. "Thank you so much, you're a lifesaver. I'll send a Lyft for you in a couple of hours. Say, three o'clock? That should give you plenty of time to get up here with Friday traffic. And feel free to stay overnight. Stay the whole weekend, if you want."

"Thanks, I think I will." A weekend at Natasha's was like a luxury getaway. Her queen-size guest bed had the fluffiest pillow-top mattress, and the guest bathroom had one of those rainfall showerheads. She subscribed to an expanded cable package with all the premium channels, plus there was a hot tub in the backyard. And, of course, it was always fun to hang out with Izzy.

When I hung up, Trey asked, "All good?"

"Yeah. She just needs me to babysit tonight." I tossed my phone in my purse and when I looked up, we were already standing in front of the adorable blue bungalow. "I should go get ready, wash this salt out of my hair. I had a great time today."

"So did I." He smiled. "Can't wait to do it again. When can we get you out on a board?"

"I'm spending the weekend at my sister's, and I'm not sure of my work schedule next week. Text me and we'll figure something out, okay?"

"Sounds good." His mouth opened like he was going to say something else, but he quickly closed it. He cleared his throat, rubbed the back of his neck, and tried again. "I want to kiss you right now, but—" he pointed to my lips "—I know you're in pain, so…" He took my left hand in both of his and raised it to his mouth. Before he made contact, he looked at me, and said, "Is this okay?"

I nodded, and he kissed the back of my hand. His lips were soft and slightly wet, and they lingered for an extra beat before he turned my hand over and kissed my palm in the same slow, sensuous way. It sent sparks shooting up my arm, straight to my heart, and when he ran the pad of his thumb slowly over the soft spot on my inner wrist, I swore my vision got blurry. This simple gesture was arguably more erotic than any sexual experience I'd ever had in the three years I'd been with Rob.

When at last he spoke, his voice was husky. "See you soon, Bree."

"See you soon, Trey."

We held hands a moment longer, and then I turned and walked away, my arm tingling the whole way home.

CHAPTER 14

At 2:45 p.m. on the dot, Natasha called to let me know the Lyft was on its way. "His name is Zoltan and he's driving a white Hyundai. He'll be there in eight minutes."

"You could've texted me that information."

"Just go wait downstairs before you mess up my rating."

I grabbed my overnight bag, double-checking that I'd remembered to pack a bikini for that hot tub goodness, and hustled out the door. As soon as I got to the curb, Zoltan pulled up, then whisked me out of PB and up the I-5 toward Encinitas.

Friday traffic being what it was, we didn't get very far on the highway before slowing to a bumper-to-bumper crawl. A glance at Zoltan's GPS said the trip was going to take almost an hour, so I whipped out my phone to pass the time.

Instagram came through with its usual eye candy: a latte

with a feather pattern etched into the foam; a book in a blanket-lined basket; a bikini model holding a surfboard on a white-sand beach, turquoise waves gently lapping the shore. That particular photo had over four thousand comments, and there were ten different sponsors tagged—everything from the hat on her head to the polish on her toes. I wondered if that was the kind of quality content Shayla served up.

I was dying to know what Shayla looked like, but it would be hard to find her on Instagram; a quick search showed over a hundred influencers named Shayla (or Shay), a handful of which were verified. So I did what any normal person in the twenty-first century would do, and I googled her.

The search phrase "Trey Cantu Shayla" returned approximately twenty-one thousand results. From this, I learned her last name was "Miller," and she was drop-dead gorgeous. I also learned that she and Trey had spent a lot of time getting photographed in public together. There were photos of the two of them cuddling on the beach, posing in front of step-and-repeat banners, and cozying up on what looked like nightclub banquets. In one, they were sharing an extremely sensual kiss.

This was torture. I needed to stop.

But before I closed down the browser window, one of the search results caught my eye. An article from SurfBuzz.com detailing an incident that happened almost two months ago, in Sydney. Naturally, I clicked it to read more.

CANTU CAN'T DO: WSF Suspends Trey Indefinitely for Tweetstorm

By Dax Ruffin, SurfBuzz Staff Reporter

After a Twitter tirade against the World Surf Federation, Trey Cantu has been expelled midway through the Sydney Surf Pro and indefinitely suspended from all future WSF events until a full investigation can be completed.

During Wednesday's Round Two heat against Zander Nakamura, Cantu was slapped with an unsportsmanlike interference call, resulting in the loss of half of his lowest scoring ride—a significant blow to Cantu, whose ranking has been slowly slipping all season. Upset by the call, Cantu stormed from the ocean, swore at Nakamura and the judges, then tweeted the following:

@treycantusurf
Disgusted with the call today. WSF is more concerned with commercial opportunities than protecting the integrity of the sport. Judges no longer reward competitors for technical competence, but for ass-kissing abilities and star power. In short: Fuck this shit.

According to Article 180 of the WSF Rule Book, any comments broadcast from social media accounts "disparaging the sport of surfing or causing harm to the WSF image" are grounds for "immediate expulsion or suspension upon the first offense." This is the latest in a series of disappointments for the once-revered Cantu, who'd won two championships in previous WSF World Tours.

Attempts to contact Cantu for comment have been unsuccessful. At the time this article went to press, Cantu had deleted all his social media accounts. Nakamura has remained silent on the incident, though his girlfriend—and Cantu's ex—Shayla Miller tweeted, "I hope Trey finally gets the help he needs."

Yeesh. This was a mess I had not been prepared to deal with. Turns out I'd been right when I suspected Trey had been involved in some sort of scandal. Though, frankly, I was having a hard time picturing how this could've gone down. The vision of a screaming, angry, unsportsmanlike Trey was incongruous with the Trey I'd been introduced to. With me, he had always been gentle, supportive, soft-spoken. Was he secretly some rageaholic? Or had this been an isolated incident, spurred on by a broken heart?

Either way, that tweet from Shayla did not instill confidence. What kind of "help" did he need?

This escape from PB couldn't have come at a better time. When the car pulled up in front of Natasha's house, I left all thoughts of Trey and Shayla behind, intent on spending the weekend relaxing and enjoying my family.

Izzy answered the door and immediately vaulted into my arms. "Auntie Bree!"

"Hey, Iz! It's so good to see you."

I wrapped my arms around her slender little body, closing my eyes as I nuzzled the crook of her neck. It was hard to believe over six years had passed since I first saw her at the hospital, wrapped up like a burrito in a Plexiglas bassinet. I'd been too nervous to pick her up, afraid I might break her, but Natasha had trusted me completely. She sat me down in the vinyl visitor's chair and placed newborn Isabella in my arms.

As soon as I felt the weight of Izzy's warm, wiggly body, I was suddenly no longer afraid. How could there be fear in a world where something as perfect as this tiny little human existed? And my sister had created her! After everything Natasha had endured, she'd still managed to build this beautiful life for herself. A home, a family, a purpose. In that moment, for the first time since our mom died, I felt like the possibilities for my future were endless, too.

Needless to say, the feeling was fleeting. But I still thought my niece was perfect. Possibly the most perfect person in the entire world.

"Are you ready to have fun tonight?" I asked.

"Yes!" Her eyes lit up as she looked at me. "Mommy got me a new Lego set—Princess Ariel's castle! Wanna build it with me?"

"You bet." Natasha told me Izzy had recently discovered *The Little Mermaid* and was a full-fledged Ariel fangirl now. Apparently, she'd even redecorated her bedroom in a splashy mermaid theme. "I can't wait to see how your room looks."

"Isabella, what did I tell you about answering the door without someone around?" Natasha descended into the hallway, carefully negotiating the stairs in her portrait collar satin gown and peep-toe stilettos. At the landing, she smoothed a hand over her chignon, assuring every last hair was in place. "You never know who could be ringing the doorbell."

"I knew it was gonna be Auntie Bree," Izzy muttered, then slithered out of my arms and ran toward the kitchen.

"You look amazing," I said to Natasha.

"Thanks!" She struck a pose and did a little spin. "I don't have many excuses to play dress-up, so I decided to go all out tonight. What happened here?" Natasha gestured to my lips.

Goddammit. "Nothing. Just an allergic reaction to new lip gloss. It's better now."

"Okay. Well, come, let me show you a few things in the kitchen before Al and I leave."

I followed her down the hallway and into the L-shaped kitchen which was easily bigger than my entire apartment, and a lot neater, too. Every surface gleamed, from the stainless steel appliances to the marble countertops. The glass doors on each cabinet revealed meticulously organized contents: perfectly aligned stacks of plates and bowls; glassware sorted by size and color; an expensive-looking soup tureen that must've been there just for show. The smart fridge hummed extravagantly in the corner.

Natasha led me straight to the wall beside the pantry, which she referred to as her "kitchen command center." There was a blackboard, a whiteboard, a calendar, two corkboards, a letter bin, a key ring, and a hand-painted distressed wooden sign above it all that said The DeAngelis Family.

"All the important phone numbers you might need to know are right here." She pointed to the chalkboard, where she'd written out not only the number for Izzy's doctor and dentist, but also for the banquet hall hosting the gala as well as her and Al's own cell numbers, as if those weren't already stored in my contacts.

"Here's the money for dinner," she said, indicating the envelope she'd pinned to the corkboard containing two twenty-dollar bills, next to which was a flyer for Flippin' Pizza. Then she opened the pantry door and switched on the light. "If Izzy wants a snack, she can pick anything from the fruit baskets, the veggie bins, or from this bottom shelf here." I caught a glimpse of a row of wicker baskets with printed labels like Granola Bars, Gummies, Fruit Pouches, and Crackers before she cut the light and closed the door again.

All this hyperorganization made life easy in a lot of ways, but it also felt a little constricting. There was all this pressure to keep things neat and tidy. The tiniest water spot on the faucet or misaligned basket in the pantry would stand out like an eyesore. In my excitement to hit up the hot tub, I'd forgotten about the stress that often arose from maintaining my sister's pristine household.

Al walked in, looking dapper and chipper, as usual. "Hey, Bree! Thanks for covering at the last minute."

"No problem, I'm happy to help."

"You're the best." He brought me in for an affectionate brotherly side hug before grabbing his keys from the kitchen command center and turning to Natasha. "Ready, baby?"

"Yes." She nodded, then turned to me. "Bedtime's at eight. Read her a chapter from *The BFG* and make sure she brushes her teeth."

"I will, Mom," Izzy said, a tinge of annoyance in her voice.

"Don't worry," I said. "Everything will be fine. Have fun tonight."

With a kiss and a hug, they were out the door, and within minutes, Izzy and I were huddled on the floor of the den, assembling a 220-piece Lego set. When that was done, we ordered pizza, and in a stunning act of defiance and bravery, I told Izzy it was okay to eat dinner in the living room while we watched *Wreck-It Ralph*. By some miracle, the couch cushions escaped sauce stains, though the movie lasted a bit longer than I'd anticipated, and she wound up getting to bed twenty minutes late. Fortunately, I remembered to make sure she brushed her teeth.

As we snuggled up in her new mermaid-print comforter, on top of frilly pink pillows, beneath a gauzy blue canopy, I reached for Izzy's copy of *The BFG*. It was resting on the nightstand between a ceramic lamp and a jewelry box covered in seashells. The box looked achingly familiar. I knew I'd seen it somewhere before, but the memory was fuzzy, as if looking through frosted glass.

"Where'd you get this box, Iz?"

She shrugged. "Mom brought it home one day when we were redecorating my room."

I picked it up, opened the top. It was filled with plastic beaded bracelets and brightly colored hair clips. The red felt lining was peeling around the edges and it had a musty sort of smell, like dust had been collecting in its fibers for years.

Suddenly, the memory came into sharp focus.

"This was my mom's box," I said, remembering quite clearly where it used to sit in the middle of her dresser. She used it as a catchall—a miniature junk drawer, of sorts—and when I was a kid, I liked to poke around in there to see what I could find. There was never anything super interesting, mostly dry cleaning receipts and extra buttons. Once I found a packet of Life Savers.

This was one of the many, many things I'd thought Natasha had gotten rid of in her clean sweep of Mom's belongings. To see it here, in Izzy's bedroom, was jarring.

"This belonged to Grandma?" she asked.

"Yeah." The word came out raspy, my throat unexpectedly thick. "Your mom didn't tell you that?"

Izzy shook her head, seemingly unperturbed.

I ran my fingers over the shellacked scallop and dove shells. "Does she ever talk about Grandma at all?"

"Not really. I know she died before I was born, and that she was a schoolteacher."

"That's all?"

She thought for a second, then nodded. This depressed me to no end, that Izzy didn't know the wonderful, beautiful, funny, quirky, interesting person her grandmother had been. There was so much she needed to know, so much I wanted to tell her. But when I tried to conjure up stories to share, I realized most of my memories had that frosted-glass fuzziness to them.

I was beginning to forget her.

The only memories I could reliably access were the tangible ones. The ones I'd secretly stored under my bed.

"She liked to read Danielle Steel novels," I said. "And she baked the best chocolate cupcakes with peanut butter frosting."

"Those sound good."

"They *were* good."

"How did she die?"

"Uh…" The room echoed with the sound of my nervous swallow. If Natasha hadn't told Izzy how our mom had died— a surprise brain tumor, followed by unsuccessful surgery—I wasn't about to divulge that information. It wasn't my place. "You'd better ask your mom about that."

"She never talks about her."

I wanted to say *I know*, but I didn't. Instead, I put the trinket box back on her nightstand and gave it an affectionate pat. "Well, at least you've got a little piece of her beside you all the time."

Then I cracked open *The BFG* and lost myself in the story of an orphaned girl who goes on to become a courageous, international heroine with the help of a big, friendly giant.

CHAPTER 15

After that, I needed a drink.

I was never one to drink alone, but this day had been like a roller coaster, and a glass of wine in the hot tub sounded like the perfect way to quiet my brain and settle my nerves. So once Izzy fell asleep, I did a thorough tidying up—loading the dishwasher, polishing the countertops, vacuuming errant pizza crumbs from the living room carpet—then slipped into my bikini and popped open a bottle of Riesling.

Hopefully, it wasn't an expensive one. With over two dozen bottles in their wine fridge, though, they probably wouldn't mind even if it was. I didn't understand why they had so many bottles, anyway. I'd never even seen Natasha finish an entire glass of wine.

With the bottle in one hand and a stemless wineglass in the other, I made my way to the backyard, where the hot tub sat beside an elevated deck. The water glowed blue and ethereal from the built-in lights. I cranked up the jets and stepped inside, then served myself a heavy pour, and allowed the hum of the motor and splash of the bubbles to drown out the noise in my head.

In light of all her "they're just things, Bree" talk, I couldn't believe Natasha had saved our mom's trinket box. Not that I begrudged her—I had a box of Mom's belongings under my bed, for crying out loud—but it was so antithetical to the decluttering principles she always preached. It wasn't like her to save things for sentimental value without putting them to immediate use. Where had she been storing it all these years? And was there more where that came from?

Before I knew it, my wineglass was empty, and as I poured myself another round, my limbs felt loose and limber. Lying back against the reclining wall of the hot tub, I stared up at the stars and the bright crescent moon and the tops of the palm trees silhouetted against the sky. It was so beautiful, so picturesque.

So totally Instagrammable.

Given the swell of emotion I'd been through today—the swimming, the surf scandal, the resurfacing of the long-lost trinket box—I wasn't feeling particularly glamorous or inspired. If I were to hashtag my current mood, it would be something along the lines of #confused or #bummedout or #tiredaf.

But when it came to Instagram, my actual mood didn't matter. As I was quickly learning, Instagram wasn't about authentic emotion. It was about fantasy and facade, about crafting a narrative to entertain and engage. To make people want what you had, or more accurately, what they *thought* you had.

A picture of this wine bottle next to the hot tub with all the blue lights twinkling off the green glass would make for some A+ quality aspirational content. Who wouldn't wish they were sitting here, getting tipsy, while dozens of jets blasted their backs with warm, frothy water? No one!

So I whipped out my phone and Instagrammed it.

....

Hot tub + Riesling + balmy San Diego night = #friyay perfection. 🍷

....

And because alcohol had dulled the edges of my inhibitions, I decided to tag @vitalvineyards, the wine brand that made this Riesling. There was nothing inherently strange or bold about this; people tagged brands all the time. But influencers always tagged them for advertising purposes, to let everyone know this was an official collaboration, especially if they added the #collab hashtag to their post.

Which I did, after the fact.

Look, it was a lie, but it was a small lie. The simple truth was that if I wanted to start getting more freebies, I was going to have to up my game.

Put another way: I'd have to fake it till I made it.

By pretending this bigwig wine brand chose to collaborate with me, I could build some credibility in the nano-influencer sphere, and potentially attract more (and better) sponsors. No more toxic makeup. Maybe I'd eventually get paid with money instead of free products. Or at the very least, maybe the products I'd get for free wouldn't leave a rash on my face.

I stayed in the hot tub for a good long while, basking in the brilliance of my clever yet completely harmless deception. After draining my second glass of wine, I cut myself off. Even though Izzy was asleep, I was still on babysitting duty. If she woke up from a nightmare, shit-faced Auntie Bree wouldn't be much comfort.

Just then, a loud slam emanated from somewhere inside the house. I sat up, prepared to jump out and towel off before escorting Izzy back to bed. But through the sliding screen doors, I saw Natasha totter into the kitchen, looking slightly unsteady on her feet. She made eye contact with me, then broke out in a wide grin, yelled, "Let me get my suit on!" and disappeared out of view.

If I didn't know any better, I'd have thought Natasha was drunk. But Natasha didn't get drunk. It was part of her type A control-freak personality to always have her wits about her, to always stay in command of her faculties.

Al sauntered into the kitchen, hanging his keys on the command center with a worn-out expression on his face. Then he looked up and spotted me, waving before coming out into the backyard. "Hey, Bree. How'd things go with Izzy tonight?"

"Fantastic. She fell asleep a little late, but that was my fault. How was your gala?"

Through a great, gaping yawn, he said, "Eh. It was a networking opportunity. Nothing too exciting."

"Natasha seems like she had a good time." I didn't want to mention what I was really thinking, but Al said it for me.

"She's drunk." He tittered, evidently amused. "I can't blame her. It was four straight hours of orthodontia talk. She needed to entertain herself somehow."

I couldn't help but laugh. "I don't think I've ever seen Natasha drunk before."

"It doesn't happen often. Open bars are a dangerous thing."

Right on cue, Natasha flung the sliding screen door open

with such force it went flying off the track and toppled over onto the concrete. She stared down at it, unmoving. "Oh, shit."

Al chuckled. "Don't worry, honey, I got it."

As he bent over to pick it up, she palmed his ass. "Thanks, hot stuff." Then she came over, empty wineglass in hand. "Fill 'er up, lil' sister."

The words came out slurred. With a meaningful glance toward Al, I asked, "Are you sure that's a good idea?"

"Don't look at him," she said, slipping into the hot tub beside me. "He doesn't control me. I'm fine. I've had, like, three drinks. I can handle a glass of—" She squinted at the bottle. "I don't even know what this is. Riesling? Whatever. Pour!"

I obeyed her command because what was I supposed to do, say no?

Once Al had righted the screen door, he gave it a few test slides and called out, "I'm going to bed, hon."

"Can you check on Iz while you're up there?"

"You got it," he said, then disappeared inside.

"How was she tonight?" Natasha asked me, taking a huge gulp of wine.

"Wonderful, as usual. We put together that whole Lego set, then watched a movie before she went to bed."

"Isn't her new mermaid room cute?" Natasha said. "Izzy picked out the comforter set herself."

"It's adorable." My mind flashed back to the trinket box, the musty smell of the peeling felt. "I saw you put a little reminder of Mom in there."

Her face screwed up into a question. "What're you talking about?"

"The trinket box on Izzy's nightstand." When she still looked confused, I added, "The one covered in seashells."

"That? I got that at HomeGoods two weeks ago."

"But it looks so much like the one Mom used to keep on her dresser."

"I have no idea what you're talking about, but it's a pretty generic box, Bree. They're probably mass-produced in some factory somewhere."

Natasha sipped her wine dismissively and I felt crushed by the weight of my hopeful naiveté. Naturally, she was right; it was a common, unremarkable, and inexpensive item. Of course she'd bought it at HomeGoods. Of course she hadn't stowed Mom's belongings away, untouched, for over a decade. She wasn't like me, with the secret memorial under my bed.

"Oh!" Natasha cried, her drink sloshing over the side of her glass in excitement. "I meant to tell you. I took your advice and started an Instagram account."

"Cool! How's it going so far?"

"Great! I wasn't sure what I was doing at first, so I signed up for this Instagram boot camp with Demi DiPalma and powered through all the lessons in one day."

"I didn't realize she taught an Instagram boot camp."

"She teaches everything. She's a genius."

"What kind of stuff did you learn?"

"Strategies for building an audience, tips for creating quality content, tricks for improving engagement. That sort of thing."

"Sounds really useful." Maybe I should've taken that course myself. I grabbed my phone from where it rested on the deck beside the hot tub. "What's your Instagram handle? I'll follow you."

"@declutterwithdeangelis. All one word."

I pulled up her profile and gasped. "You have over twenty-five thousand followers."

"Mmm-hmm." She nodded over her wineglass, as if this wasn't completely astonishing. Meanwhile, @breebythesea had 223 followers, and I'd felt like every single one was a triumph. Until now.

"How did you get all these followers so quickly?" And what was I doing wrong?

"I bought them. Well, most of them."

I'd heard of this practice—paying some third-party company to give your account a big batch of followers, mostly bots who were programmed to interact with your account on an automated schedule. "Demi DiPalma told you to buy followers?"

"No," she said, "I figured that one out on my own. Right after I started the account, I got a DM from someone called BuyFollowersNow or MoreFollowers4U, something like that. Anyway, I paid them $250 and an hour later, I had twenty-five thousand followers."

"But doesn't that defeat the purpose of using Instagram to boost your business? You're trying to reach actual people who could turn into paying customers."

"Yeah, but it's impossible to gain any traction without a little help. People want to follow people who are legit, and the only way to prove you're legit is to have a lot of followers. It's a total catch-22. By pretending I already have a big following, I'll be able to attract real people who are genuinely interested in my work."

"Right." Instantly, I thought of the picture I'd just posted, the wine bottle with the bogus #collab hashtag. "Fake it till you make it."

"Exactly!" After another huge gulp of wine, she asked, "So, what's going on with your action plan? You started telling me about it last weekend but then we were interrupted. You said you made a vision board?"

"A virtual vision board—on Instagram, actually—and it launched me into this whole new venture of being a nano-influencer." I could see she was about to ask what that was, so I headed her off at the pass. "It's like a regular influencer, but on a smaller scale."

"How many followers do you have?"

Too embarrassed to speak the actual number out loud, I said, "Not nearly as many as you. I can't afford to buy followers. Right now, I'm mostly focused on trying to pay my rent. I've been working with HandyMinion all week, though, and it's been good. If I keep it up, I think I'll stand to make way more than I did when I was with GrubGetter."

She set her wineglass down on the side of the hot tub and sighed that same exasperated sigh she gave whenever she was about to lecture me on the importance of "aiming high" and "never giving up" and "choosing happy."

"Let's back up a second. How did you define your aspiration? What did you write in the first action item?"

"I didn't actually define one." Another exasperated sigh. "I couldn't think of anything I really wanted to do or be. All I could see when I did that creative visualization exercise was a perfectly curated Instagram feed."

She cocked her head, thoughtful. "Well, maybe the fact that you've manifested this nano-influencing thing into your life is a sign from the universe that you should continue down this path. But you shouldn't settle for 'nano' anything. You should aim for greatness. What's your Instagram niche?"

"Niche?"

"It's the category you're looking to dominate. A lot of the big ones are so oversaturated right now, it'll be hard for you to stand out in something like travel or beauty or fashion. You should pick a niche that's less common, but still profitable. I bet you could make a killing on something like cooking in small spaces. How to make the most of your tiny appliances in a kitchenette. Gourmet meals in a microwave, or whatever."

"But I don't know how to cook."

"Well, you can learn as you go. Fake it till you make it, right?"

It was difficult to envision myself making anything aside from organic pasta bowls in that miniature microwave. Not to mention, I had no interest in trying. "I'm not sure."

"So how do you plan to monetize your account?"

It was becoming increasingly clear that I had not thought this process through. "Um, I was hoping brands would give me money."

"Yeah, but for what? There are different ways of earning money as an Instagram influencer. You could charge a flat rate per post or earn commission through affiliate links. You could also create your own product to sell. Oh!" She snapped her fingers, spraying droplets of water in my face. "You could compile a bunch of your recipes into an ebook!"

"I don't think the whole 'cooking in small spaces' thing is the right niche for me."

"Then what is?"

A thin coat of sweat was forming on my upper lip. This hot tub was suddenly stifling. "I don't know. I guess I haven't really given it enough thought."

"You told me you read *The Aspirational Action Plan* from cover to cover."

"I did! And aside from defining my aspiration, I followed the manifesting process to a T. I made the vision board, I said my affirmations. I put positive thoughts out into the world, and I cleared away negative energy."

"But you don't have any sort of strategy to set you up for success."

"The book didn't say anything about strategizing."

"It was implied. Positive thinking is an important part of the process, but you can't expect the universe to just hand you things without working for them. It's a self-help book, not a magic spell."

Was Natasha so drunk she'd forgotten the conversation we'd had last week? "Those were the exact words you used. You said, *This book is like a magic spell.*"

"That was a figure of speech." She hiccupped. "Besides, a magic spell can only work if the conditions are right. So let's help you establish the perfect conditions. Pick a topic you'd like to focus on. It can be related to one of your special skills, or interests, or maybe a passion you've always wanted to pursue."

There was that word again: *passion.* "I don't have any passions or interests, and my only special skill is delivering food. I doubt that would be a lucrative Instagram niche."

"How can you say you have no passions or interests? That simply can't be true."

"It is."

Natasha shook her head. "Everyone has a passion. I remember you used to be so into reading. You always had your nose in a book. What about bookstagramming? I heard that's huge."

The sad truth was I hadn't read a book for pleasure in years. I'd started a few, but hardly ever made it past the first chapter. When I was a kid, I'd often curl up in the corner of the couch for hours, finish a whole novel in one sitting. Usually, my mom would be in the other corner, totally engrossed in a book of her own. It was a thing we did together, reading. Every night, same spot. A bond forged in mutual, satisfied silence.

After she died, though, it was hard to get back in the habit. I hadn't even wanted to sit on that couch anymore, let alone crack open a book. The only reading I'd ever done was assigned by my teachers, required for class.

If Natasha felt like Mom's death had extinguished the fire inside her, I felt like my fire had never even been ignited. Not properly, anyway. I'd been fourteen, still trying to figure out exactly who I was, what I liked, what I wanted out of life, and when she died, it was like I'd stopped trying. The burden of daily living zapped me of all my energy. There was nothing leftover to stoke the flames of a burgeoning passion.

So I kept my head down, did my schoolwork, and went to college. It was a path that had been laid out for me, an easy one to follow without thinking too much about it. It wasn't until much later, after I'd bombed out and accrued an absurd amount of debt, that I realized it was the wrong choice. A choice I'd made on autopilot. Like every other choice I'd made in my life.

"I don't know. Honestly, I haven't really read much since Mom died." My voice was heavy with unshed tears. "I've made so many mistakes in my life, Natasha, I don't even—"

"No." Natasha's eyes were like flint. All of a sudden, she sounded very sober. "We don't look back, Bree. That's not where we're going."

Instantly, I straightened, blinking until my vision was clear. My sister had no patience for self-pity or dwelling on the past. If I was looking for sympathy, I wouldn't find it here.

"Now," she continued, "if you want to be an Instagram influencer, then you can be an Instagram influencer. We will figure this out together. Give me your phone."

She held out a sopping wet hand and, without asking why, I placed my phone in it. After a few seconds of silent tapping and scrolling, she said, "Your new name is Bree by the Sea?"

I nodded.

"That's good, we can work with that. Focus on a laid-back, coastal vibe." More tapping and scrolling. "The photos are all right, but you can do better. Have you heard of Lightroom?" When I shook my head, she said, "It's a comprehensive photo editing app. It's got color correction, retouching, all that good stuff, but it's way better than the free apps you've been using. I'll install it for you, you can use my account for presets. What app are you using to generate hashtags?"

My blank stare was all the answer she needed.

Natasha spent the next twenty minutes applying everything she'd learned in Demi DiPalma's Instagram boot camp to my account. She installed apps and made tweaks to maximize discoverability, improve analytics, schedule posts for optimal engagement, and enhance the quality of my content.

The whole time, I kept wondering if being an influencer was something I actually wanted to do, or if it was just another one of those autopilot decisions. I'd spent so much time coveting the lives of random strangers on the internet—or, rather, the way they'd *portrayed* their lives—that it was all I could see when I closed my eyes.

"There." With a triumphant smile, Natasha handed her

phone back to me. "It's not a full-fledged strategy, but it's a very strong start."

"Thanks," I said, and I meant it. Even if I felt conflicted about the direction my life was taking, I was genuinely grateful to have Natasha's help in course correcting. "You're always saving my ass."

"It's my job." The corner of her mouth twitched, and for a moment, it seemed as if she might cry. Instead, she ran a hand over her now-bedraggled chignon and cleared her throat. "It's late and Izzy's got soccer in the morning. I should go to bed."

"Right. Me, too."

While Natasha killed the jets, I grabbed the empty wine bottle and glasses, and we headed inside, leaving puddles in our wake. A quick kiss good-night and we retired to our respective bedrooms. I enjoyed a long, luxurious rainfall shower before snuggling into the fluffy comfort of the pillow-top mattress. With the covers pulled up to my neck, I whipped out my phone to do a final presleep social media check.

No.

There was no way.

I refreshed my Instagram profile three times, just to make sure it wasn't some bizarre glitch. But every time, the same number showed up. It was real. It was amazing.

@breebythesea had 25,223 followers.

CHAPTER 16

The follower count changed everything.

When I woke up the next morning, all my posts had hundreds of likes. Some of them even had thousands. There were dozens of new comments, many of the generic "**Love your pics!** ♥" variety (which were, admittedly, nice to read), but also several requests for collaborations from various brands. And no random Kissy Face lip glosses or FRANGELICO shoes, either—most of these were brands I'd actually heard of. I said yes to every offer because how could I say no? This was what I'd said I'd wanted. It was time to welcome the abundance.

Of course, my payment for all these collaborations took the form of free products, which was great and everything, but it wasn't gonna pay the bills. So in the Lyft home from Natasha's on Sunday afternoon, I signed up for a full week of HandyMinion jobs.

I mowed lawns. I filed papers. I scrubbed toilets. Once, I woke up at 4:30 in the morning to wait in an hour-long line at the new PB Donut Shop before they sold out of those gourmet crullers that Eater.com had made famous. I performed each assignment with care and precision, and I earned five stars every single time.

I also got a text from Trey: **Whenever you're ready to paddle out, let me know...**

The truth was, I didn't feel ready, and I didn't know if I ever would. But I did want to get back out there in the water, to recapture that feeling of weightlessness and delight.

Plus, I wanted to know what the hell was going on with that article I read in *SurfBuzz*. Naturally, I wouldn't come right out and ask him, "Are you a rageaholic?" but I needed some sort of reassurance that he wasn't going to go all green and hulky at the slightest provocation. I decided to take a morning off of work to find out.

> How's Friday again? Same time, same place?

You got it. 👍

Midweek, the #collab packages started rolling in, so it was time for me to implement my newly updated and well-thought-out Instagram strategy.

Natasha had told me to focus on a "laid-back, coastal vibe," so I decided to stage all my photos at the beach. It wasn't quite a niche, but it was a theme, and that was good enough. My plan was to implement a content calendar, posting one picture per day at peak times of engagement as identified by the analytics app she'd installed. To use my time wisely, I would shoot photos in batches and edit them all at once, then schedule their uploads in advance.

Even though I intended to take all my photos at Law Street Beach, I was going to geotag them at different beaches around San Diego. Yes, it was another little lie, but it was an easy way to reach a wider audience. No one had to know I never actually went to Coronado Island or Oceanside Pier. For the most part, sand and surf looked the same in every town.

Late Wednesday afternoon, after a long day of scrubbing shower grout with a toothbrush, I slapped on a full face of makeup, blew out my hair, and dragged a big bag full of freebies to the beach. As I hustled down Beryl Street, eager to catch the golden hour for the brief period of perfect lighting, my phone buzzed with a text from Mari.

What're you up to rn? Got something for you.

Omw to Law Street Beach. Meet me there in 15?

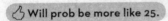 Will prob be more like 25.

Perfect. Instead of relying solely on precariously posed selfies, Mari could take a few full-body shots, too. I'd been worried about how to pose with those FRANGELICO shoes—turned out, in real life, they were pretty ugly—but a panoramic photo that minimized the shoes and maximized the setting would work wonders.

Hump day was busy as ever at the beach, with people lying on blankets, wading in the water, and jogging along the shore. Toward the far end, in the shadow of some big boulders, there was a fully dressed couple holding hands and leaning against a shopping cart filled to the brim with overstuffed bags. The beach was a haven for the homeless, and while the occasional uppity tourist complained to the lifeguards about their presence, for the most part, it was a place where everyone peacefully passed the time.

Like any good Instagrammer, though, I would have to pretend I was the only person here. That the beach was my private photo studio, with no other sign of human life for miles. I found a relatively untouched stretch of sand, well south of the lifeguard tower, and dropped my bag of collab goodies at my feet.

First up, I'd tackle the small nonwearable items, things I could hold in one hand while taking a photo with the other: a phone case, a tube of hand lotion, a bottle of kombucha. Those heavy-duty rubber gloves I'd worn all day did an excellent job of protecting my freshly painted manicure, an iridescent blue polish I'd chosen to go with my beachy theme.

I held up each item, angled correctly to get a good view of the label or pattern or whatever the brand manager asked me to feature, and I snapped a slew of photos. Some with waves in the background, some with sky. Then I put each product down in the sand, arranging shells and rocks around them in interesting patterns, and snapped some more. Sometimes, I included props of my own, like sunglasses and flip-flops. A particularly pretty piece of dried-out kelp accessorized the green tube of hand lotion nicely.

While setting the stage for the kombucha shoot, I spotted Mari trudging toward me over the sand, with a giant bag slung over one arm. She waved, smiling, but as she grew closer, her eyebrows knotted together.

"What's all this?" Leaning down, she picked up the kombucha and read the label out loud. "'Detox your adrenals with this powerful miracle elixir.' What does that even mean?"

"I don't know." Feeling instantly defensive, I snatched the bottle back.

Her eyes traveled from the kombucha to the hand lotion to the half a dozen other items spilling out of my tote bag. "Oh. This is one of those nano-influencer shoots, isn't it?"

"Technically, I'm not a nano-influencer anymore because I've gained more followers. I'm now a micro-influencer. But yes, it is a photoshoot."

"Are you getting paid to shill this crap?"

"It's not crap!" Well, not all of it was crap. That hand lotion was actually really luxurious. "And yes, I'm getting paid, if you count the free merchandise as payment."

"But you're not getting paid in actual cash?"

"No." With Mari's negative attitude, I wasn't sure if she'd be willing to help me get the photos I needed. But the sun was rapidly setting and there were only a few quality minutes of golden light left in the day. "Would you do me a really quick favor? I need a couple of full-body shots, but I can't get them on my own."

She smirked. "Will I be getting compensated for my photographic skills?"

"You can have these after I'm done modeling them." I pulled the FRANGELICO heels from my tote bag, and Mari made a dry-heaving noise.

"Those are the fugliest shoes I've ever seen."

"I know. I'm thinking maybe you could shoot them from far away."

"Like outer space?" She looked around the beach and

pointed at a cluster of large rocks in a secluded corner. "You could stand on a rock and I could shoot you from below."

"Good idea. Thanks." I wiggled out of my cover-up, so I was wearing nothing but a string bikini, then slipped on a pair of sunglasses and a wide-brimmed hat. Stepping into the shoes, I pointed my toe and said, "What do you think?"

With her eyes on my feet, Mari said, "I think you're lucky I love you, because this is utterly ridiculous."

After the shoes, I modeled a white T-shirt that said PLAY SLAY ROSÉ in huge black block letters, followed by a fairly nondescript cross-body bag. When we were all done, I put my cover-up back on and packed away my stuff. "Thanks so much, Mari. I really appreciate it." Nodding to the plastic bag she'd brought with her, I asked, "What's in there?"

"Oh, that's why I wanted to come by and see you. It's Rob's drone. I told you I'd return it."

"You didn't have to. He's never used it and it's not like he's coming back anytime soon. Wanna keep it?"

"Nah. That video didn't perform as well as I thought it would, so..." She dragged her toe back and forth through the sand, watching the patterns shift, avoiding eye contact. Clearly, she was still riding a wave of self-doubt.

"Are you working on anything else right now?" I asked.

"I haven't been feeling particularly inspired lately." I opened my mouth, but she interjected before I could get any words out. "If you're going to suggest I look to this Demi DiPalma woman for inspiration, it's a hard pass. You know, I googled her after we talked the other day. She's a scam artist."

Here we go again with the scams. "Look, I know her ideas seem a little out there, but—"

"They're a *lot* out there."

"That doesn't mean they don't have value."

"Demi DiPalma has no credentials whatsoever. She's not a certified life coach, she's a 'lifestyle guru.' There's a big difference. Actually, I'm pretty sure she was a social media manager for some marketing firm before she hit it big with her vlog, which should tell you something."

"It tells me that she's hardworking and ambitious and built a successful business from the ground up all by herself."

"Really? Because it tells *me* that she's good at manipulating people into giving her money. You know those Demi DiPalma–brand essential oils she sells on her website that she claims will help 'manifest abundance'?" She rolled her eyes, as if she couldn't stand how gullible some people were.

"That's pretty condescending, Mari. Even if you don't believe in it, it's not right to look down on someone who does."

"It's not about looking down on people. Believe whatever you wanna believe. But she charges a 50% markup on everything in her shop, simply because she slaps a label with her name on it. Her expensive 'boot camps' are a joke, too. They're really just glorified PowerPoint presentations filled with links to other sources on the internet. And don't get me started on the jade egg."

"What's the jade egg?"

With a sigh of disgust, she picked a stone up off the sand and held it aloft. "It's a four-hundred-dollar rock you stick in your vagina."

"Um…why?"

"According to your girl Demi, to 'detoxify negative sexual energy.'"

"It sounds like a yeast infection waiting to happen."

"Exactly." Mari squeezed the stone in her hand and took a

deep breath. "Look, I'm not saying that energy isn't real, and I'm not ragging on people who subscribe to that philosophy, either. If that works for you, then that's great. I just think it's pretty shitty to market a bunch of wildly overpriced items to people who are down on their luck or full of self-loathing or just plain desperate to change their lives. She takes advantage of people in their worst moments, and for that, she's a scammer."

I thought back to the very first sponsored post that showed up in my Instagram feed a couple of weeks earlier. In it, Demi DiPalma had asked if I was struggling to make ends meet, mere moments after I'd searched Google for a way to earn fast cash. Clearly, I'd been targeted, and then instantly directed to her website, where I could buy a "No Excuses" T-shirt for $39.99. So maybe Mari had a point.

Maybe I was being taken advantage of.

Then again, I'd made some big, positive changes in my life since I'd read *The Aspirational Action Plan*, hadn't I? I chucked Rob's crap out of my apartment, I started Bree by the Sea, I swam in the ocean with a hot surfer, for crying out loud!

"Fair enough," I said. "But it's not an all-or-nothing kind of thing. You can take the parts that work for you and leave the rest. I don't have to buy stuff from her shop to recognize that her ideas have merit."

"*Do* her ideas have merit?"

"Yes, of course!" Pointing to my bag of freebies, I said, "There's the evidence. My Instagram account is totally taking off, and it's all because I followed her advice." Desperate to prove my point, I whipped out my phone and showed her my Instagram profile. "See for yourself. Over twenty-five thousand followers."

Mari took my phone and studied my feed before casually flicking her thumb through my followers list. Then she handed it back to me and said, with an air of disgust, "They're all fake."

"What?" The air was suddenly sucked out of my lungs, but I tried very hard not to flinch. Of course I knew what she was talking about. The real question was, how did she know they were fake?

"They're all bots, Bree. It's obvious. Half of them have the same stupid profile photo." The smug sense of superiority on Mari's face made me feel like a total failure. "You think this kind of thing doesn't exist in the YouTube world? For twenty bucks, you can get a thousand subscribers. No savvy person actually does it, though, because it's completely fraudulent and destroys your credibility. Was this one of Demi DiPalma's brilliant ideas?"

"No, it was Natasha's idea."

"Wait, *Natasha* believes in this shit?" She furrowed her brow. "I'm surprised. She's so levelheaded."

"Yes, she's levelheaded, and yes, she believes in it because it's not fraudulent. It's a common practice that a lot of influencers use. A way to kick-start my career and—"

"Your career?" Mari laughed. "Bree, this is not a career. This is a scam."

"Everything's a scam to you."

"No, only scams are scams to me, and what you're doing is a scam. Not to mention, it's self-absorbed and shallow and fake. You're a better person than this. You could be pursuing something totally worthwhile—helping people in need, creating works of art, contributing to the world in some meaningful way—and instead, you choose to devote your time to shilling a bunch of crap to people who probably can't even afford it. Crap you don't even use yourself." She kicked my tote bag for emphasis, sending one of the FRANGELICO shoes rolling off into the sand.

She had a point. I would never wear these hideous shoes, so why was I trying to convince someone else to?

The sad fact is, I was doing it for the likes. I wanted the attention, the praise, the validation from someone—anyone, even random strangers on the internet. I wanted people to tell me I looked amazing, gorgeous, anything other than mediocre. I didn't even care if it was a lie, or if it was coming from a bot that was preprogrammed to spit out canned compliments on a regular schedule.

How pathetic.

On the other hand, who was Mari to judge me for my choices? After all, it's not like she devoted her life to feeding the homeless or saving the planet. She was trying to be a social media star, too.

A hot, molten anger built up in my chest until it erupted like a volcano over my tongue. "What are you doing that's so important and meaningful, then? You record yourself complaining and you upload it to YouTube. How is that a worthwhile pursuit?"

For a moment, she looked gutted, as if I'd plunged a dagger into the pit of her stomach. Then the hurt vanished and was immediately replaced with flared-nostril fury.

"I'm making people laugh," she said. "Real, actual people. Not bots I paid for in bulk. I'm giving them a piece of myself—a true, authentic piece of myself—and I'm not lying to them about who I am or what I do or what I like or don't like. And yeah, not everyone laughs. The comments I get aren't all fawning and flattering like yours are. But at least they're real."

As Mari turned her back on me and began to walk away, I had the sudden urge to lunge at her, wrap my arms around her waist, beg for her forgiveness. What I'd said was callous and hurtful, something she didn't deserve, especially not after all the hard work she'd put into her comedy over the years. I'd lashed out because I was feeling defensive. And I was feeling defensive because everything she said to me was true.

I didn't want to be an Instagram influencer. I wanted the influencer lifestyle—at least, the lifestyle as it was portrayed in the typical influencer feed. But it was all a carefully curated narrative. The lifestyle I coveted was a lie.

Before I could find my voice, Mari was already gone, walking briskly up the ramp toward Ocean Boulevard. In all our years of friendship, we'd never had a fight this bad, where one of us stormed off in anger. I needed to apologize to her, to make this right. But I'd wait until we both cooled off, and I could speak without shame strangling my vocal chords.

The sun was just disappearing beyond the horizon now. I stood still, staring at it, trying not to blink, anxious to catch a glimpse of the elusive green flash. Maybe if I wished hard enough, if I believed with all my heart, if I tuned my attention to the exact right frequency, then the universe would deliver it to me.

I watched until the last speck of light was extinguished, and the sky was nothing but an endless dusky blue expanse. No green flash. Time to pack it up and go home.

With my tote bag full of freebies hanging off of one arm and the plastic bag containing Rob's drone slung over the other, I plodded up the beach toward the street, feeling sorry for myself. Then I passed by the homeless couple and felt stupid for wallowing in self-pity. No matter how bad I had it, at least

I still had my apartment. It may have been shady and illegal and possibly in imminent risk of an electrical fire, but it was a roof over my head. A safe space with a bed and a minifridge and a box full of memories of my mom.

The couple propped a sign against their legs: Anything Helps. I didn't have any spare change or extra food to give them. But I did have all the stuff in these two bags.

I approached them with a smile on my face and placed the bags on the sand in front of them. "This is for you guys."

They looked at each other, then one of them peered inside the tote bag. She removed the bottle of kombucha and read the label out loud. "'Detox your adrenals.'"

"It's a health drink," I said. "At least, I think it is."

At the same time, her partner opened the plastic bag and removed the drone, turning it over in his hands. "What is this?"

"A camera drone." When he squinted in confusion, I added, "It works, I just don't need it anymore. I figured maybe you guys could sell it or something..."

As the words came out, I winced at my privilege. It was so easy for me to post something on Craigslist or eBay without a second thought. My ubiquitous internet access and permanent address were something I took for granted. I'd thought I was doing a good deed here, but were these two bags of crap actually going to help them, or was I simply adding to their already immense burden?

"I'm sorry," I said. "If you don't want this stuff, I can take it back. I didn't mean to give you a bunch of useless things."

"No," she said, still rooting around in the tote bag. "This is great. Thank you. We'll find a way to sell everything." She paused, then pulled out the shoes, inspecting them with a grimace. "Except maybe these."

"They're ugly, I know."

"Very."

Despite having shed two bags and ten pounds' worth of stuff, I left the beach feeling heavier than before. It took an enormous amount of effort just to press the crosswalk button at the corner of Mission Boulevard, where I waited for the traffic to come to a stop.

"Bree?"

A tall, lanky guy was suddenly standing beside me. He gave me this goofy smile, and when I didn't immediately say hi, he pointed at his chest, like I should already know who he was. Granted, he did look vaguely familiar, but so did half the people in Pacific Beach.

"It's Colton," he said. "From Doobie Den."

Ah, Doobie Den. Rob's old dispensary. I hadn't spent much time there—I'd tried to avoid visiting him on the job. Sometimes it couldn't be helped, though. Like whenever he forgot his wallet, which was disturbingly frequently.

Now that I had context, I recognized Colton. He was the guy who was always standing slack-jawed behind the glass case of pipes and bowls. Frankly, I was surprised he knew my name.

"Hi," I said.

"How's Rob?" Clearly, Colton hadn't gotten the memo.

"I wouldn't know. He's in Peru."

"Nah, man. He came back a while ago." He stood there, eyes glazed over, scratching his temple like it hurt him to think.

"No, he's still very much out of the country."

Colton shook his head. "Nah, he's in LA or something. I saw it on Instagram."

This guy had no idea what he was talking about. Rob had

deleted his Instagram before going to the Amazon, as part of the Divine Mother Shakti's technology ban. Still, he took his phone out of his back pocket to scroll through it, presumably looking for photographic evidence that Rob was, indeed, in Los Angeles. Annoyed as I was, it was also kind of funny to see the confusion on Colton's face as he searched for an account that no longer existed.

"Yeah, here he is."

He held his phone out so I could see the screen, which was tiled with square photographs of Rob. Except it was a better version of Rob than I'd known. This Rob had gotten a haircut and shaved off that scraggly chinstrap beard he'd been sporting for the past two years. His right arm was sleeved in brand-new tattoos, and he posed in front of iconic LA landmarks, like the Capitol Records Building and the Hollywood sign, gazing off into the distance, straining to appear introspective.

This Rob looked suspiciously like he was trying to be an Instagram model.

"What the fuck," I muttered, and something like understanding dawned on Colton's face.

"Oh, shit." He lowered his phone, eyes wide and fearful. "You guys broke up, didn't you?"

The light at the other end of the crosswalk flashed from a red hand to a white stick figure. Colton mumbled a half-hearted, "Sorry," then ducked his head and bolted across the street. As eager as I was to get home and process this discovery in solitude, I couldn't lift my feet off the ground. They felt nailed to the sidewalk.

The light flashed red again and cars sped up and flew past,

obscuring my already blurry vision. My head ached, straining to wrap itself around this new and bewildering information.

Rob was back in California.

And he was an Instagram model.

CHAPTER 17

@robmccrory_official.

That was his Instagram name. Not sure why he felt the need to append an "official," though. I doubt there was anyone trying to impersonate him. He did have a pretty big audience—over fifty thousand followers—but when I scrolled through the accounts, a bunch of them had the same profile picture. Seemed Rob knew how to pay for fake fans, too. And with his parents' money, he could afford to buy a lot of them.

I couldn't get over how good he looked, though. He'd started styling his hair and wearing nice (and probably free) clothes, and that permanent paunch he'd had ever since I'd known him was miraculously gone. In fact, he had a six-pack now. Apparently, he'd been doing a lot of crunches in the Amazon. Or maybe that only started once he got to LA. His Instagram account was only a month old, but who knew how long before that he'd been stateside? Whatever he'd done, it was clear he'd turned his life around, at least in the physical sense.

Other than his revamped appearance, it was hard to tell exactly what was going on, because the photos were typical curated Instagram perfection. Rob standing on Santa Monica Pier, modeling sunglasses. Rob hiking Runyon Canyon, modeling quick-dry shorts. Rob with his arm around a hot woman, both of them modeling swimsuits. Everything hashtagged #collab. A narrative crafted explicitly for likes.

Any question of where he was living or why he was in LA was answered as soon as I saw the photo of him lounging beside a sun-drenched infinity pool. The geotag simply said Brentwood, Los Angeles, but I knew he must've been at his parents' house. I'd never been there—I'd never even met his parents—but I'd seen pictures of and heard stories about that house, and specifically that pool. The endless, jobless summers he spent sunbathing there, possibly in that very same lounge chair. The booze-soaked parties he'd thrown in high school when his parents were away on yet another trip. I'd envied his carefree teenage experience, so different from my own.

Looking back on it, I suppose that was part of what had drawn me to him in the first place. After all those years I'd spent stressed-out in the wake of my mother's death, his blithe attitude was refreshing. Rob came from wealth, a degree of affluence I couldn't properly wrap my head around, so he wasn't tainted by those pervasive feelings of uncertainty and doubt, the fear that the rug could be pulled out from under you at any moment. His trust fund was more than a safety net; it was a crutch.

Of course, he couldn't get all of his money at once. It was doled out in monthly payments—his "stipend," as he referred to it. The payments were generous, far more than I was making as a GrubGetter. They would've been even higher had he chosen to stay in college, but against his parents' wishes, he'd dropped out of USC in the middle of his sophomore year and settled for a smaller payout so he could move down to PB and bum around aimlessly by the beach.

When I met Rob, he was in the midst of this postadolescent rebellion, rejecting his parents' posh lifestyle in favor of—as he called it—"slumming it," which entailed many months of smoking weed and couch surfing in various acquaintances' beach houses. Then, one night, he and I locked eyes across a crowded Garnet Street bar.

Coincidentally, that was the same night I'd puked in the Jack in the Box parking lot. After I caught my breath and wiped my chin, he took me by the hand and kissed me, despite how horrible I must have tasted. I immediately took him back to my apartment above the garage, and he stayed there for the next three years.

He didn't need to live in that apartment with me. He could've easily afforded to live somewhere nicer, somewhere legal with a full kitchen and a functioning electrical system. There was a part of me that hoped he might eventually decide to upgrade us both to a legit apartment, one I couldn't qualify for on my own with my shoddy credit score and irregular income. But he liked where we lived. He said it was "cool." Which, to him, meant it would absolutely horrify his parents.

I really liked having him around, though. A live-in boyfriend made me feel special, like I wasn't a total failure if I could snag a guy who wanted to share my bed every night. Plus, splitting the bills with him every month allowed me to (finally) start making payments on my student loans. After he moved in, I stayed current on that debt. Until seven months ago, when he abruptly decided our apartment wasn't "cool" after all and ditched me for the Divine Mother Shakti. Now he was back by his parents' pool, looking finer than ever, and I was merely a footnote in that poorly planned and best-forgotten phase of his early twenties.

Not to mention, I'd defaulted on my loans.

I hated him.

Though I really had no right to. He'd been honest with me about everything—who he was, where he came from, what he wanted, why he stayed. Deep down, I knew he was wrong for me, but in my desperation to be coupled up, I ignored all my misgivings. Instead, I imagined we were something that we weren't.

And where did that leave me? Standing on a street corner, scrolling through Rob's new-and-improved Instagram account, wondering if an ayahuasca trip through the Amazon might help me turn my sinking ship around, too.

Unfortunately, I didn't have a stipend to pay for a flight to Peru. So I tucked my phone away and walked home through a fog of frustration. Because it figured: just when I thought I'd finally gotten over Rob, declared him irrelevant and placed him firmly in my past, he came bounding back into the present day, stunting my progress with memories of his inertia.

When I reached the blue bungalow, I stopped, resting my hands on the white picket fence out of habit. On a normal day, I'd try to daydream away all my bad feelings by pretending this house was mine. But this wasn't a normal day. And I didn't want to pretend anymore.

Trey's wet suit hung from the eaves, swaying ever so slightly in the breeze. Through the sheer curtains hanging in the windows, I could see there was a light on, not in the front room, but somewhere in the back. Maybe the kitchen? I wasn't sure of the floor plan, since I'd never actually been inside the house. The tours I'd taken had all been imaginary.

In that moment, more than anything, I wanted something real.

My body moved so fast, my brain could hardly keep up. Before I could register what was happening, I opened the gate, walked down the front path, and pressed my fingertip to the doorbell.

Trey opened the door, and his smile flooded the front porch with light. "Hey there."

"Hey there." Now that I was here, I had no idea why, or what to say. This was awkward, wasn't it? Me, showing up unannounced and with no good reason.

Trey didn't seem to think it was awkward, though. He simply invited me in with a casual sweep of his arm. "Come on in."

This was it. My chance to see the inside of the home I'd lusted after for so many years. How many times had I refreshed the Airbnb page to study the photographs, or stood at the curb creating a fictional life for myself within these walls? In my fantasies, I'd crossed the threshold a thousand times. I didn't think it would ever happen in the real world.

And now it was.

In a way, I'd manifested my dreams.

I stepped into the foyer, and Trey closed the door behind me, asking simple questions I couldn't properly comprehend. Not because he wasn't being clear, but because I was too distracted. This foyer…it hadn't been part of the photo gallery. I didn't even know it was here. Cute hall tree, though.

"You okay?" Trey's look of concern snapped me back to reality.

"Yeah, totally fine. Sorry, I was just..." I waved my hand in the air, gesturing to the ceiling, the walls, the floor. "Taking it all in. I've only ever seen the inside of this place on Airbnb."

"Oh. Well, let me show you around." He stepped into the living room and I followed close behind. "It's nothing special, really. It's actually pretty small."

"It's lovely," I said.

But he wasn't lying. It *was* pretty small. A lot smaller than it looked in the photos. All the furnishings were there as I remembered them, but they were closer together than I had envisioned. The whole place was cramped.

Lovely, but cramped.

And now that I took a closer look, perhaps not quite as lovely as I initially thought. The couches were flat, not fluffy, and one of the cushions was stained with something that looked kind of like guacamole. The ash-wood floors were scuffed and scratched. There was a huge dust bunny under the coffee table, the top of which was covered in boxes of surf wax and what appeared to be a broken longboard fin.

"Ah, it's a bit of a mess right now." Trey followed my gaze and his cheeks went red. If he considered this messy, I was never letting him see my apartment. He might have had it condemned.

"Not at all," I said. "It looks a little different from the pictures on the website, though."

"Yeah, I hired a real estate photographer, some friend of a friend who knew how to angle the shots so the rooms looked nice and big." He shrugged. "I guess it's kind of deceptive, but no one ever complained the place was too small or anything."

"It's not too small, it's perfect. It's a hell of a lot bigger than my apartment, that's for sure." Of course, that wasn't saying much.

I crossed the room, peeking across the breakfast bar into the kitchen, checking out the stainless steel appliances, the rustic wood dining nook. All the details I'd seen online were accounted for.

So why did I feel like something was missing? It wasn't anything I could put my finger on, either. It was abstract and indiscernible, like a coat of shellac had been peeled away from every surface, every cabinet, every piece of furniture.

"Did you go swimming again?" Trey asked, eyes glinting. He remained lustrous, despite it all.

"No, why?"

He pointed to my legs, where grains of sand clung to my skin. "Looks like you came from the beach."

"Yeah, but I didn't go swimming." No way was I going to tell him what I'd really been doing: standing on a rock in fugly shoes, posing with a bottle of kombucha, picking a stupid fight with my best friend over buying fake followers. How ridiculous. I was embarrassed to even admit it to myself.

You know what my problem was? I spent too much time in my head. Wanting, wishing, dreaming, visualizing. I lived in worlds that didn't really exist, worlds I'd crafted from Instagram feeds or Airbnb listings or articles I read on SurfBuzz. com. I needed to spend more time in the real world, having real conversations with real people.

"I googled you."

Oh, shit. I didn't mean to say that out loud.

There was no unsaying it, though, and now I had to elaborate, since Trey was giving me major side-eye.

"Don't look at me that way," I said. "I told you, this is a normal part of human interaction."

Trey breathed deeply, blew it out slowly. "Okay, then. What did you find?"

"Lots of pictures of you and Shayla."

He cocked a brow, as if to say, *What else did you expect?*

"I also found an article. About what happened in Sydney."

His Adam's apple bobbed on a swallow. "'Cantu Can't Do.' That the one you're talking about?"

I nodded. "Look, I don't mean to pry, and I know this competition was in the past, but—"

"You *are* prying." His voice was suddenly cold. "And you're right, the competition was in the past. I'd like to leave it there."

This was a frosty side of Trey I'd never seen before. "There were some things in that article I found concerning. It raised some larger questions and—"

"It has nothing to do with you."

The temperature seemed to have plummeted all of a sudden. The air was so sharp, every breath stung my nostrils. Trey's ears were a shocking pink, his jaw muscles tensed. We were alone in a house together, and that article had everything to do with me.

"Are you a rageaholic?"

Instantly, his expression went from stony to stunned. "No. Geez. Is that what you—" He scrubbed a hand through his hair and winced like he was in pain. "It's that quote from Shayla, isn't it?"

"Yeah. I mean, look, if you need help and you're getting it, that's great. I just want to know the truth about what happened before and what's happening now." *And if I should be worried about anything happening in the future.*

With a heavy sigh, he collapsed on the couch, head in hands. I sat beside him, at arm's length. The guac stain sullied the space between us.

"She said it to make me look bad. Like I deserved what she did to me, cheating on me all those months." He looked up, out the front window, then in my eyes. "It wasn't true. I don't need 'help.' Not any more than anyone else needs it, anyway."

"Then what was up with the unsportsmanlike conduct and the screaming at the judges and the tweetstorm?"

"The unsportsmanlike conduct was an unfair call. When you're surfing in a tournament, you're at the mercy of the judges. What they say goes. But it's all subjective, and even though they say they don't play favorites, they do.

"Anyway, in this heat, they said I interfered with Zander's wave, but I didn't. He screwed up and made it look like it was my fault. This wasn't the first time he'd pulled something like that, either, and I could've contested it, but...I guess I'd just had enough."

His eyes drooped, all iciness gone, replaced with lukewarm detachment. Obviously, there was more to the situation than a couple of biased judges. Zander and Shayla were still dating, and as far as I knew, Zander was still competing in the tournament, still traveling the world, with Trey's ex-girlfriend on his arm.

Those were details I wasn't going to ask about, though, because in that sense, he was right, it had nothing to do with me. Still, I couldn't help but wonder, "Do you regret it? Now that you've been suspended from the competition."

He thought for a moment, then said, "Yes and no. I regret losing my cool, but I don't regret speaking the truth, even if the truth wound up getting twisted for clickbait." He shot me another quick side-eye, and my stomach clenched with guilt.

Suddenly, I realized my phone was still in my hand, my fingers locked around it as if it was a lifeline. I loosened my grip and tossed it on the coffee table, eager to distance myself from all these virtual worlds that didn't really exist.

"And," he continued, "I don't care about being disqualified since I was gonna quit anyway. My scores had been tanking all season, and it wasn't always because of favoritism. My head wasn't in the game. I needed...a break."

I slid a couple of inches closer to him, covering the guac stain. "You must've been under a lot of pressure. The competition at the pro level, I can't imagine how fierce it is."

"It wasn't the pressure that broke me. It was the posturing. Suddenly, my whole world was about maintaining an image. I wanted to live my life without every little movement being scrutinized. That's something Shayla never understood.

"So when they made the call to disqualify me, I didn't bother to fight it. I just packed up my board and came home." Trey's eyes danced around the room, surveying the exposed ceiling beams and pale blue walls. "It's weird calling this home, though. I've never actually lived here."

"You haven't?"

"Nah. Back when I won my first tournament, about four years ago, I used the money to buy this house as an investment property. As soon as I got the keys, I hired a decorator to make it look nice and popped it up on Airbnb. I figured I'd make a nice chunk of change renting it out and then come live here when I retired. Or maybe sell it for a profit. Never thought I'd be here now." Regret flashed in his eyes.

"Well, I'm glad you are." It was a bold move saying some-

thing that unabashedly earnest, but Trey rewarded my bravery with a smile.

"I'm glad I'm here, too."

The space between us on the couch grew smaller. We were
maybe a thigh's width apart by now. "You know, this is my
dream home."

Trey looked predictably confused. "It is?"

"It is. Sometimes, when I'm feeling really bummed out, I
like to stand outside by the fence and fantasize about what it
would be like to live here. It always makes me feel better."

Uh-oh. From the expression on Trey's face, I had clearly
gone too far in the oversharing department. His mouth
opened, slowly, like he wasn't quite sure what to say next.

"Bree." My name on his breath was golden. "You're one
of the most interesting people I've ever met."

I guffawed. That was the last thing I'd expected him to say.
"I assure you, I'm the opposite of interesting. In fact, a well-
respected professor once told me I was 'acutely mediocre.'"

"That professor's an asshole. Mediocre people don't conquer
a lifelong fear of the ocean by wading right into the oncoming
waves. They don't ask difficult, uncomfortable questions to
get at the truths they need to hear. They're more concerned
with looking cool than being real. You're the furthest thing
from mediocre, Bree. You're extraordinary."

Extraordinary.

That single word was better than any five-star rating I'd
ever received. Better than Level Ten Minion or Top Grubber
status. It was the abundance.

"My lips are feeling better," I said, my voice barely above a
whisper. "In case you were wondering. Totally healed."

Trey's mouth curved into a wry smile. "Good to know."

The space between us disappeared. I closed my eyes and tasted his salty-sweet lips, and as one big, strong hand reached up to cradle the back of my head, there was only one word to describe the sensation spreading through my body, across my skin, down to my bones.

Extraordinary.

CHAPTER 18

The bedroom exceeded expectations. While the rest of the bungalow may have lacked luster, everything contained within these four walls shined like a diamond. Though I'm pretty sure that glow had nothing to do with the furnishings and everything to do with Trey. His luminous body, his generous heart. He was simply incandescent.

That kiss he'd planted on my hand the other day was merely a taste of the pleasure to come. In his bedroom, there weren't just sparks; there were full-blown flames. His fingertips on my skin, his palms on my flesh, his mouth on mine—each touch was the strike of a match, building a heat within me I'd never felt before. He discovered nerve endings I didn't know existed, revived atrophied muscles, paid careful attention to parts of my body and soul I'd neglected for so long.

For the first time, I felt worshipped. Extraordinary.

Now it was the morning after, with sunlight melting through the translucent window shades and those newly discovered nerve endings still tingling. I felt spent from my lips to my toes. Used, in the very best way.

I'd awoken to find Trey missing, and my heart sagged. Even though I knew surfers often got up at the crack of dawn to catch the morning's first waves, it was still disappointing to find myself alone, without an explanatory note inviting me to make myself comfortable and assuring me he'd return as soon as he was done.

Then a clatter arose in the kitchen, the distinct sounds of a pan scraping the stovetop and a whisk whipping up batter. A loud sizzle, followed by the smell of buttery sweetness, and it finally hit me. Trey wasn't surfing. He was making me breakfast.

It was difficult to wrap my head around it, and the longer I lay there staring up at the ceiling fan, cocooned in what felt like trillion-thread-count sheets, the harder it was to believe. But this was happening. I was here, in my dream home, with my dream guy cooking me dream breakfast after an extended evening of dream sex. Sometimes, dreams do come true.

Trey's phone was propped in a charging stand on his night table like an alarm clock, the time visible on its screen: 7:35. Fortunately, my first job didn't start until nine. I had at least another hour to bask in this brilliance before returning to the colorless drag of reality.

The smells emanating from the kitchen grew stronger, and my salivary glands worked overtime. With all the distractions of the previous evening, I hadn't eaten dinner. Not that I'd minded, but now my stomach was angry and demanding compensation. I scanned the room for my clothes before remembering I'd abandoned my dress and bikini somewhere in the living room (we'd gotten things started on the couch). So I did that totally cliché thing you always see in movies, and wrapped myself up in a sheet, bunching the ends in one hand and holding it against my chest.

Man, this sheet was so soft. It put the linens on Natasha's guest bed to shame.

With quiet steps, I made my way down the hall, padding into the kitchen just as Trey turned away from the stove, holding a frying pan in one oven-mitt-covered hand. He smiled at me. "Good morning, beauty."

I smiled back. "Good morning yourself."

He was shirtless, gliding around the kitchen in boxers and bare feet. When he tilted the pan toward a serving dish, I gasped when I saw what slid out of it.

My reaction made him wince. "Do you not like French toast? If not, I can make you eggs or oatmeal or whatever else you'd like."

It took a second to find my voice. "No, I love French toast. It's my favorite breakfast food, actually."

"Good, because it's my specialty. I like to coat it in a coconut crust."

When Trey turned back to the stove, I pinched the fleshy inner part of my forearm, hard. The pain was sharp, and most definitely real, which meant I was wide-awake and standing in this room. This moment—the one I'd fantasized about just a couple of weeks ago, eating coconut-crusted French toast in this kitchen—was actually happening.

I had manifested my dream into a reality.

"Grab a seat." He motioned toward the breakfast bar, where he'd laid out two matching place settings, forks on the left, knives on the right. There was a carafe of orange juice beside a pitcher of maple syrup, and the creamer and sugar bowl were a matching set, with identical palm trees painted on the side. And now that I took a closer look, those same palm trees were also painted on the lips of the plates.

"Love the dinnerware." I tied a knot in the sheet to hold it in place, then slipped onto a stool as he poured steaming coffee into a palm-tree-embellished mug. "You're a regular Martha Stewart."

"Not really," he said. "My decorator picked it all out. Said it added charm to the Airbnb rental."

"Your decorator was correct." I held the coffee cup under my nose and took an intoxicating sniff. "This smells like heaven."

"It's Kona."

"Fancy." Kona coffee was grown exclusively on the Big Island of Hawaii, making it one of the most expensive—and delicious—coffees in the world. This was no economy-sized Folgers, like I stocked in my kitchenette. This was luxury.

"Do you ever think you'll move back to Hawaii?" I asked, as he flipped a piece of bread in the frying pan.

"Definitely in the future, but not for a while. A few months ago, my parents moved out to California—my dad had a job opportunity he couldn't pass up. They're in Orange County now, about an hour north of here. I love the island, but I wanna be near my parents, especially as they get older. You know what I mean?"

"Sure." I did, but I didn't. Aging parents were a concern I'd never have to deal with.

As if sensing where my mind had wandered, he asked, "Your sister lives in San Diego, right?"

"Yeah, in Encinitas."

"Is the rest of your family here, too?"

"Nope." I took a huge mouthful of coffee so I wouldn't have to elaborate. Nothing killed a cheerful, flirty moment like talking about your dead mom and absent father. I wasn't interested in making things awkward or uncomfortable. I simply wanted to enjoy the sex hangover.

Fortunately, there was a sudden buzzing sound coming from somewhere in the living room, distracting us both from the question at hand. I peered across the breakfast bar and saw my phone vibrating on the coffee table, its screen lit up with an incoming call.

"That's probably my sister," I said, making no move to get up from my stool. "She calls all the time, even though she knows I hate talking on the phone. I don't get why she can't send a text, instead."

"My mom is like that, too." Trey slid the final piece of French toast onto the serving platter. "She says it's because she needs to hear my voice. That's how she knows I'm okay."

I'd never thought of it that way, but as soon as Trey said the words, they rang true. It's not like Natasha didn't know how to text; she texted her friends and clients all the time. I'd seen her. Maybe she called me because she needed to know I was okay. After all, she was always telling me it was "her job" to take care of me, which usually translated to her saving my ass. Kind of like a substitute mom.

At once, I felt ashamed for ignoring her call, and guilty for giving her grief in the past. With one arm holding the sheet tightly to my chest, I hopped off my stool and crossed the room. By the time I reached my phone, it had already stopped buzzing, but when I checked my missed-call logs, it wasn't Natasha.

"I was wrong." I tossed the phone onto the couch beside my discarded bikini bottoms and returning to my spot at the counter. "It was some restricted number. Probably spam."

"I've been getting a lot of those lately." Trey pulled a silver shaker from a cupboard and dusted each slice of French toast with powdered sugar. Martha Stewart, indeed. He surveyed his tablescape, beaming, then looked at me. "Please, dig in, before it gets cold."

The first bite was rich, tender sweetness, a perfect balance of crisp crust and chewy dough. So much better than my usual breakfast of protein bars, or on occasion, store-brand Pop-Tarts. Licking syrup off my bottom lip, I said, "This is incredible. Where did you learn to make this?"

"Mostly trial and error, though I did borrow heavily from Alton Brown's recipe." He leaned in, as if letting me in on classified information, and whispered, "The secret is warmed honey."

"You're totally Martha Stewart."

The pride on his face couldn't be disguised. It was adorable. "Cooking is one of my hobbies. One of the perks of ditching the tour is that now I can spend more time in the kitchen."

I stuffed another massive bite of bread in my face. "What's on the menu for lunch? I might come back if it's as good as this."

"Unfortunately, I won't have time to cook any more today. I've got lessons lined up from ten until five with only a few twenty-minute breaks in between."

"Wow. SurfRack's really working you hard, huh?"

He shrugged. "They let me set my own schedule. I like

being out there all day, teaching other people to love the ocean." His eyes suddenly lit up. "Speaking of which, we're still on for tomorrow morning, right?"

"Absolutely. I'm working today from nine until six, but tomorrow morning, I'm all yours."

Trey's cheeks flushed a little, and with the cutest little nose-scrunch, he said, "You know, I feel like an asshole for not knowing this already, but what do you do for work?"

"Right now, I'm a HandyMinion."

"What's that?"

"Um, I guess you could say I'm sort of a handygal? I do whatever odd jobs people need me to do. Yard work, furniture assembly, housecleaning. That sort of thing." Shame and self-doubt cropped up instantaneously. "It's not very glamorous."

Trey raised an eyebrow. "Glamour's an illusion. Trust me."

I thought of all the #glamorous Instagrammers, their perfectly framed photographs, how easy it was to buy an audience. Were Shayla's followers bought in bulk, too? Was anyone really living out their #goals, or was it all an elaborate ruse?

"You're right," I said. "But I do wish I was doing something a little more fulfilling. Working toward a meaningful goal, instead of living task to task. I just don't know what that something should be."

"Well, what are you passionate about?"

Here we go again.

"Nothing," I said. "There is absolutely nothing I'm passionate about." He opened his mouth to respond but I held up my hand to stop him. "There isn't. I've tried so many times to figure out what my passion is, and I've always come up empty. I know that must seem crazy to someone like you, with such a serious passion for surfing."

"Oh, surfing isn't a passion." He swallowed a big bite of French toast and shook his head. "It's a way of life. My passion is actually teaching people to surf. Spreading that way of life to others."

Interesting. "How did you figure that out?"

"By doing it." He shrugged one shoulder. "It started out in Hawaii. A few years back, when I was on break from tour, one of my childhood friends opened a surf school in the touristy area. He was still getting it off the ground, so I taught a few lessons here and there, just to help him out. I didn't think I'd actually enjoy it, but I did. Watching someone ride their first wave...it's like I'm reliving that magic all over again."

His eyes got this faraway look, and he added, "I've never said this out loud, but one of my secret dreams is to start a surf school for kids in tough circumstances who don't have the money to pay for lessons. Like a nonprofit or something. I feel like getting those kids out in the ocean could change their lives forever."

"Wow. That's a really noble goal."

He shrugged again, finishing off the last of his breakfast. "It's not about being noble, it's about doing what's right. The world is an unfair place, and so much is out of our control. I like to think about what I can do to help level the playing field, even if it's something small."

Starting a surfing nonprofit to benefit underserved children didn't seem small by any stretch of the imagination, but Trey was nothing if not humble.

"Anyway," he continued, "that isn't my point. My point is that there's definitely something you're passionate about, even if you don't know what it is yet. Don't put too much pressure on yourself to figure it out, though. It's all about what makes you feel your feelings."

I nodded, but I wasn't totally convinced. Right about now, the only thing making me feel my feelings was the memory of last night. My insides went soft as I flashed back to scenes from the bedroom, and the urge to pin him against this breakfast bar overwhelmed me.

But before I could make a move, he was on his feet, dishes in hand. "We'd better get cracking so we're not late for work."

When I reached for the juice glasses, Trey chided me. "Leave cleanup to me. You go get dressed." Then he kissed my lips and started loading the dishwasher.

I studied the curve of his ass as he bent down to slide plates in the bottom rack and realized he was quite possibly the perfect man. He could cook, he could surf, he cared about disadvantaged kids, he knew his way around a California king bed *and* a dishwasher. Plus, he was patient and supportive, letting me move at my own pace without giving up on me—in both the bedroom and the ocean.

More than anything, he was genuine. Or at least, he seemed genuine. It would be easy to doubt him, easy to fear his intentions, but I was choosing to trust that he was who he appeared to be. Maybe this is what it meant to choose happy.

Because I certainly felt happy as I grabbed my bikini and dress and wandered into the bathroom. When I looked in the mirror on the back of the medicine cabinet, it was my own happy face smiling back at me. It was like that selfie I'd taken after Trey had saved me from the stingray. Another vision manifested into reality.

I emerged from the bathroom fully dressed, replacing the

sheet on his bed before returning to the living room, where Trey was straightening the pillows on his couch.

"Your phone was buzzing again," he said.

My call log showed another restricted number. "These spammers are out of control."

"Whatever you do, don't answer any unexpected calls from Slovenia. I did that once and wound up with a two-hundred-dollar charge on my phone bill."

Trey stood up and turned to me, caressing my upper arms while gazing into my eyes. "This was great. Thanks for coming over."

"Thanks for having me."

"You're welcome here anytime." His voice was a growl, so low and so close I could feel it in my chest. I sank my fingers into the thick, dark hair at the nape of his neck and his mouth touched mine and it was a struggle not to drag his perfect ass back to bed.

But I had a job to do, so when our lips parted, I reluctantly headed toward the door.

Trey followed closely behind. "I'll see you tomorrow, bright and early. I'd suggest we meet tonight after work, but you need a solid eight hours of sleep if you're gonna surf in the morning, and we both know that won't happen if we're together."

In the foyer, I slid my feet into my flip-flops, then spun around to plant another kiss on his pillowy lips. "You're right about that."

He wrapped his hands around my waist and pulled me toward him so our hips pressed together. "Does eight work for you?"

"Eight's perfect."

With a last kiss, we said our goodbyes, and I headed down

the path toward his picket fence with a smile on my face. After a night of phenomenal sex, it was hard not to feel like things were looking up.

Though they weren't looking up for everyone. Because as I walked the few feet home, I saw a car parked at the curb, a woman sleeping in the front seat, the back seat packed with what looked like all her worldly belongings. Trey was right, the world was an unfair place.

So what could I do to help level the playing field? I certainly didn't have the money to start a nonprofit, but maybe I could volunteer for one. When I got home from work, I'd search VolunteerMatch for an opportunity.

You know what I was not going to do? Waste another second of my time or energy on trying to become an Instagram influencer. In fact, I was tempted to delete my account altogether. It was self-absorbed and shallow and fake, just like Mari had said.

My brief foray into Instagramming had been completely misguided, and I couldn't allow it to drive a wedge between me and my best friend. I needed to fix this, immediately. As soon as I opened my front door, I flung myself onto the futon and whipped out my phone, ready to text and make up. But a notification from the HandyMinion app stopped my thumbs in midair:

Urgent Message for Minion BREE: Your worker account has been suspended.

CHAPTER 19

There must have been some mistake.

I'd passed the quiz during the onboarding process, and I knew what it took to be a good HandyMinion. I never swore on the job, I was polite to all my clients, I had a five-star average rating, for crying out loud! There was no reason my account should have been suspended.

But as I read the email waiting for me in my inbox, it became increasingly clear that this was not a mistake. This was intentional. It was happening. And I was totally screwed.

To: Bree Bozeman
From: HandyMinion Service—Do Not Reply
Subject: Account Suspension

This message serves to inform you that your HandyMinion worker account has been suspended until further notice. All

outstanding jobs have been reassigned to alternate Minions. Please contact support at the phone number listed below for more information.

It was salt in the wound to make me talk on the phone in this state. After waiting on hold for what seemed like an eternity, a human being finally came on the line to explain why I'd been ousted.

"Section 19g of the HandyMinion Terms of Service states that you shall keep your PayPal account active at all times to ensure timely compensation."

"My PayPal account is active." *Isn't it?*

"We received word this morning that your PayPal account has been frozen."

My heart launched into a complex gymnastics routine, using my ribs as a springboard to flip and twist and turn around my chest. "What? Why?"

"Ma'am, we're unauthorized to share additional details. You'll have to speak to a PayPal representative for more information."

One thought crossed my mind: hackers. Possibly the same Slovenian masterminds who'd scammed Trey out of two hundred dollars. They'd pay. They'd all pay!

Though right now, the only pay that really mattered was my own. "I don't understand why this has to impact my HandyMinion account. Why can't I continue to work while I sort this all out?"

The customer service representative continued in an apathetic, monotonous drawl. "Without a PayPal account, we have no way to disburse your earnings, ma'am."

"Can't you send me a paper check?"

There was a pause. Perhaps they were thinking it through.

As I mentally praised myself for being solution oriented and unconventional, they cut in with, "Ma'am, this is the twenty-first century."

So, that would be a no.

My heart was getting tired of bouncing around. It slowed to a steady, deafening beat that caused my eyes to water. Each *thump* brought a fresh wave of tears.

"What do I do now?"

"As I said, you'll need to contact PayPal, ma'am." This customer service rep had no sympathy for my wavering voice. To be fair, they probably dealt with people's personal crises all day long. I imagined, in a job like this, you had to shut down your emotions just to get through the day. "When PayPal has reinstated your account, you can go through the HandyMinion application process again."

"What do you mean, the application process? I'll still retain my existing account, right? Like, my rating and status will remain intact when this is all sorted out?"

An exasperated sigh came through the receiver, sounding strikingly similar to Natasha's. "You'll need to start over again, ma'am."

"Start over." The thumping in my chest deepened, growing louder, more insistent, rattling my whole body. "But why?"

"Section 15f of the HandyMinion Terms of Service states that all HandyMinions who lose their worker privileges must—"

That was it. I couldn't take any more corporate blather. My thumb slid to the end-call button and I immediately started scouring PayPal's website for a contact number, which they did not make very easy to find. After wading through several layers of FAQs, I unearthed a toll-free number, tapping the digits into my phone with trembling fingers. Several touch-tone menus stood between me and a human, but when I finally got her on the phone, I screamed, as if being assaulted, "My account has been hacked!"

Except it hadn't been hacked.

"We received a court order on May 15 requiring us to restrict access to your funds."

"You froze my account?" I couldn't believe what I was hearing. "Is that even legal?"

The rep didn't answer my question. There was typing in the background, fingertips slamming on keys. "I'm sending you an email with the details right now. You'll need to contact the plaintiff at the phone number provided."

"How can you do this?"

Another exasperated sigh. "Section 21b of the PayPal Terms of Service states—"

I didn't wait for her to finish. Instead, I hung up and opened my email, reading the details of the court order. Case number V-38472-SJ498H-2 had been filed yesterday in the US District Court for the Southern District of California, and the plaintiff was listed as EduLender, Inc.

Turns out you can't ignore your student loans for the better part of a year without there being some serious repercussions.

The universe had not sent positive energy to scrub away my debt. On the contrary, my debt had grown, snowballing into a terrifying monolith made of compound interest and late fees that threatened to squash my credit score beneath its bulk. Access to both my PayPal and my checking account had been restricted by this court order, and according to the unfriendly phone rep at EduLender, the only way to get it back was to speak to a lawyer. Not sure how they expected me to pay for a lawyer when they'd removed all access to my money, but I'm also not sure that they cared.

Fuck.

Remember when I said things were looking up? Scratch that. Things were down. Way down. If there were a floor below a subbasement, that's where I'd be, huddled in a dank, dark corner.

Where were those great golden beams of sunshine Demi DiPalma had talked about? I'd followed her manifesting process, I faked it all the way, but now my life was arguably worse than it was before I read *The Aspirational Action Plan*. Mari was right about that, too. Demi DiPalma was full of shit.

For the next few minutes (or possibly hours, it was hard to tell time in my pit of despair), I sat on the futon, staring into space, trying to pinpoint the exact moment my life became unmanageable. Maybe there was something inherently wrong with me. I'd always blamed my numerous failings on childhood traumas, my missing dad and dying mom, but the fact was, Natasha had been through those same traumatic events— even worse, she'd had to upend her whole life to take care of me!—and she turned out fine. More than fine, actually. She was close to perfect. Meanwhile, I couldn't even maintain an active HandyMinion account.

Then, as if sensing my struggle from clear across San Diego County, Natasha's name appeared on the screen of my buzzing phone.

Under normal circumstances, I'd have declined it. But I found myself thinking about what Trey had said, how his mom needed to hear his voice to know he was okay. And though I wasn't feeling particularly okay at the moment, surely I could fake it for Natasha. The woman had dropped out of college to be my substitute mother. The least I could do was offer her a little peace of mind.

Deep breath.

No crying.

I am a fierce, fearless warrior.

With a plastered-on smile, I shrieked, "Hi!"

"Wow, you sound perky. What's wrong?"

"Nothing!" My voice was about twelve octaves too high. I cleared my throat and tried again. "What's going on?" Still a bit shrill, but a definite improvement.

And it seemed to appease her because she took off chattering at full speed. "Well, my Instagram is blowing up. Lots of new followers—real followers—so I'm feeling like it might be time to start putting my long-term plan into motion."

"What's your long-term plan?"

"Getting a book deal." She said it as if I should have already known, as if book deals were so easy to come by. "I started writing a proposal centered around a highly specific organizing concept—how to maximize wall space beyond simple shelving. I'm talking door storage, pocket strips, command centers, the whole shebang."

"Cool." I had no idea what a pocket strip was, nor was I in the mood to ask. "That's great."

"Are you okay?"

"Yeah, totally." Oh, shit. I was warbling.

Natasha didn't buy it. "What's wrong? Tell me now."

I opened my mouth to assure her it was nothing, but instead this sad little whimper came out. There was no faking it now, no pretending everything was okay. My throat swelled and the tears flowed. "I've made so many mistakes."

Her breath crackled through the airwaves, irritated static. "What do I always say about not looking back, Bree?"

"I'm not looking back!" The words came out sharper than I'd intended, framed by sobs. "I'm looking right in front of me. And the outlook is grim, Natasha. It's really fucking grim."

"Okay, you're spiraling. Take a deep breath and shift your mindset. Try a positive affirmation from the back of the book. What about the whole 'fierce, fearless warrior' one?"

Affirmations, my ass. "My accounts were all frozen today. Bank, PayPal, everything."

"What? How did that happen?"

I was deeply ashamed to admit the truth. Natasha would never have gotten herself in a situation like this; she was too careful, too organized, too put-together. Her income and expenses were logged neatly in a spiral notebook with the words Budget Like a Boss stamped on the cover. She was current on all of her bills, with a credit score in the high eight hundreds. If she knew I'd shoved my past-due notices into a box and abandoned them in Rob's old storage unit, she'd be horrified.

But what choice did I have? Lying would do me no good. She'd see through it, anyway. I was not okay, and there was no convincing her otherwise.

"I stopped paying my student loans when Rob moved out. They issued some court order to put a hold on my assets, not that I have much for them to hold. The bigger problem is that I can't get paid, so I can't work, and now I have to talk to a lawyer and I can't afford that and…"

My words faded into whimpers. In a quiet, stoic voice, Natasha asked, "Where are you?"

"At home."

"I'll be there in twenty minutes."

She ended the call and I glanced around the room, instinctively feeling like I should straighten up before she arrived. The apartment was a wreck, as usual. Even the kitchenette, which I had cleaned so carefully, had reverted to its previous state of disorder and disrepair. Those pink peonies that had once looked so perfectly Instagrammable on the windowsill, the ones I'd taken as a sign from the universe of better days ahead, were now wilted and brown and dead. There wasn't much water left in the vase, and what remained was mucky, filled with fallen petals and slime. The perfect metaphor for my life. Always starting with high hopes, always ending with some unsightly mess.

I should've cleared it away, washed the vase, thrown the flowers in the trash. But I couldn't bring myself to get up off the futon. I'd rather deal with Natasha's criticism than exert the enormous amount of effort it would take to rise to my feet and cross the room. So I sat there, staring off into space again, and didn't move until I heard her knock at my front door.

Natasha burst in with a Tupperware full of leftovers— "Stuffed peppers! They're keto, but I swear they taste good"— and a plan of attack.

"One of Izzy's classmates, her mom is an attorney. She specializes in intellectual property law, but she has a friend who's a debt lawyer. I didn't even know that was a thing, but apparently, they handle all sorts of collections violations and bank lawsuits. They can even help you consolidate your student loans and reduce your overall interest. I sent her an email explaining the situation and I'm waiting to hear back."

"How much does she charge?"

She ignored my question, crossing the room to put the peppers in the minifridge. When she caught sight of the flowers, she froze. One fingertip grazed a shriveled bloom, sending petals cascading to the sill below.

"Were these peonies?" she asked. "It's hard to tell now that they're..."

"Yeah. I bought them for Instagram. I thought if I put a vase full of pretty pink flowers on my windowsill and took a picture, it would somehow change my life. Like I could wish my dreams into reality. So stupid."

She spun on her toes, hands on her hips, scowl on her face. "Don't say that. It's not stupid. It's true that you need a strategy, but the power of positive thinking is—"

"I have nothing, Natasha!" For the first time I could remember, my sister looked taken aback at my words. "I've been creating vision boards and clearing away negative energy and repeating these same, shitty affirmations over and over again. And none of it works for me. I'm a failure." I slumped forward, my spine as limp as the stems on those lifeless flowers. "I always have been, and I always will be."

At once, she was sitting beside me, my hands wrapped in hers, her eyes fixed on mine. "You are not a failure. Do you understand me?" She spoke sternly, but there was an undercurrent of doubt to her words. "You'll get through this. Let me loan you some money so you can get by until this whole thing is sorted out."

"We both know I'll never be able to pay you back."

"So don't pay me back. I don't need you to."

"And the debt lawyer. I'm assuming you plan to pay for that, too?"

Her silence was all the answer I needed.

"I can't let you."

"Yes, you can. Why are you fighting me on this?"

"Because." *Because you've already done more for me than you ever should have.*

"That's not an answer. Be honest, Bree. Do you really have any other choice?"

There was that question again. The last time she'd asked it, I watched my Civic get dragged away down the street, never to be seen again. I'd already lost my car, my job, my bank account. What would I lose next, my home? Probably.

Unless I chose not to.

"Can you drive me to a storage unit?"

Her face was a mask of worry. "Why? What does that have to do with anything?"

In a flash, I was opening the junk drawer. At least this much had stayed neat. Orange key ring in hand, I said, "Rob left some stuff behind at the StoreSmart in Mission Valley. It's *our* stuff," I quickly amended, knowing Natasha would never willfully take part in a storage unit heist. "We just didn't have the room for it here, and I forgot all about it once he moved out. I want to get it now and sell it for extra cash."

Yes, this was a complete one-eighty from my earlier stance. Stealing was wrong, and I knew I shouldn't do it, but I decided that I was okay with it now. Because even though I hated Rob, I was no longer fueled by spite or resentment. This was sheer desperation.

Besides, he was cavorting around LA, being Insta-famous and lounging by his parents' pool, while I was in serious danger of losing my home. He didn't care about all those pristine electronics collecting dust on the side of the freeway, and if he did, he could always buy more without a problem.

Frankly, this seemed to be the most logical choice. The best choice.

"Fine," she said. "But I need to be back in Encinitas by two thirty to pick Izzy up from school."

"I'll be quick."

We sped down the highway in Natasha's Audi, the ride so smooth and quiet, like the wheels were hovering an inch above the asphalt. "Do the back seats fold down?" I asked.

"Yes." She glanced at me sideways. "What exactly are you planning to bring home?"

"I'm not sure yet." *As much as I can fit in the car.*

She shifted in her seat. "Listen, the whole reason I called you this morning was to tell you about this thing I saw on Instagram."

Ugh. Instagram.

My stomach squeezed into a tight little ball, but I managed to keep a straight face. Natasha had just spent $250 to boost my following. How could I possibly tell her I was already so disgusted with the whole endeavor that I wanted to delete my account? I couldn't. So I didn't.

"This weekend," she continued, "there's this incredible event taking place in Palm Desert. Demi DiPalma's Semiannual Synergy Summit."

"I saw the ad for it. It costs twenty-five hundred dollars a ticket."

"Not anymore. The price was slashed in half. I guess not enough people signed up or something and they're trying to fill the spaces at the last minute. Anyway, I reviewed the agenda and there's a workshop on how to get your book published, given by Demi herself. She's so successful and so influential, if I could get my proposal in front of her, it could be huge. So I'm gonna go. The timing couldn't be more perfect since Al and Izzy are doing Daddy-Daughter Adventure Camp in Temecula this weekend."

"Cool." Truthfully, the idea sounded a bit far-fetched to me, but I wasn't going to doubt Natasha. She had a way of making the impossible seem possible.

"Why don't you come with me?" I shot her a death stare and she said, "My treat, obviously. There are going to be a lot of informative workshops and chat sessions. Maybe you could reset your intentions and get inspired again. Redefine your aspiration."

Ugh. Aspirations.

"I'm not sure I believe in anything Demi DiPalma has to say. You didn't achieve the things you did because of a vision board and some chanting. You achieved them because you're naturally organized, you had a strategy, you're smart and talented. You've got it all together."

Her knuckles grew white against the steering wheel. "It may seem that way, but I'm not as pulled-together as you may think I am."

"Well, you're more pulled-together than me."

She raised her eyebrows and gave a reluctant little grunt. It was kind of hard to argue with that.

"Don't you think she tries to sell ideas that are way too good to be true?" I asked. "Like that four-hundred-dollar jade egg she has on her website."

"Oh, the jade egg works. Trust me on that one. It was worth every penny."

Aggressively blocking the image of Al and Natasha detoxifying their negative sexual energy together, I pressed on. "But her whole business is based on taking advantage of people when they're down. Charging excessive amounts of money for things that aren't actually proven to be effective. Mari said she's a scammer."

"Mari?" She gave a condescending click of her tongue. "You know I love her, but she's been working in the same coffee shop now for a decade. She's not exactly the pinnacle of ambition."

I bristled. "She has a YouTube channel, too."

"Yeah, and it hasn't gone anywhere. She's exactly the same as she was when you met her. She hasn't evolved at all. I'm just saying, consider the source before you take someone's advice. Do you trust Mari's judgment more than you trust mine?"

That was a no-brainer. Of course I trusted Natasha's more. She was older, more experienced, had a stable job and family and luxury car.

"Even if you're still skeptical of Demi DiPalma," she continued, "the change of scenery will do you good. When was the last time you got out of San Diego?"

"I have no idea." Truly, I couldn't remember. Maybe some time in college? High school? I rarely had a reason to cross county lines.

"Then come with me. It could shift your mindset and potentially change your life." She added, as if it were an incentive, "Plus, there'll be plenty of Instagrammable moments."

Images of the event's website floated through my mind. The glamping tents, the farm-to-table dinners, the beautiful views of the desert. Opportunities like this were few and far between.

"Okay."

"Great." Natasha flipped her blinker and turned off the highway at Hotel Circle. "Because I already bought you a ticket."

CHAPTER 20

Natasha's car sagged under the weight of Rob's belongings. His snowboard, his PlayStation, his Oculus VR headset. I'd crammed it all in like some sort of packing engineer, not wanting to waste a single square inch of her interior. I even strapped his untouched Firewire surfboard to the roof rack.

"Did this stuff really belong to the both of you?" Natasha asked, her eyes slivers of doubt as I reached for a baseball jersey signed by Cody Bellinger. "I don't remember you ever being a Dodgers fan."

"I got into them while we were dating," I lied. "Rob gave this to me as a birthday gift."

Which reminded me, I should grab that yoga mat, too.

While doing a final sweep to see if there was anything else worth taking, my eyes fell upon my Bankers Box of old college memories. I had a sudden urge to throw it open and stomp on the contents, tear them to shreds, burn it until there was nothing left but cinders and ashes. Because college is what got me in this mess. The pursuit of higher education didn't improve my status or prospects. It had turned me into a desperate thief.

With one hand, I popped off the cover, revealing all those unpaid student loan bills I'd thrown in at the last minute. Maybe this debt lawyer would need to see them. I gathered the huge stack in my fist, then lowered the gate to the storage unit and made my way back to the car.

Natasha was already in the driver's seat, writing furiously in a spiral-bound notebook. When I slid into the passenger side, she slapped it closed. "Making last-minute tweaks to my book proposal," she said, answering a question I didn't ask. "It's amazing how quickly the ideas have been flowing. What's that?"

She pointed to the envelopes in my hand. Instinctively, I clutched them tighter, not wanting her to see, but it was pointless since she already knew the truth. I fanned them out, their faces stamped with angry red ink, screaming URGENT and PAST DUE and FINAL NOTICE.

Natasha gasped. "How long have you been ignoring these?"

"I told you, since Rob moved out." Though had it been longer? Even when he was around, I was never really on top of my bills, never quite sure of when I paid or how much. It was all too overwhelming, too many zeroes on my outstanding balance. And since I knew I would never, ever get ahead of my debt, I found it so much easier to fall behind.

"Why didn't you ask me for help?"

There was no good way for me to answer this, so I didn't. I just collected the envelopes into a neat little stack and stared out the window as we took off down the highway. Soon, we passed by Mission Bay, with all the enthusiastic outdoorsy people running and biking and swimming, but this time, I didn't feel envious. All I felt was deep fatigue. The need to go home and crawl into bed and never come out.

Natasha pulled her Audi down the alley behind the triplex, where we could unload by the garage door and take the back gate to get to my apartment. Not only did this save us time and steps, but it also helped me avoid the possibility of running into Trey out front. I wasn't in the mood to see him right now, not with thousands of dollars' worth of ill-gotten goods. He'd undoubtedly ask me why I had a surfboard if I was so afraid of the ocean, and then I'd have to fake my own death and move to Mexico to avoid admitting to him that I stole it from my ex-boyfriend's storage unit.

Although faking my own death and moving to Mexico sounded like a pretty sweet way to get me out of this crippling debt situation. I'd keep that in my back pocket in case this lawyer couldn't help me.

Natasha gave me a quick kiss and said she'd call me later with details about the weekend trip. "I'll drive us. I'm thinking we'll leave midmorning tomorrow but let me check the traffic forecast first."

As she walked out the door, I called, "Thanks for the ride!" and turned to face the massive pile of stolen property in the middle of my apartment floor. There was a moment's hesitation in which I second-guessed this decision. Technically, what I was about to do was illegal, and I already had one outstanding court case to deal with. Did I really want to bury myself deeper?

Then I remembered Rob's Instagram posts. His sleeve of tattoos and his brand-new six-pack. How he posed with a hot bikini model up in Brentwood. How he'd been "slumming it" down in PB with me.

That was all the motivation I needed to fire up the Craigslist app and start posting. I approached it methodically, carefully. There was a science to selling things on the internet; that much I'd learned from my stint as an influencer. I had to manipulate the photos, making the products look light and bright and flawless. I had to craft compelling copy, using keywords I knew people would be searching for. I had to develop a narrative for each posting—something to convince the buyer they didn't just want this item, they needed it.

Most important, I had to emphasize that these transactions were cash only. No Venmo or PayPal or anything else that could potentially be frozen by a court order.

The electronics all sold pretty quickly. Within minutes of posting the Oculus VR headset—"Hardly used! Still in original packaging!"—I'd had five requests and was even able to finagle a bit of a bidding war. Most of the items were sold to whomever could pick them up first, though. Since I was heading to Palm Desert the next morning, I wanted to clear out as much as possible before I left. I asked people to meet me outside, in the alley by the garage, so I wouldn't have to let any strangers into my house.

There was less demand for Rob's other stuff, though, which wasn't much of a surprise. No one wanted to buy a used snowboard in the middle of spring, and there were already so many surfboards for sale in this town, Rob's Firewire got lost in the crowd. To improve the chances of a sale, I changed the price, making it the cheapest available surfboard on Craigslist. It was probably too low, but frankly any cash was better than no cash, and my strategy worked, because moments later, my inbox lit up with a request. Someone named Dan-O would be swinging by this evening at around 7 p.m. with a crisp stack of twenties in hand.

The only item I didn't bother to post was an Italian-leather briefcase. It was in mint condition, wrapped in tissue paper and nestled into the original box. Google told me it was worth eight hundred dollars brand-new, but there was one little problem I hadn't noticed when I'd first grabbed it from the storage unit: a monogram burned into the leather—RJM for Robert Justin McCrory. Putting aside the obvious issue of low demand for a briefcase with someone else's initials, this would also be a definitive way to trace the item back to Rob, and therefore, me. Best to shove this back in storage whenever I got the chance.

Which was a big waste, really, because I was sure Rob never had any intention of using this briefcase. According to the card that was still taped to the inside of the box, it had been a high school graduation present from his father, who'd apparently envisioned his son proudly swinging this around the hallways of some Hollywood law firm. Rob told me his dad always wanted him to follow in his footsteps, but Rob didn't want to be an attorney. He didn't want to be anything, really. He was directionless and passionless, just like me.

In the end, that was the only thing Rob and I had in common: we were both aimless college dropouts, searching for meaning in a confusing and competitive world.

Even though I knew it was dangerous, even though I knew it was not where I was going, I closed my eyes and took a moment to look back. What if I had not allowed the criticism of a single bitter professor to decide my fate? What if I'd chosen to ignore him, to soldier on, to pick a major—any major—just to eke out a diploma and get a degree? So many more doors would've opened for me. So many more choices would've been available. I'd have a stable job, I'd live in a better apartment, I never would've wasted my time with Rob...

Though maybe that was just an excuse. After I dropped out, I could've easily chosen a different path besides GrubGetter and stoner boyfriend. A college degree was not a requirement to live a stable, happy life. Natasha was living proof of that.

My phone buzzed in my hand and I opened my eyes to see a YouTube notification on my screen.

Marisol Vega Hates Everything just uploaded a new video!

I tapped the notification to load the YouTube app. A still image of Mari filled my screen, her face contorted into a rehearsed cynical scowl, overlaid with the words: **SELF-HELP GURU...OR SCAM ARTIST?**

Oh, boy.

The video played, and there she was, sitting in her usual desk chair with an overstuffed bookshelf in the background. *The Hunger Games* was visible just over her left shoulder, the same copy she'd had since we were tweenagers, with a cracked spine and dog-eared pages. After all these years, she was still the same Mari. And, unlike Natasha, I didn't think that was such a bad thing. In fact, it was pretty great.

On my phone screen, she held up a stone—the same stone she'd picked up at the beach the other day. With a stern expression, she stared into the camera. "What if I told you this rock had magical healing powers? That it could manipulate the energy around you to improve your mental, physical, and emotional well-being? And what if I told you that to activate its powers, all you had to do was—" the camera quick-zoomed into her face here "—stick it in your vagina?"

I laughed so hard, I snorted.

"You'd probably tell me to get bent," she continued, tossing the stone to the side as the camera angle widened. "And you'd be right to do it. There are only two people whose advice you should take about what to stick in your vagina—your gyno and that very helpful store clerk at Déjà Vu Love Boutique. Yet every day, people are spending hundreds of dollars on vagina rocks peddled by self-help gurus—" she put air quotes around that phrase "—who have huge Instagram followings and no actual professional qualifications."

Mari steepled her fingers and leaned back in her chair, appearing to be lost in deep thought. "It really got me thinking, you know? Like, maybe I've been doing my life all wrong. All I do is record myself complaining and upload it to YouTube. What's the point of that? Who am I really helping?"

This sounded uncomfortably familiar. My tongue felt thick in my mouth, remembering our fight, the words I'd spat at her in anger and shame.

On the screen, she leaned forward again, a huge smile spreading on her face. "And that's when I realized—it's time for a change. I'm hopping on the self-help bandwagon and getting a piece of that sweet vagina-rock money. Say goodbye to YouTuber Marisol Vega, and say hello to Marisol Vega, lifestyle guru!"

For the next four minutes and twelve seconds, Mari ranted hilariously about overpriced essential oils and cultural appropriation, while deftly weaving in incisive commentary on our society's collective obsession with self-improvement and how it conflicted with our need for external validation. How we derived our self-worth from likes, follows, ratings, and stars instead of finding it within ourselves.

"I fall victim to it, too," she said, in a rare moment of on-camera vulnerability. "In fact, just the other day, I thought about quitting YouTube because my subscriber count has been at a standstill for weeks. And frankly, you people aren't always very nice to me in that comments section.

"But then I realized I'd be miserable if I quit. I love creating these videos, and I'm not gonna let anyone steal that joy from me. I'm just gonna keep striving to be better at this, to turn out the best work I possibly can. Because I'm all about self-improvement, but I'm not doing anything just for the likes."

It was the realest version of Mari I'd ever seen on YouTube. It was also my favorite of all her videos. By a long shot.

Our fight on the beach had been less than twenty-four hours ago, but it felt like it had been ages. We never went this long without corresponding; normally, we would've exchanged a dozen texts by this point in the day. It was time to put this disagreement behind us, so I whipped out my phone and made the first move.

> I just watched your video. It was amazing.
> Honestly, the best one you've ever done.
> No exaggeration.

Thanks. 😊
I wanted to try something a little different.
I was actually afraid you'd be mad at me.
Since I quoted you and everything...

> Not at all.
> You're 100% right.

> I'm sorry for everything I said.

So am I.
I hate being mad at you.

> Me, too.
> I love you.

I love you, too.
Now that we've buried the hatchet,
do you think I could borrow that drone again? Lol

> Um... I don't have it anymore.
> It's a long story.

Rob didn't come back for it, did he?

> Ha! Hell no.
> But I do have a funny/horrible Rob story to tell you.

Wanna hang out tomorrow & fill me in?

> Spending the weekend with Natasha.
> Let's catch up on Monday. ♥

There was no way in hell I was telling Mari where Natasha and I were actually spending the weekend. After watching that video, I felt extra ridiculous about even partaking in this charade. Even though I wasn't paying my own way, my presence alone would be a show of support for Demi DiPalma and her scam artistry.

The more I thought about it, the less I wanted to go to

Palm Desert. And, frankly, I didn't think Natasha should go, either. Everything she'd achieved had been because of her own hard work and strategic planning. She didn't need to fork over thousands of dollars to become a success, because she already was one. As for her book proposal, there must've been plenty of legitimate ways to pursue publication without going through Demi DiPalma.

I was so worked up about it, so replete with indignation, it drove me to do something completely out of character: I pulled up Natasha's number in my contacts list, and I pressed Call.

She answered on the second ring, her voice tight with concern. "Bree?"

"Yeah, hi."

"What is it, what's wrong?"

"Nothing, why?"

"What do you mean, why? Since when do you ever call me? You always decline my calls and tell me you hate talking on the phone." I opened my mouth to respond, but she interjected. "Anyway, I'm glad you called, because I was actually just about to call you. I got an email from Nazanin Ansary—she's the debt lawyer I was telling you about. I'll forward it on. Basically, she said she's out of town right now but she can meet with you first thing on Monday to help you get your accounts back."

"Wow. That's great, thanks."

"Her office is in Encinitas, so I figured if you wanna stay here on Sunday night, I can drive you there in the morning after I drop Izzy at school. We'll probably get back late on Sunday, anyway."

"Right. About that, I—"

But she didn't let me get a word in edgewise, launching forward into her plans for the next day. "I'm thinking I'll send a Lyft for you at, like, nine. Then we can hit the road at ten so we can arrive in time to settle into our tent before the introductory Passion Powwow."

"Okay. But don't you think—"

"Oh! And I forgot to mention, I just found out we got upgraded to an UltraLuxe tent. I'm not totally sure what that entails, but I know it's gonna be amazing. I really can't wait for this weekend. We've never spent time together like this, just the two of us."

I wasn't quite sure what she was talking about, because my entire adolescence consisted of time together, just the two of us. She must've been able to read my mind, because she quickly added, "I mean, I know there's been a lot of you-and-me time over the years, but there hasn't been much quality you-and-me time since you went away to college and I got married, and we've *never* taken a you-and-me vacation. This is gonna be really special."

Well, shit.

Clearly, this trip meant more to Natasha than I thought it did. It wasn't simply an overpriced self-help retreat in the Coachella Valley. It was a chance for sisterly bonding. Only a total asshole would suggest canceling now.

"I'm looking forward to it," I said, resolving myself to suck it up and deal. It was only two days in the desert.

Instead of goodbye, Natasha said, "They're going to have a hot tub, so don't forget to bring a bathing suit." Which reminded me I needed to pack a bag. I should've swiped that rolling Samsonite suitcase from Rob's storage unit when I had the chance.

As I tore through my closet in search of an old duffel bag I knew I'd used in college, my phone buzzed with a text message from Trey: **Meet outside at 8AM? I've got an extra board for you.**

Double shit.

With everything else going on today—and there was a whole lot of "else" going on—I'd forgotten all about my private surf lesson. This morning, Trey was all I could think about; now he was the furthest thing from my mind. I frantically tried to figure out a way to make it work, but if the Lyft was coming for me at nine, there was no way I could squeeze in a surf lesson beforehand.

> Trey, I am so sorry, but I won't be able to make it.
> Something came up with my sister. Totally last-minute.
> Need to be in Encinitas first thing.
> Will be there all weekend.

> No worries, I get it.
> Family first.

> Can I get a rain check? Next week?

> Absolutely. 👍
> Hope everything's ok with your sis.

Disappointment settled over me like a lead blanket. I wanted to get back in the water with Trey, more than anything. The highlight of my day—my week, my year!—had been waking up this morning in the house of my dreams, with the man of my dreams cooking me the breakfast of my dreams.

I couldn't deny there was power to all that creative visualization. Without it, I wouldn't have conquered my fear of the ocean, wouldn't have waded into the waves like a fierce, fearless warrior. I wouldn't have knocked on Trey's door last night, either.

Positive energy followed positive thoughts.

So I resolved to keep my thoughts positive this weekend, and make the most of this rare and precious time alone with my close-to-perfect big sister.

CHAPTER 21

The duffel bag wasn't in my closet. It was stuffed beneath my bed, crammed behind my box of memories in a dusty, wrinkled lump. When I straightened it out, a dust cloud exploded in my face, causing a series of violent sneezing fits. Worse still, I discovered a crucial seam had burst, so anything I put in the bag would promptly fall out the bottom.

As I kneeled on the ground, wondering if I could roll into this retreat with my belongings in a garbage bag, I remembered my junk drawer, and more important, the electrical tape I knew was inside. Good thing I'd held on to it. A few wide, overlapping strips mended the hole in the duffel quite nicely. It certainly wasn't #glamour or #goals, but I wasn't concerned with impressing anyone. Not anymore.

I did want to wear something nicer than my usual uniform of joggers and T-shirts, though, so I combed through my closet looking for outfits that would be appropriate for both farm-to-table dinners and chanting circles. Problem was, I didn't have much. My maxidress was an obvious choice, even though it was still a bit rumpled from spending last night on Trey's floor. There was a red body-con dress I'd worn exactly once, the night I met Rob on Garnet Street. Not exactly suitable for a retreat in the desert, but I tossed it in my bag, anyway; it'd be perfect negative energy to burn in the ceremonial firepit.

The most promising find was a cute romper with a strappy back in a flowery print. It almost reminded me of those pink peonies—before they died, of course. I'd bought it a while ago, an impulse purchase during a rare trip to Forever 21, but the price tags were still dangling from the sleeves. There weren't many opportunities for me to wear an outfit this adorable, but it seemed perfect for this weekend. Hopefully, it still fit.

I wiggled out of my clothes and stepped into the legs, hoisting the top of the romper up over my hips. As I attempted to slip my arms through the sleeves, the straps in the back got all tangled up, and I realized it was on backward. My boobs protruded awkwardly through the straps that were supposed to be stretched across my shoulder blades. I caught a glimpse of myself in the mirror hanging on the back of my closet door and couldn't help but laugh.

It was all very funny until someone knocked on the door.

A quick check of my phone revealed the time—6:38. Dan-O wasn't due to pick up the surfboard for another twenty minutes, and he'd told me he would text when he arrived. I'd explicitly asked him to stay outside, in the alley by the garage, not climb the stairs to my apartment and knock on my door. Why was it so impossible for people to follow simple instructions?

Well, I wasn't gonna answer the door, especially in this state, with my boobs hanging out of this romper like some sort of BDSM sub ready for a play party. With the dead bolt firmly in the locked position, I reached for my phone. I'd simply text Dan-O and tell him to go wait downstairs, like we'd *initially agreed upon.*

Except I didn't even have a chance to pull up his number, because all of a sudden, the room echoed with the distinct scratch of a key in a lock and I watched in horror as the dead bolt handle turned to the left.

What the hell was going on? Who even had an extra key? Was it my landlord? Had my Venmo payment for the rent not gone through because of this damn court order?

There was no time to think it through. As soon as the front door cracked open, I dove into my closet, seeking cover behind the narrow rack of clothes. Hangers went flying off the pole, fabric collapsing in a puddle at my feet. I clutched the bodice of my high school prom dress to my exposed chest— *why* did I still have my prom dress in here?—and tried in vain to quiet my heavy breaths.

With the closet door half-closed, I couldn't see who had entered the room. Hinges creaked, then tentative footsteps hit the laminate floor. One step, two steps, pause.

I tightened my throat, afraid the air going in and out of my lungs would give me away. Whoever it was gave a questioning hum—a distinctly male hum—and then the footsteps resumed. One step, two steps, no pause, oh, God, they were headed toward the closet. I grasped desperately for a weapon, any weapon, that platform shoe I hadn't worn since freshman year would do. With a rigid stance, I raised it up, prepared to gouge out an eye with this heel.

The footsteps stopped right outside the closet. I could see his shadow under the door, hear him clear his throat, smell his thick, skunky, familiar odor. It smelled remarkably like weed.

This motherfucker.

In a fit of unforeseen fury, I dropped the prom dress, shoe still in hand, and shoved the closet door open, throwing all my weight behind it. The force was enough to send Rob flying backward. He grunted, then lay there a moment, staring up at the ceiling. His reflexes had always been poor.

Finally, he sat forward, rubbing the back of his head. "Ow! What the fuck, Bree?"

"What do you mean, 'What the fuck?' I should be the one asking that question. What the fuck are you doing here?"

The asshole had the nerve to smile. "I'm home, baby."

I couldn't believe I hadn't made him hand over his keys. "This isn't your home. You left, remember? You said you were going to find yourself in the rainforest."

With some effort, he got to his feet, then his eyes bulged lecherously as he took in my outfit. "You getting into bondage now? I like it."

I was so angry I didn't bother to cover my boobs. I just pointed to the door. "Get out."

He ignored my demand, instead scanning the mess strewn around the apartment. "Yo, is that my surfboard?"

The lie came quick. "StoreSmart called me the other day and said I needed to empty out your storage unit or they'd auction it off. Said the bill hadn't been paid in three months."

"That doesn't make sense, it's on autopay out of my bank account. Why did they call you and not me?"

"You got rid of your phone before you went to the Amazon, remember? I'm assuming you got a new number now that you're back?"

He nodded, as if this made perfect sense, though in reality, I doubt Rob had been smart enough to list me as a backup contact for his storage unit. "Right."

"Why are you here?"

Rob's eyes got soft. Almost weepy, really. He took a step toward me and I backed up, instinctively lifting the shoe in my hand as a threat. *Don't come closer.*

A deep inhale, a dramatic exhale. "Because I miss you."

Well, that was unexpected.

I dropped the shoe on the floor at my feet, feeling cold and completely exposed. My eyes fell upon the box with the contents of my car. It had been living on the floor since Natasha brought it over. The hoodie sat on top; I snatched it up and quickly zipped it on over my backward romper. It smelled like mildew.

If Rob had returned three weeks ago telling me how much he missed me, I would've fallen into his open arms and forgotten about everything that had gone down. But things were different now. I was over him.

No, more than that. He repulsed me.

For the first time since he'd arrived, I took a good, long look at him. He didn't appear nearly as polished as he had in his Instagram photos. His hair was mussed, and his chinstrap was growing back, and his Pink Floyd T-shirt had a hole in it. From the bulge above his waistband, it seemed like his six-pack was gone, too.

Though maybe he never had a six-pack to begin with. Maybe his muscles had been digitally airbrushed. Another Insta-scam.

"If you missed me so much, then why didn't you call me when you landed in LA?" Rob opened his mouth, ready to protest, but I said, "I saw your Instagram, Rob. I know you've been back for quite some time."

He nodded, acknowledging defeat, then carelessly pushed aside the duffel bag and sat down on the bed. My clothes crumpled beneath his weight.

"In the rainforest," he said, fingers stroking his chin in an approximation of thoughtfulness, "I confronted some hard truths about myself. The Divine Mother Shakti told me that at the root of all my problems was my broken relationship with my parents. So I went back to LA with a fresh set of eyes and an open heart, prepared to focus one hundred percent of my energy on healing that relationship. That's why I couldn't call you. There wasn't enough space in my soul."

What a bunch of bullshit. "But there was enough space in your soul to start an influencer account?"

"That was a business move. It required a totally different soul energy."

I clasped my hands together tightly to keep from throttling him. "So, what now? You've healed things with your parents and now you want to heal things with me?"

"I didn't heal things with my parents." He picked at his ragged cuticles. His nails were bitten down to the quick, and for a second, I almost felt bad for him.

"What happened?"

"They started in on the whole college thing again, and I'm just not about that life, you know? It's like they want me to be someone I'm not."

I nodded, my sympathy growing. Sure, Rob came from money, but his parents weren't exactly warm and fuzzy. From what he'd told me, they were hardly ever around growing up, always distracted with work or social obligations or trips abroad without him. They didn't spend much quality time with him, getting to know him or nurturing his spirit. Which was probably why he turned out the way he did.

"But it made me realize how perfect you are for me," he continued. "You let me be who I am, and I let you be who you are. We don't try to change each other. We're so good together."

He stood up and walked toward me, one hand reaching out for mine. I didn't reach back. Instead, I wrapped my arms around my chest, holding myself for support.

"That's not a good thing," I said. "When you love someone, you should encourage them to aim high. Challenge them to be better."

A lazy smile spread across his unshaven face. "You don't need to be any better, baby. I think you're perfect just the way you are."

An endearing sentiment, if it hadn't been coming from Rob. "You told me living with me was 'slumming it.'"

He laughed, like this was all some big joke. "You know what I meant by that."

"No, I don't. Honestly, enlighten me, because—"

An incessant buzzing distracted me from finishing my sentence. I crossed the room, to where my phone sat amidst the clutter on my coffee table. The screen lit up with an incoming call from a 619 number I didn't recognize. I swiped it to voice mail, but then saw I'd received two text messages from the same number.

Hey, it's Dan-O. I'm here for the surfboard.

You home? I'm outside by the garage.

"Goddammit."

"What is it, baby?" Rob put a hand on my shoulder, which I instantly brushed away. I needed to get rid of Dan-O, immediately. My thumbs typed frantically, telling him there was a change of plans, that he couldn't have the surfboard tonight. But before I hit Send, there was a knock at the door.

Rob threw me an accusatory look. "Who's that?"

"I don't know." My high-pitched voice didn't sound particularly convincing to my own ears, but Rob seemed eager to play big hero man.

"Stay here." Slowly, he approached the front door, his fingers curled into a shaky fist. As he turned the knob, he cocked his arm, ready to throw the first punch. I flashed forward to our twin mug shots, taken later this evening, after we were arrested for a Craigslist bait-and-switch scam.

"Don't!" I yelled, at the exact moment Rob flung open the door.

Dan-O stood on the landing, his eyes filled with fear. He threw his hands up to shield his face. "I don't wanna hurt you man, I'm just here for the surfboard!"

Rob squinted, arm still cocked. "Yo, don't I know you from somewhere?"

Peering through his fingers, Dan-O studied Rob's face. Then he lowered his hands and said, "Didn't you work at Doobie Den?"

"Yeah. Oh, wait, now I remember. You always ordered the Afghan Kush. Dan-O, right?"

He sighed with relief and lowered his hands. "Right."

In one smooth movement, Rob transformed his fist into a high five, and these two had a touching reunion in my doorway, as if I wasn't standing there in a hoodie and a backward romper. "Good to see you, man."

"Same, same. Where you been?"

"Around. Did a little traveling down to South America, then LA for a while, and now I'm back in SD for good. Just talked to Colton, I'm gonna pick up a shift at the Den tomorrow."

"Just like old times."

"No doubt!" Rob laughed, overjoyed to begin his life again. The same life he'd been living before he'd gone to the Amazon in search of a change. So much for deep spiritual growth.

"So, where's the surfboard at?" Dan-O asked, rubbing his palms together.

The smile on Rob's face faded slightly. "What are you talking about?"

"The Firewire. From Craigslist." He peered over Rob's shoulder, spotting the board propped up against the wall. "That's the one from the picture, isn't it?"

Rob looked at the board, then back at Dan-O, then slowly, painfully, he turned his gaze toward me. Any hope I may have had that his pot-addled brain couldn't put two and two together was dashed as soon as he said, "That's the one, but it's not for sale."

Dan-O made a confused sound. "But, the ad—"

"Yeah, man. The ad was wrong." With a smarmy smile, he swung his gaze back toward Dan-O. "Big misunderstanding with my girlfriend."

"I'm not your girlfriend anymore," I said.

Dan-O looked from Rob to me with an expression halfway between confusion and terror. "Uh, okay."

"Sorry about that, man. Come in tomorrow and I'll hook

you up with some Sour Kush Kids." He extended his hand for another bro slap, before Dan-O hightailed it down the stairs. Then Rob spun around, a clarity on his face that I don't think I'd ever seen before. "You've been selling my shit?" When I didn't answer, he pressed on. "What else have you sold?"

"Some electronics."

"My PlayStation?" I nodded. "My Oculus?" I nodded again. "Even my camera drone?"

"No, I didn't sell that." Which was the truth; I'd given it away.

He raked his hands through his hair. "What the fuck, Bree?"

I knew what I did was wrong. I knew I should've said I was sorry and paved the way toward redemption. But in that moment, at the end of what felt like the longest day of my entire life, there was no remorse. Only resentment.

"You left! You just picked up and moved out without caring about how it would affect me."

"Last I checked, we weren't married. I'm twenty-eight, this is my time to go out and explore the world. I went on a journey to find myself."

"Well, you didn't find anything new. You're the same loser you always were."

"*I'm* the loser?" He gestured to the mess all around us. "I'm not the one selling my ex-boyfriend's shit on the internet to pay rent on some shithole apartment."

"Well, we don't all have Daddy's trust fund to pay our way through life. Some of us have to hustle to keep our heads above water." It was the first time I'd ever acknowledged his trust fund out loud. From the way his mouth hung open, I couldn't tell if he was shocked or shamefaced.

But the next words he spoke were pure fire. "You wanna talk about my father? Fine. Once he finds out what you did, I'm sure he'd be happy to see you in court."

My face burned thinking of his dad, the big Hollywood attorney. His money, his power. He could crush me like a bug.

Even if things were tense between him and his parents, even if they hadn't "healed their broken relationship," they'd always have their son's back. They still gave him money, still welcomed him into their Brentwood mansion every time he needed a soft place to land. The last thing I wanted to do was face them in court. I had enough legal woes at the moment.

"I'm sorry." The words were forced, strained, but they had to be said. "The stuff is gone now, though. I can't get it back. You can have all the money I made from it, but I don't have anything else to give you. I lost my job, my car died, and my bank accounts are all frozen. So I'm not sure what your dad would accomplish in court. Unless you want to throw me in jail."

I handed him the cash I'd accrued from the evening's sales, wondering what kind of sentence my crime carried, what kind of prison I'd end up in. How could I ever tell Natasha what I'd done? What I'd made her an accomplice to, without her knowing?

Rob pocketed the cash, then dug the heels of his hands into his eye sockets, as if trying to scrub away everything he'd seen. "No," he said, then dragged his palms upward over his forehead. "Of course I don't want to throw you in jail."

He moved toward the futon, then threw himself down, sending stacks of clutter tumbling toward the floor. On top of it all was a small padded envelope, the one my Kissy Face lip gloss had been delivered in. It was torn open and emptied out; I should've tossed it in the garbage last week, but like everything else in my life, I chose to throw it on top of an ever-growing mess and deal with it at some later, undetermined time.

Right now, Rob picked it up, turned it over in his hands. "Bree by the Sea," he said. "What's that?"

"It was a failed experiment."

"Instagram?"

I didn't answer. In retrospect, the whole thing was so stupid and embarrassing, I didn't want to acknowledge it had happened.

"Can I stay here tonight?"

At first, I thought he was joking. One look at his face, though, and it was clear he was a hundred percent serious. "No."

"Please?"

"Do you honestly think I'm going to have sex with you after everything that has happened? We didn't even have sex when we were together."

At least he had the courtesy to blush. "I'm not...that's not what I meant. I just need a place to stay tonight, that's all."

"Go to a hotel."

"I can't."

"Why not? There are a dozen hotels within a half-mile radius. Pick one, walk up to the front desk, and hand over your father's credit card."

"I don't have my father's credit card anymore." He started picking at his cuticles again. "My parents cut me off."

This should've been a sweet moment of schadenfreude. But there was no pleasure in seeing Rob slouching on my futon, with messed-up hair and chewed-up nails, his forehead streaked with worry lines. All I could see was a failed Instagrammer, a college dropout, a guy without a passion or a plan.

Plus, if he really wanted to, he could still send me to jail.

"Fine," I said. "I'm going to Palm Desert for the weekend, anyway. You can stay here while I'm away, but when I get back on Monday, you'd better be gone. Understood?"

He nodded, and I whipped out my phone to text Natasha: **Think you could send that Lyft to me now instead of tomorrow morning?**

Thirty seconds later, the phone rang. "Is everything okay?"

"Yeah, it's…" I glanced over at Rob, still holding that padded envelope in his hands, his expression vacant and altogether sad. "I'll explain when I get there."

"Hold on a second." There was a minute of silence, then, "Shaun, white Mazda. He'll be there in six minutes."

She hung up before I could say thanks. I sprinted to my bed and threw my clothes in the duffel bag. As I headed for the bathroom to grab toothpaste and a razor, Rob said, "When are you leaving?"

"A car is coming for me now." I tossed my toiletries in a Ziploc and chucked them on top of my clothes, then zipped it up and slipped on my flip-flops. All at once, I remembered I was still wearing this backward romper and mildewed hoodie, but I'd sort that all out once I got to Natasha's.

I grabbed my purse from where I'd thrown it on the floor, and as an afterthought, tossed my copy of *The Aspirational Action Plan* inside. Maybe I'd find a way to put it to good use this weekend. Like selling it secondhand.

With my hand on the doorknob, Rob asked, "Before you go, do you know where my bong is?"

"The six-foot one?" When he nodded, I said, "It's not here."

He cried out, horrified, as if I'd committed an act of murder. "You sold that, too?"

"No. I tried to, but no one wanted it. Someone swiped it when I left it on the street."

I slammed the door behind me, then made my way to the curb, where Shaun was already waiting in his white Mazda. As we drove away, I cast a longing glance at Trey's blue bungalow. There was a light on in the living room—now I knew for sure it was the living room. Then I closed my eyes and imagined myself curled up on the couch beside him. A quick, beautiful daydream to sustain me through the weekend.

CHAPTER 22

"I can't believe he had the balls to come back."

If Natasha was using the word *balls* before noon, it was a sure sign she was furious. She'd been ranting about Rob's balls, nerve, gall, and audacity almost nonstop since I showed up on her doorstep the night before. At first, I appreciated the solidarity. But now we were more than halfway through our journey to Palm Desert, and I was officially sick of rehashing it.

Eager to change the subject, I asked, "Did you ever figure out what the UltraLuxe tent upgrade is all about?"

She shook her head, eyes fixed firmly on the road. "I haven't had time. Why don't you check it out now? There's probably a description on the website."

I whipped out my phone, happy to finally see a full set of bars; cell service had been spotty on this trip. Before we entered another dead zone, I pulled up demidipalma.com and navigated to the Synergy Summit section. Under "Accommodations," there was a photo of the UltraLuxe tent. And it looked ultraluxurious.

"Wow, this tent is gorgeous," I said, zooming in to get a closer look. With hardwood floors and an en suite bathroom, it only vaguely resembled a tent.

"I think they said it was more of a yurt."

"Whatever it is, it's nicer than my apartment." There were two queen beds piled high with stacks of fluffy pillows. I could already envision myself curling up under that downy duvet, closing my eyes, and drifting off to the soundtrack of the desert. "We're gonna get such a good night's sleep."

"We're gonna have the best time." Natasha reached across the console and squeezed my hand. In profile, she was beaming. Happy to get away, to pursue her dreams, to spend time with me. I squeezed back, grateful for this opportunity.

My other hand buzzed. There was a notification on my phone, a DM from @kombucha_king, the brand of kombucha I'd posed with at Law Street Beach before deciding to trash this whole influencer idea.

Hi Bree by the Sea,

We hope you're enjoying your complimentary bottle of Krazy Adrenal Detox Kombucha! We're writing to remind you that, as per the influencer agreement you electronically signed on May 12, you are required to publish a sponsored Instagram post featuring a photo of the Krazy Adrenal Detox Kombucha, with the hashtags #kombuchaking, #kombuchadetox, and #peacelovekombucha, within seven days of receipt.

If you choose not to partake in our collaboration, please return the kombucha at your own expense as soon as possible. Failure to comply with our agreement may result in legal action.

Peace, love, and kombucha!
The Kombucha King Team

Legal action over a five-dollar bottle of kombucha? Peace and love, my ass.

"Goddammit."

I didn't realize I'd spoken the word out loud until Natasha asked me, "What's wrong?"

"Nothing. I just forgot to post something to Instagram."

"An ad for one of your collab partners?"

"Yeah." Though it was a pretty toxic partnership, since they were already threatening to sue me. A shiver went through me at the thought of another court order. And if Kombucha King was coming after me, then eventually the other brands would, too. The ugly shoes and the hand lotion and the phone case. I'd given all of it away to that couple on the beach, so I couldn't return them. @breebythesea couldn't die until I'd fulfilled my influencer obligations.

These past couple of days, I'd been ignoring my Instagram notifications, indifferent to the likes and comments that I'd once found so validating. Now I wondered if maybe I'd missed some other threatening message.

With a flick of my thumb, I scrolled through them, scanning for mentions of lawsuits or contracts. Among the hundreds of meaningless notes from my loyal bot followers was a comment from @vitalvineyards, that wine brand I'd tipsily tagged in a fake #collab post last week.

Under my beautiful photo of a Riesling and a hot tub, they posted a comment.

Thank you for the tag, and we're glad you're enjoying our wine! But we must make it clear: this post is not an official collaboration with Vital Vineyards, and this account is not an approved Instagram Partner.

Ugh. So much for faking it.

Eager to get my obligations over with as soon as possible, I returned to my home screen, ready to upload the first of several photos. An error message appeared: **couldn't refresh feed.** The bars on my phone were gone, replaced with a sad letter *X*.

"Shit," I said. "We drove back into a dead zone."

"Use the scheduler I installed. You can pick your photos and set filters and captions and tags and all that. As soon as you get service again, they'll post automatically."

I scrolled through my home screen, looking for the apps she'd installed last weekend, when we were sitting in the hot tub. Naturally, they were all neatly organized in a subfolder titled Instagram Helpers. I'd never actually gotten around to using any of them.

"InstaScheduler," I said, tapping the bright purple icon with an IS in the center. "You're a genius."

"Not really. It was featured in that Instagram boot camp I told you about. You should really take it, Bree. I can give you my log-in information."

"Maybe." I flashed back to what Mari told me about Demi DiPalma's so-called boot camps. She said they were overpriced scams with no original information, but Natasha had clearly learned a whole lot from hers.

That being said, I had no intention of taking it. Because as soon as I scheduled these collab posts, I was done with Instagram for good.

As I swiped through my photos, searching for a halfway decent shot of the Krazy Adrenal Detox Kombucha bottle, Natasha asked the question I'd been hoping to avoid. "So, how's the whole influencer thing going, anyway?"

Suddenly, my phone slipped from my grip, tumbling onto

the rubber mat at my feet. "Oops!" I bent over to pick it up, taking my time down there, trying to figure out the best way to answer. This wasn't the time to admit I was giving up on the influencer game. I'd tell her eventually, of course, but not now, before our extra-special sisterly bonding weekend.

For now, I'd keep my answers short. The less I said, the better.

"Good."

I popped back up, phone in hand, and resumed my swiping. But Natasha wasn't done with the questions. "Has the increased follower count helped you at all? Have you been able to grow any real followers organically?"

No. "It's been slow going."

"What about your metrics? Have you seen any improvement with your engagement?"

I have no idea what you're talking about. "I don't think so."

"It doesn't sound like you're taking this very seriously, Bree."

"It's not that I'm not serious. But the whole Instagram business model seems sort of arbitrary, doesn't it? You can spend lots of time researching hashtags and choosing your aesthetic and everything, but success is completely out of your control. You just have to hope the right person sees you at the right time. It all boils down to luck."

"Luck is what happens when preparation meets opportunity." Ah. Time for some aphorisms.

"I don't know what that means."

"Arm yourself with all the information you possibly can, come up with a solid strategy, and when the opportunity for success arises, it's yours for the taking."

"That seems awfully idealistic."

A serene, self-satisfied smile spread across her face, like she had all the answers and I was being needlessly combative. "Bree, I'll just say this—whether you think you can, or you think you can't—you're right."

She was probably right, but I'd heard enough pearls of wisdom for one morning. With an irritated sigh, I turned back to my phone and set upon the tedious task of scheduling these Instagram posts. Meanwhile, Natasha put on a podcast about tackling digital clutter. Forty minutes later, we pulled into a dirt parking lot for the Palm Desert Polo Club, where a large banner demanding we CHOOSE HAPPY pointed us in the direction of Demi DiPalma's Synergy Summit.

Any lingering tension dissipated the moment we stepped out of the car, swept away on the soft desert breeze. We pulled our bags from the trunk—Natasha had replaced my janky duffel with a LeSportsac tote the moment I'd arrived at her house—and headed toward the crowded registration table. After swiping Natasha's credit card ("for incidentals"), a chipper young woman named Saffron handed us thick welcome packets and gave us directions to our temporary home in tent #12. "Make a left at the saguaro. You're the third yurt on the right."

As we walked the path toward our tent or yurt or whatever it was, my chest felt all light and fluttery. I recalled the photo from the website, how luxurious it was, and felt the excitement grow inside me like a rising ocean swell. When we reached #12 and flung back the curtain that served as a door, though, all the excitement drained away with the force of a rip current.

The tent was tiny. And there was only one bed.

"This can't be it." Natasha backed out onto the path and waved at a woman holding a clipboard and a button that said

Official DiPalma Tribe Member. "Excuse me, I think we were assigned the wrong yurt. We were supposed to be up-graded to the UltraLuxe."

The woman gave my sister a withering look. "I don't work here."

"Oh, sorry." She pointed to the button affixed to her shirt. "I just saw that and assumed you were a staff member."

"They're giving these out to everyone. They're in the welcome packets." She glanced over our shoulders and into the tent. "That's gotta be the UltraLuxe, though. I'm in a standard and it's probably a third of the size."

The woman was right. After dragging our bags back to the registration desk, we were told that yes, tent #12 is indeed an UltraLuxe, and no, they did not have any availabilities with two separate beds. "The website clearly states that the photos are merely examples and actual furnishings may vary," Saffron said, in a decidedly less chipper tone.

Natasha's shoulders slumped slightly on the walk back to our tent-yurt, so I tried to cheer her up, giving her a playful nudge with my elbow. "We'll just have to cuddle extra close tonight."

She looked at me, eyes wide, a sad smile on her face. "Like we used to do."

It hadn't occurred to me before, but as soon as she said the words, I knew exactly what she meant. Memories rushed in like a flash flood: Natasha and I, snuggled together in my tiny twin bed, my damp face buried in the crook of her neck. We slept that way every night for about six weeks after our mom died. I'd been too afraid to sleep alone.

"At least this time, it's a queen-size bed," I said.

We pulled back the tent flap and surveyed the room again. "Actually, that looks more like a full."

The rest of the room was fine, if not exactly what I'd classify as "ultraluxurious." The floor consisted of some raw wooden planks covered in a threadbare Persian rug. The bed was not covered in fluffy pillows, as advertised. There was a distinct odor of sewage wafting in from the en suite bathroom, which looked suspiciously like a double-wide porta-potty.

There was a dresser, though, and a luggage rack, so while Natasha set to work unpacking, refolding, and organizing her clothes, I stretched out on the bed and reviewed the contents of the welcome packet: an Official DiPalma Tribe Member button, a PopSocket with the words "No Excuses" stamped in gold foil, an Official Synergy Summit Program, and about two dozen flyers advertising small businesses run by members of the "Tribe." In other words, every woman at this retreat.

Including Natasha.

"These are cute." I held up the Declutter with DeAngelis postcard, printed with a photo of Natasha above her Instagram handle and her "Choose Happy" catchphrase, which I now knew she'd borrowed from Demi DiPalma. On the other side, she'd written a short biography, in which she proclaimed herself, "Author of the upcoming book *Work Your Wall Space!*" But there was one sentence that threw me off balance.

"It says here you're a UCLA graduate."

She flinched ever so slightly, then resumed folding her underwear into careful thirds. When she spoke, her voice was low. "I *did* go there."

"Yeah, yeah. Of course." This was certainly not an issue I wanted to push, but Natasha was on the defensive.

"Like I said before, luck is where opportunity meets preparation." She placed her clothes inside the top drawer of the distressed wooden dresser and closed it with a little too much force. "Landing a book deal is extremely competitive. You have to be able to stand out in a crowd."

"Definitely." I regretted ever mentioning it. So what if Natasha told a little white lie? It's not like this was some official résumé. Besides, the "DiPalma Tribe" was all about faking it till you make it. Lying about having a college degree was the ultimate fake out.

Part of me wished I'd thought of doing that years ago. If I had, maybe my PayPal account wouldn't be frozen right now.

Natasha folded the luggage rack with a loud slap, then placed her suitcase on its side next to the dresser. "We should get going. The Passion Powwow started five minutes ago."

I made no move to get up off the bed, instead reaching for the program that listed the times and descriptions of every event so I could see what this Passion Powwow was all about. It was printed on page two.

Join us in the Hacienda courtyard for a chance to share your visions, affirm your goals, and elevate your energy levels. The perfect way to kick off your SYNERGIZING weekend in the desert!

Well, that didn't clear anything up.

But Natasha seemed pumped. She stood in front of the full-length floor mirror, fluffing out her hair and straightening her skirt. Her body was practically vibrating; any elevation in her energy levels, and she'd probably blow the roof off this shoddily constructed yurt.

It was hard to stay cynical when she smiled at me, though.

There was so much hope and desire and drive in her eyes. For her, I'd stay positive. And if energy really did follow thought, maybe I'd even find myself a passion at this powwow.

CHAPTER 23

In my humble opinion, the Passion Powwow was misnamed. It should've been called the Hashtag Hoedown because the entire space had been transformed into one giant Instagrammable experience.

There were multiple stations arranged explicitly for photo ops—balloon bouquets, step-and-repeat banners, life-size cutouts of Demi DiPalma, an eight-foot-tall Plexiglas champagne flute filled with plastic balls for "bubbles"—and judging by the number of phones pointing and snapping, they were all being put to good use. Signs were posted all around instructing Instagrammers to hashtag their posts with #synergysummit and #dipalmatribe—which would probably start trending, given how long the lines were. Hashtag, upload, repeat ad infinitum.

Here, the influencers were out in full force. People posed with handbags, furry boots, someone even had a curling iron, as if she were casually doing her hair in the open desert. When one woman in a paisley catsuit draped herself around the trunk of a Joshua tree, pouting and arching her neck, someone to my left sniggered. "Who does that girl think she is, Shayla Miller?"

The name was jarring, out of context, but it jogged my memory. Instantly, I remembered what Trey had told me yesterday morning as we filled our bellies with syrupy French toast: glamour's an illusion. Seeing all these influencers sucking in their stomachs, waiting their turns to take the same tired pictures against the same tired backdrops, made me realize he was right.

I pulled my phone out of my purse and texted him: **So bummed to miss out on our surf lesson this morning. Can we catch up on Monday night?**

As soon as I hit Send, Natasha was behind me, thrusting me in the direction of the step-and-repeat banner. "Go take a picture."

"No, I'm good."

She snatched my phone from my hand and gave her signature exasperated sigh. "You say you're having trouble growing an authentic following, but you're not taking advantage of crucial Instagrammable moments like these."

Rather than argue in a public space where anyone could livestream my business to the entire world, I complied with Natasha's request. In fact, I chose to make a fun game out of it, laughing and jumping and posing like a fool. There was a big bowl of glittery confetti on a table next to the banner, so I grabbed a great handful and tossed it in the air.

"That was perfect!" With a gleeful expression, Natasha

tapped at my screen, while I stared at the glitter being swept away on the desert breeze with a feeling of deep remorse.

"Do you think that confetti is eco-friendly?" I asked, but she simply handed my phone back and strolled away to schmooze with some other guests.

I wandered off toward the far end of the courtyard, where there was a massive spread of Demi DiPalma–brand items for sale, arranged artfully on tables. Journals, T-shirts, decals. A huge stack of books, including *The Aspirational Action Plan*. The jade egg was displayed on a pedestal, like the Hope Diamond.

Then there were the crystals and oils, the talismans to manifest abundance. I'd always been skeptical, but now that I was here, I had to admit there was something sort of magical about them. An energy that radiated off the table. It could've been all in my head, I guess, but wasn't every tangible thing in this world simply a reflection of our thoughts, our feelings, our sensory input?

It was a heavy thought. The kind of thought Rob would perseverate on for hours after he smoked too much Afghan Kush.

A woman stepped up to the display beside me and ran a finger over a smooth green stone. Back and forth, as if she was rubbing an oil lamp and hoping for a genie to appear. The movement mesmerized me, and she must have felt me staring, because suddenly her finger froze on the crystal and she turned toward me with wide, watchful eyes. Quickly, I looked down, feigning extreme interest in an essential oil diffuser.

"Excuse me," the woman said. "Aren't you Bree, from Bree by the Sea?"

I was floored. If a complete stranger recognized me from

Instagram, then perhaps my nano-influencing had been more effective than I thought. Is this what celebrities felt like?

"Yes." I smoothed a hand over my hair, trying desperately to play it cool. "That's me."

She smiled with her mouth closed, her lips pressed together firmly. Those lips looked familiar, or maybe it was the color. Sort of an iridescent puce.

"Hi," she said, extending her hand for a shake. "I'm Leanne Whitely, the owner of Kissy Face Lip Gloss."

"Oh. Nice to meet you." This was unusual, the CEO of a cosmetics company attending a desert retreat with the commoners. "Are you giving a presentation or running a workshop or something?"

"Me?" She laughed heartily, revealing a speck of Burgundy Wine on her front tooth. "No, no. I'm here to make some connections, spread the word about the brand. Your post was fabulous, by the way. Thanks so much for the collab."

"It was my pleasure," I said. "Please give my thanks to your social media manager for reaching out to me."

Another laugh, like I was the funniest person in the desert. "Sweetie, I'm the social media manager. And the manufacturer. And I package and ship and do all the other hundred-thousand things it takes to run a small business." She laughed again, but this time it was fainter, more resigned. "I'm still in the 'faking it' phase."

"Right." That explained why she chose me to advertise her product. I wasn't a nano-influencer. I was a nobody. "May I ask why you chose me to participate in your ad campaign?"

"Well, I was scrolling through the DiPalma Tribe's Instagram stories one night and saw they'd shared your photo. You said you were working through your *Aspirational Action*

Plan and manifesting your dreams, so I knew we were on the same journey. And when I clicked on your profile—" she gestured vaguely to my face "—obviously, you're gorgeous, and you'd posted this wonderful photo that looked like you were dreaming of a kiss. Naturally, I thought you were a perfect fit."

The photo in question was the one I'd taken right after Trey had delivered me home via piggyback. I really was dreaming of a kiss.

"Can I send you my newest color for another collab?" she asked. "It's called Grape Escape."

Looking at the earnest expression in Leanne's eyes, knowing how hard she must be working to achieve her dream, the kindest thing I could do right now was tell her the truth. "I sort of had an allergic reaction to your lip gloss."

"A rash?" I nodded and her face drooped. "Dammit. You're the third person to tell me that. There's something wrong with my formula." She dragged the palm of her hand across the back of her neck. "I just mixed up a whole new batch, too, and now I've gotta throw it away. What a huge waste of money."

I almost considered telling her the rash wasn't so bad, but that wouldn't have done her or her business any favors. "I'm sorry."

"It's not your fault. Obviously." Her fingers found the green stone again, stroking it as if it held the secret solution to all her problems. "My luck's been so bad lately. Maybe I should invest in one of these crystals to turn it around."

It was a small stone, no bigger than a golf ball. The sign beside it read "Green Aventurine, the 'stone of opportunity,' boosts creativity, wealth and prosperity. $199."

That was a costly little golf ball.

My thoughts went to Mari, how she said Demi DiPalma

was a scammer because she took advantage of people in desperate situations, people who were down on their luck and eager for a change. What would she do in this situation? Probably start chucking these crystals in the trash while shouting curse words at the top of her lungs. That wasn't really my style, but there was no way I was letting Leanne walk away without giving her an alternate perspective.

"My sister says that luck is what happens when preparation meets opportunity." I pointed to the sign, my fingernail tapping against the hefty price tag. "Maybe you'd be better off investing that money in preparing a new formula, so when a huge influencer wants to rep your brand, you can seize the moment."

It felt good to be the person doling out the advice instead of the one carelessly ignoring it. Unfortunately, Leanne didn't share my sense of satisfaction.

"I didn't ask for your opinion." She raised one manicured hand and waved it wildly, gesturing to my entire being. "You're giving off a lot of negative energy right now."

She whirled around in a lavender-scented cloud, her hair swishing in my face before she stalked away. Talk about negative energy.

This seemed as good a time as any to find Natasha, so I wove my way through the crowd of DiPalma disciples, all of whom appeared remarkably similar: white skin; thin frames; long, wavy hair painted with expensive-looking highlights. They all seemed vaguely familiar, like maybe I'd seen them on Instagram during one of my many leisurely scrolls.

After a moment of searching, I spotted Natasha standing beside a curtain of colored streamers hanging from a rolling clothes rack. Yet another manufactured photo op that looked ridiculous in real life but amazing on the internet. She was chattering away to two girls, and from the expressions on their faces—and the phones in their hands—they clearly wanted her to move out of the way so they could take a picture and move on to the next station.

As I approached, Natasha handed over one of her business cards, the ones with Choose Happy brush-lettered on the back. "If you ever feel you need some guidance on how to minimize your digital clutter in order to maximize your impact on Instagram, please give me a call. I do phone consultations!"

One of the girls took the card while the other one drawled, "Okay, thanks."

Natasha turned, catching sight of me instantly. She waved, smiling, and closed the gap between us. Over her shoulder, I saw the girls roll their eyes.

Bitches.

"Why do you look so surly?" she asked.

"People here are weird."

An exasperated sigh. "Stop being so negative." She pulled the program out of her purse and perused the schedule. "Look, there's a seminar in the pavilion now—The Four Pillars of Purposeful Power. Come with me."

While I would've preferred to collapse facedown on the bed and lose consciousness, this weekend was ostensibly about sisterly bonding, so I said, "Sure."

I followed along behind her, but I didn't make it very far before my phone buzzed with an incoming call. When I saw Trey's name splash across the screen, my body hummed with excitement. Sure, I hated talking on the phone, but this was *Trey*. I was hungry for the sound of his voice. So without

thinking it through, I told Natasha to go ahead without me—
"I'll meet you there in a minute!"—and swiped to answer.

"Hey there."

"Hey," he said. "Sorry to bother you at your sister's, I just wanted to hear your voice. How are you?"

The hum intensified. "No bother at all. I'm great. What's going on with you?"

"I'm on a break between lessons and I was thinking about what we talked about yesterday morning. About the nonprofit I want to start."

"Cool." I wound my way through the maze of photo ops, passing a woman posing with one arm wrapped around the cutout of Demi DiPalma while grasping *The Aspirational Action Plan* in her other hand. "Have you come up with some ideas?"

"Yeah, actually. I started googling around to see what kinds of organizations already—"

A series of shrieks ripped through the courtyard.

"What was that?" Trey asked.

"Nothing. Just some kids playing. I'm at the park with my niece. You know how it goes."

In reality, that eight-foot-tall champagne flute had toppled onto its side, sending hundreds of plastic balls flying across the courtyard. It didn't appear anyone had been seriously injured, or even mildly scraped, but the collective reaction was one of sheer terror. Women went running in every direction, as if the cheap plastic display was in danger of imminent explosion.

"Go on," I said, trying in vain to move past the mess.

"Okay. Well, I was thinking—"

More screaming. This time because someone tripped over

one of the runaway balls, taking down someone else's tripod, on top of which sat an expensive-looking ring light. The owner broke out in hysterics, dropping to her knees and cradling the equipment like a newborn baby.

This Passion Powwow was rapidly becoming the influencer equivalent of the Hindenburg disaster.

"Are you sure everything's okay over there?" Trey asked.

The frenzied chatter around me was at fever pitch. People were yelling about selfies and followers and broken phone screens. This was not playground conversation, and it wouldn't take long for Trey to catch on.

"Actually, you know what, I'm so sorry but this is a superbad time. I should really go. We'll talk when I get home, okay? I really want to hear all about your ideas."

"Sure, no problem."

There was a hint of disappointment in his voice, and I wanted to tell him to forget it, I was wrong, this was a great time to talk! But before I could form the words, he'd already ended the call.

What a disaster. Why hadn't I just sent him to voice mail?

I walked toward the exit in a fog of regret, so distracted I accidentally bumped into a woman taking a selfie next to a cactus. She lurched forward, narrowly missing a face-first collision with its spines. As she screeched, I held my hands up, ready to gush with apologies. Then she rounded on me, and I realized she was one of those girls who'd rolled her eyes at my sister.

"Watch where you're going!" she yelled.

For a moment, I considered shoving her straight into the cactus. Instead, I took a deep breath and thought of an insult that would sting far worse than the prick of those needles.

"I've seen you on Instagram, and your aesthetic sucks."

She let out a horrified gasp, and I walked away without looking back.

CHAPTER 24

The catastrophe of the Passion Powwow was soon forgotten, and the rest of the day rolled on in a cloud of chanting circles and chakra balancing, oddly juxtaposed with workshops on conscious financial investments and breaking through the glass ceiling in the workplace. It could've been an inspirational experience, except each session was capped off by an in-your-face sales pitch.

Need more help figuring out where to put your money in the stock market? Buy Demi DiPalma's *Guide to Women and Finance*.

Want to feel fierce and fearless when you walk into a job interview? Wear this underwear with NO EXCUSES printed along the butt.

Does your energy feel out of whack? Install a Demi DiPalma–brand infrared sauna in your home. Sign up for the payment plan today, and there's no interest for the next six months!

Credit cards were being swiped left and right. It made me wonder if this retreat was really designed to be restorative and educational, as advertised. The way I saw it, it was basically a pop-up shopping mall in the middle of the desert.

I didn't say anything about it, though. Mostly, I stayed quiet, letting Natasha chat up prospective connections while I hung in the background, trying not to emit too much negative energy.

Finally, at six o'clock, it was the moment I'd been waiting for: a sumptuous farm-to-table dinner. I changed into my romper (straps positioned correctly across my back, this time) while Natasha put on a gauzy, floral wrap dress, and we made our way to the Hacienda courtyard, which had been transformed into a beautiful outdoor dining space.

Picnic tables and benches were arranged in rows, beneath globe lights strung between freestanding poles. There were bottles of rosé sweating in silver buckets on every table, and each place setting was topped with a sprig of creosote. It was golden hour, and the surrounding saguaro and sagebrush created an ethereal atmosphere that was positively Instagrammable.

There'd be no hashtagging for me tonight, though, since I'd left my phone back in the tent, plugged into the charger. Natasha had huffed when I told her I'd be offline for the duration of our meal but didn't push the issue. By this point, I think she'd grown tired of telling me what to do.

We chose the last two open spaces at the end of a picnic table filled with chatty women, all of whom had that same vaguely familiar look about them. As soon as we slid into our seats, Natasha slipped easily into the conversation already in progress, sipping sparkling water and being her effervescent self. Meanwhile, I reached for the rosé.

Dishes were passed around family style: warm flatbread and sharp cheese; herbed salad with seared tuna; the most tender charbroiled steak I'd ever tasted. This meal was undoubtedly the highlight of the trip, a welcome change from my steady diet of ramen and protein bars. I savored every morsel, detaching myself from my surroundings. The conversation around me faded into an incomprehensible din. Though more than a few times, I did hear Natasha mention her business, her book proposal, how she was looking for a publisher.

While the waitstaff cleared our dinner dishes away, I wiped my mouth in anticipation of dessert. The crowd around me grew a bit louder, raucous but in a reserved kind of way. One woman a few seats down from us had clearly had more than her fair share of rosé, though, and her subtly slurred voice surged above the rest.

"I just want to say how amazing it is to be here with all of you strong, fierce, warrior women this weekend!" Wine sloshed over the top of her glass as she raised it above her head in a wobbly toast. Natasha and I shared an amused glance as the woman continued her drunken soliloquy.

"When I'm at home, I don't feel *seen*, do you know what I mean?" A couple of women murmured in agreement here. "I have dreams inside of me that are unmanifested and my husband just doesn't understand. But you ladies do. Because you're my tribe!"

There was sparse, halfhearted applause. Natasha kicked me under the table to silently ask, *Can you believe this is happening?* But I couldn't take my eyes off this woman, addressing complete strangers as if they were her closest friends. It was fascinating.

The longer I looked at her, the more familiar she became. Did I follow her on Instagram? No, I'd seen her in person before. Maybe I'd done a HandyMinion job for her. Or had I delivered her chicken?

It hit me at once, like a tidal wave. She had her hair down instead of in a messy bun, and she'd traded her No Excuses T-shirt for a peasant dress, but there was no mistaking it. This was Andrea T.

Eddie Trammel's wife.

My first instinct was to shield my face, not wanting to be recognized as the ditzy delivery girl whose piece-of-shit car broke down in her driveway. The woman who'd forgotten the chipotle ranch dressing, much to her husband's dismay. So I ducked down behind a large centerpiece covered in succulents.

"What are you doing?" Natasha whispered, not wanting to attract attention to my odd behavior.

Ignoring her, I peered at Andrea through two fleshy aloe leaves. She wasn't looking in my direction; she barely registered my presence. And it occurred to me that, even if she did, she wouldn't have recognized me. The rare customer who actually committed the face of their delivery person to memory could never place it out of context.

For example, I once ran into a regular Chicken Coop client at the beach—someone who ordered the same six-piece and biscuits every Friday night, like clockwork—and when I greeted her by name, she looked at me like I was a serial murderer, then ran in the other direction. It was like we existed on their doorsteps, or not at all.

A sad state of affairs, for sure, but in this moment, it

brought me great relief. I sat up, just as the waitstaff brought around dessert: grilled stone fruit shortcakes topped with fresh whipped cream. Under normal circumstances, I'd be in heaven. Now, I barely tasted it, my mind too consumed with the past, the present, my failures, my all-consuming mediocrity. How a weekend in the desert wasn't going to change any of that.

The woman to my left released a heavy breath, clearly tired of listening to Andrea T.'s boozed-up babble. In an effort to rein in the conversation, she said, "Has anyone else seen this video that's all over Twitter?"

Most everyone shook their heads, and someone asked, "What video?"

"Ugh, yes, I saw it!" Andrea groaned. "And I wish that girl would crawl back in the hole she came out of."

"What video?" Natasha asked this time, ever fearful of being out of the loop.

With a look of disgust, the woman next to me explained. "This girl was ranting about lifestyle gurus and how they're scam artists and how Demi DiPalma is, like, a fraud."

My ears pricked. "Are you talking about, 'Self-Help Guru or Scam Artist?'"

"I don't remember the name of it, but she spent, like, a ridiculous amount of time bad-mouthing the jade egg. But it's like, how can you judge something you've never even tried? So uneducated." She shook her head, deeply disappointed.

On the one hand, I was thrilled that Mari's video had gained enough momentum to be described as "all over Twitter." On the other hand, the women at this table didn't seem to understand what it was really all about.

"I think you're missing the point."

As soon as I opened my mouth, Natasha kicked me under the table again—this time, as a plea to stay quiet. But I couldn't.

"Actually," I continued, "she was probably trying to comment on how our desire for self-improvement makes us easy targets for people who want to take advantage of—"

"Demi should sue her!" Andrea piped up. "Take her for everything she's got!"

More furious kicking. My shins would be bright purple in the morning.

"Technically, she didn't mention Demi DiPalma by name," I said, "so I don't think there would be much of a case there. But I do think her perspective has merit, and it might be worthwhile to consider before we dismiss it out of hand."

The woman next to me seemed to be chewing on this thought, but Andrea snorted wetly, her mouth filled with a heaping scoop of shortcake. "Whatever. I'm not gonna take advice from that stupid loser."

That stupid loser?

At once, I lost all feeling in my lower legs and all sense of ladylike decorum.

"Her name is Marisol Vega, bitch, and she's more brilliant than you could ever hope to be."

Scandalized gasps erupted at the sound of the B word. Someone broke a wineglass at the other end of the table, and it was possible a vinyl record scratched somewhere in the distance. A beat of stunned silence, then another. Finally, Andrea spoke up, in a calm yet condescending tone. "You know, you're giving off a lot of negative energy right now, and I don't appreciate that."

Natasha launched herself off the bench and grabbed my wrist. Through her teeth, she snarled, "Let's go."

We marched back to the tent, my sister leading the way in stony silence. I couldn't recall her ever being this mad at me. When we were safely inside, she lowered the flap, tossed her purse on the bed, and spun around. "I can't believe you did this."

"Did what? Called someone out for insulting my friend? She was talking about Mari, you know that, right?"

"I know who she was talking about."

"And do you know who that woman is? Eddie Trammel's wife." At her blank stare, I said, "My old physics professor. The one who—"

"Oh, enough. I'm so tired of hearing about him. He's not the reason you dropped out of school, and you know it."

"What?"

"You dropped out because you can't make a decision to save your life. You're so afraid of making the wrong choices that you make no choices at all. You give up before you even get started. And then you wonder why your life is in the state it's in."

The words fell on me hard, like a brick being tossed out a twelve-story window. They left me dumbstruck and disgruntled. They hurt because they were true.

Five majors in three years. A complete inability to commit to a path. Afraid to try, afraid to fail. Opting for a swift emergency exit as soon as I had an excuse.

I wasn't mediocre, I wasn't passionless. I was afraid.

There was nothing to say in response. Natasha was right. But she wasn't finished.

"You've had opportunities I haven't, Bree, and you don't even appreciate them. You got into a great college, and you quit for no reason. I bought you all these followers for your Instagram account, and you're not even taking it seriously."

"That's different," I said. "This Instagram idea was totally misguided. It's not at all what I thought it was gonna be."

"So you're giving up on it." It wasn't a question, so I didn't give an answer. "Right. Fine, give up on another dream if you want to. But you're not the only one who has dreams, Bree. This is my dream. This—" she threw her arms wide, indicating the tent, the desert, maybe the whole world "—is my opportunity. I'm trying to make a good impression at this retreat, to get my ideas in the hands of the right people. Don't ruin this for me. Not again."

Again.

Her face flushed and she turned away, digging through her dresser drawer while I stood there trying not to cry. Never before had Natasha given any indication that dropping out of college to take care of me had ruined her life. But there it was, out in the open: Natasha saved my ass by sacrificing her dreams. And she resented me for it.

My insides felt shredded and raw. Silently, I pulled my pajamas from the LeSportsac tote bag—another prime example of Natasha saving my ass. I didn't wash my face or brush my teeth. I just changed and slithered under the covers, careful not to take up too much space.

Clinging to the edge of the mattress, I rolled over onto my side, facing away from my sister, a million light-years away from the days of us snuggling close together in my tiny twin bed.

CHAPTER 25

I slept horribly that night. Not only because of the silent tension in the air between Natasha and me, but because there was a new moon manifesting ceremony going on somewhere outside. People were chanting and singing, there were chimes and bowls and gongs. If Natasha heard it, she gave no indication. She barely moved the entire night.

After the ceremony, as the first light of dawn was breaking, I finally drifted off. When I awoke, Natasha was already gone, her side of the bed neatly straightened as if she hadn't been there at all. I glanced at my phone on the nightstand and saw it was already 10:30. According to the Synergy Summit program, I'd slept right through breakfast, which was a huge bummer, since lunch wasn't for another two and a half hours. I perused the schedule, searching in vain for snack breaks, and saw the book publishing workshop was going on right now. That must've been where Natasha was.

Hopefully, she was making good connections and would come away from this retreat with a book deal. Hopefully, I hadn't ruined things for her. Again.

The memories of last night were like a lead weight in my belly. We had never, ever argued with such vitriol. Sure, we'd had sisterly spats over the years, like that time she tried to surprise me into decluttering my apartment. By comparison, though, they were relatively inconsequential. The fight last night got to the meat of our relationship. It cut right to the bone.

Part of me wanted to pack up and go, to let her enjoy the rest of the weekend without me hanging around, mucking things up with my negative energy. But that would be needlessly dramatic, and actually make things worse. She'd worry, then come chasing after me, and wind up missing the rest of the trip she'd been so looking forward to. Which was essentially the story of our entire sisterhood. Best to stay here, lay low, keep my mouth shut.

Not that I regretted what I'd said last night. Andrea T. had it coming; the words "that stupid loser" still echoed in my ears. I scowled just thinking about it. Mari was smarter, more thoughtful, and more ambitious than anyone at that ridiculous retreat. Myself included.

But I was glad to hear her video had garnered some attention from the Twitterverse. Grabbing my phone, I pulled up YouTube to check how many views she'd gotten in the past two days and was completely blown away.

Over five hundred thousand. That was way more views than any of her other videos had ever achieved. Even ones that had been out for months rarely got above twenty-five thousand. And this had happened in less than forty-eight hours.

I texted her.

> Just saw your view count for the self-help vid and... HOLY SHIT!

I know. I kind of can't believe it.
YouTube put it on the Trending page!
I guess it struck a chord?

> Definitely! Some women here were talking about it last night!
> Apparently it blew up on Twitter?

Yeah a really popular comedian RT'd it!
Where are you btw?

> Okay, don't laugh and don't be mad.

???

> I'm at a Demi DiPalma retreat in Palm Desert.

Instantly, my phone buzzed in my hand with a call from Mari.

"I'm sorry," she said. "I know you hate talking on the phone, but I need more information and texting is not gonna cut it."

I told her the whole story: how Natasha had bought us these tickets, how I'd felt bad saying no, how I'd stayed awake all night listening to women screaming affirmations at the moonless sky. "Anyway, at dinner last night, a few women were... let's just say, less than enthused with your take on things. But there were a couple of others who seemed like they were giving it some serious thought."

"If I've convinced only one woman to refrain from putting an overpriced rock in her vagina, then I've done my job." I laughed, and she asked, "Hey, what was that funny-slash-horrible Rob story you wanted to tell me?"

The mention of Rob's name made my stomach cramp. "It's not funny anymore. Now it's just horrible. He's back."

"What?"

"Yeah, he showed up on my doorstep after I texted you Thursday night. He told me he wanted to get back together."

"I hope you told him to kiss your ass."

"I did, but it was a little complicated, since he caught me in the act of selling his stuff." Mari started to cheer, but I quickly added, "He actually threatened to sue me. Said he'd tell his dad and they'd see me in court."

"Oh, please. Like his father would waste his time on that. The man does multimillion-dollar deals, he's not gonna care that his son's ex-girlfriend sold his Xbox or whatever. It'd be cheaper and easier for him to just buy Rob new shit."

Mari made a good point. His parents seemed to express their love not so much with investments of time or effort, but with money.

Then again, they *had* cut him off.

"Well," she continued, "that explains what happened with the camera drone."

"No, actually. After you and I got into that fight, I realized how selfish and ridiculous I was being, and I wound up giving it away to this homeless couple I always see hanging out on the beach. I figured they could sell it for cash or something."

"Oh, that's Pete and Yasmin. They always come into The Bean House for free day-old pastries. Then I usually take whatever they don't eat down to the Community Resource Center on Mission Bay Drive."

"Wow. That's nice of you."

After a pause, she said, "Well, you know. They provide food and clothes and books to a lot of organizations in the neighborhood, like women's shelters and stuff. Sometimes when you're stuck in a place like that, a chocolate chip muffin can make your whole day."

"Of course." I often forgot that detail of Mari's history, the thirty days she'd spent living in a safe house with her mom, back when she was in kindergarten. She rarely spoke about it, and she was so well-adjusted, you'd never have known she had such a traumatic early childhood. But it was clearly something she'd never forget, something that inspired her to help the kids that were going through it now.

Maybe that was why she devoted her life to making other people laugh. Because her childhood was so devoid of laughter.

"Listen, let me know when you get home," she said. "Let's hang out. I miss your face."

"Miss your face, too. I'll be back in PB on Monday."

We hung up, and I hoped against hope that Rob would be gone by the time I got home. I didn't want him hanging around, filling my apartment with pot smoke and Cheetos dust. And I definitely didn't want Trey to see us together.

I considered texting Trey now, a quick "just saying hi" or something, but then decided that would be awkward in light of the way I'd rushed him off the phone yesterday. Thinking about it made my head hurt. I'd sort it all out later.

For now, I tossed my phone to the side, angry that we lived in a society where a rich kid from Brentwood got endless second chances and a storage unit full of untouched electronics, while the highlight of the day for a poor kid from an abusive home was a day-old chocolate chip muffin. Trey was right: the world was an unfair place.

And I was part of the problem, supporting charlatans like Demi DiPalma by lying around in a ramshackle luxurious tent-yurt that cost two grand a night.

What could've possibly justified the exorbitant cost of these lodgings? I supposed the private double-wide porta-potty wasn't cheap, even if it did make the whole space smell like a sewer. Still, we were posted up in a plot of dirt in the middle of nowhere, and nothing about this decor screamed "expensive." If anything, it screamed "appropriated," with a dream catcher over the bed and Tibetan prayer flags draped across the ceiling and a statue of the Lord Ganesha sitting on top of the dresser.

At least the food was good.

Just as I considered rolling out of bed to face the portable toilet, the entry flap to the tent flung backward and Natasha strode in, a stack of papers neatly tucked under one arm. Her face was a stone. She crossed the room and began rearranging items in her luggage. At no point did she acknowledge my presence.

I sat up and asked, "How did it go?"

She jammed the papers she'd held in her hand down into her bag, thrusting them with what seemed to be unnecessary force. Without looking at me, she said, "It wasn't what I thought it would be."

Uh-oh. If my big mouth got her in trouble, I'd never forgive myself. "Did you get a chance to chat with Demi Di-Palma? What did she say about your book?"

"Demi DiPalma wasn't there. They said she had a scheduling conflict and would only be available for the fire ceremony tonight." She took a deep breath, then smacked the top of her luggage closed. Finally, she looked at me. "Seems wrong, though, to plan a whole weekend for your followers and then not have the courtesy to show up when you said you would."

I nodded, hearing Mari's voice in my head. *It's because she's a scammer!*

"Anyway," Natasha continued, "she's supposed to do a meet and greet before the ceremony, so hopefully I can catch her then."

"Hopefully." I said it to be encouraging, but I wasn't optimistic. At this point, it wouldn't have surprised me if Demi DiPalma appeared only as a holographic image.

Natasha made her way back to the entrance to the tent. "I'm headed out to a demonstration on juice cleanses now, so I'll catch you later."

"Sure. See you at lunch?"

Natasha paused at the threshold but didn't answer. Then she walked out, dropping the tent flap behind her.

I flopped back down on the bed, staring at the prayer flags on the ceiling, trying to tamp down my rising nausea. So much for a special sisterly bonding retreat. I would've done us both a favor if I'd just stayed home.

Lunch was served buffet style, and it did not disappoint: chilled tomato-basil soup, miso-glazed salmon, portobello mushrooms stuffed with avocado and goat cheese. I searched the crowd for Natasha's face, but couldn't find her, so I took my plate of food back to the tent and ate in blissful silence in the middle of the bed.

That's where I stayed all afternoon. Even though I would've really liked to attend that journaling workshop and possibly check out that hot tub I'd heard so much about, I didn't dare leave the safety of the tent. It wasn't worth the risk of further aggravating the rift between me and Natasha. If I said the wrong thing to the wrong person, she might never forgive me. And given my current state of mind, I was definitely inclined to mouth off.

Shortly before dinner, Natasha returned to the tent. I pretended to be asleep while she got dressed and did her makeup because I couldn't bear the thought of another fight. When she left, my stomach rumbled, and I realized that as much as I wanted to continue to hide out all night, eating was a necessity. So I threw on my still-slightly-rumpled maxidress, grabbed my purse, and returned to the scene of last night's crime.

The tables were arranged with the same beautiful settings, sprigs of creosote replaced with sprays of peppergrass. At once, I heard the unmistakable cackle of Andrea T., already hitting the rosé and halfway to hosed.

Eager to avoid another run-in, I quickly turned away, only to spot Natasha already seated at a different, full table. She was perfectly primped and pretty, as always, but there was something slightly off. All this conversation was going on around her, and while she was making eye contact and nodding along, she wasn't talking as much as she normally would in situations like these. It was like she was dialed down a notch.

Be that as it may, she obviously didn't want to hang out

with me tonight, since she didn't save me a seat. So I found an open spot at a far table and slid into it without saying a word.

I didn't talk at all during dinner. I barely even heard what other people were talking about, either. Instead, I chose to focus entirely on my food. With the exception of tomorrow's breakfast, this was the last meal being offered at the retreat, and I intended to enjoy it. After this, I had a long life of ramen awaiting me.

Once we'd stuffed ourselves with caprese salad and mushroom risotto and grilled asparagus, the waitstaff came to pass around dessert. While waiting for my strawberry tartlet to be delivered, I tuned back in to the conversation around me.

"What are you burning?" one woman asked, referring to the fire ceremony scheduled to take place directly after dinner.

"My size 12 underwear," another woman replied. "I'll never be that big again!"

Considering I was a size 12, it was a struggle not to launch my dessert fork clear across the table like a trident and hit this lady right between the eyes.

"What about you?" It took a second to realize the woman to my left was directing the question at me. "What are you burning?"

"Oh." Despite my growing skepticism of the whole DiPalma movement, I was still drawn to the symbolic beauty of watching my old body-con dress go up in flames. "A reminder of my ex-boyfriend. The dress I wore on our first date, actually."

She smiled in solidarity. "I'm burning a gift from my ex, too."

As I devoured my tartlet, I wondered what Natasha was planning to burn, what kind of negative energy she saw standing in the way of her success. Aside from me and my negative energy, of course. I had a terrible vision of her tossing an old photo of us into the fire, and the very thought of it made my eyes prickle.

When the waitstaff appeared to clear away the tables, the group rose as one and started filing out toward the field where the fire ceremony was to take place.

It was dark. Not quite the blackness of midnight, but the sun had recently set, and with the absence of a moon to light the sky, the desert felt murky and ominous. Still, it was easy to see where we were supposed to go, because the fire glowed orange in the distance like a guiding light. As I approached, it grew brighter, more intense. The smoke was thick, and the scent clung to my hair and my skin. Wasn't a fire of this magnitude a hazard in the middle of an arid zone, with so much dry, flammable brush around?

Whatever. If these people wanted to burn down the desert with their fire ceremony, there was nothing I could do to stop them. Though it did make me think twice about chucking my dress on it. This thing was so cheaply made, it could serve as a fire accelerant.

A nervous energy buzzed among the crowd. Women clustered in small groups around the fire, clutching items to their chests, presumably their personal pieces of kindling. Natasha stood by herself, gazing into the fire. I walked up to her. "Hey."

She looked right at me, her eyes filled with something like sorrow. "I'm so sorry for what I said last night."

"It's okay, don't worry about that now." I rubbed her arm wrapped tightly around her book proposal. It trembled under my palm. "Demi DiPalma is gonna be out any minute, right? Just focus all your energy on talking to her about your book."

"Right." She breathed deeply, then choked a bit when the ash hit her lungs. "Right, that's what I'm here for."

"Exactly. We'll sort everything out later."

Truthfully, I didn't want to sort anything out. I wanted to pretend she'd never said what she'd said, to return cluelessly to the world we'd created where I was the screwed-up little sister and she was the responsible big sister who took pride in her role as the caretaker and didn't have a single regret about her choices in life.

That wouldn't be fair, though. To either of us.

A woman in glasses and a headset power walked through the crowd, yelling, "Can I have everyone's attention, please? Please quiet down for a moment so I can give instructions on how the fire ceremony will transpire."

The raucous chatter quieted to a hush, and the woman with the headset continued. "In a moment, Demi DiPalma will be joining us." A cheer erupted, then settled down immediately when the woman in the glasses raised her hands. "To ensure she has time to speak with everyone, we're going to form an orderly line. You will each have your moment to get a picture with Demi—remember to hashtag it #synergysummit and #dipalmatribe—before releasing your negative energy into the ceremonial fire. Please be considerate of your fellow Tribe members and keep the line moving at all times. Thank you."

After that touching and inspirational speech, several staff members began herding the amorphous group of women into a single row that snaked around the circumference of the fire. In front of me was Natasha; behind me was a woman so overcome with emotion, there were tears streaming down her cheeks. She clutched a rolling pin in one hand, holding it like a billy club. I hoped it was for burning and not for giving beatdowns.

Then, from the darkness, Demi DiPalma appeared. In her white-linen palazzo pants and matching tunic, she looked like some sort of goddess, radiating light and hope and comfort. Her black hair was stick-straight and sleek, her eyes blue and piercing, her skin glowing with the power of injectable fillers. She walked barefoot on the dirt, her hands clasped solemnly in front of her.

The crowd broke out in wild applause. Natasha clapped softly around her armful of papers. The woman with the rolling pin was sobbing uncontrollably.

Demi held up one hand, and silence ruled. "Hello, sweeties."

In unison, like well-trained schoolchildren, "Hello, Demi."

"I'm so honored to be here with you today, walking with you on this journey toward your truest selves. I hope this weekend has been an opportunity for you to connect with your Tribe and elevate your spirit, to dwell in possibility and inspiration. I hope you've spent time sending your desires out into the universe. Because now is the time to clear away the negative energy that is getting between you and your dreams."

"I love you, Demi!" The woman behind me held her rolling pin high, like a flashlight at a concert. Demi smiled with closed lips and nodded once to acknowledge her. Then she muttered something to the woman in the headset, and the line began to move forward.

Silently, we inched forward. I touched Natasha's shoulder in support, but she shook me off. "Sorry," she said. "I just need to concentrate. I'm rehearsing what I'm gonna say in my head."

"No problem."

This was unlike Natasha to be so nervous, but then again, she did hold Demi DiPalma in high regard. Meeting your idol, the person you've credited with changing your life, was a big deal. Even the most stolid person would probably freak out.

I watched as Demi greeted each person with a hug, a soothing pat on the back, and a smile for the camera, before directing them over to the fire. It didn't feel like they were meaningful encounters. In fact, it felt more like an assembly line. I bet the photos would look great on Instagram, though.

Finally, Natasha was up. Before she stepped forward, she turned to me, her face as vulnerable as I'd ever seen it. "Do I look okay?"

I took her in from head to toe: her wavy hair, her subtle makeup, her embroidered dress that was somehow both boho and professional at the same time. She was a work of art, my sister. A treasure.

"You look perfect," I said. And with the hint of a smile, she spun around and moved confidently toward the woman who changed her life.

CHAPTER 26

Demi DiPalma was close enough to touch. If the woman with the headset weren't creating a physical barrier with her body, I probably could've done it with ease. Not that I would have, because Natasha was standing beside her, beaming. I wasn't going to do anything to interrupt this moment.

"Hello, sweetie." Demi held out her arms and Natasha leaned tentatively into her embrace, holding her paperwork awkwardly off to one side. "How are you this evening?"

"I'm great." Her voice was wobbly and didn't sound very convincing. She cleared her throat and tried again. "First of all, I want to tell you that I'm a huge fan of your work and *The Aspirational Action Plan* literally changed my life."

She smiled and nodded, unsurprised by this outpouring of devotion.

"Anyway," Natasha continued, "I was wondering if—"

"Would you like a picture?"

Natasha flinched, totally thrown off by the request. "Um… sure."

"Saffron will take your phone." Demi pointed to the woman who'd helped us at the registration desk and was now standing at the ready as the event photographer. Natasha hesitated, then reached in her purse and handed it over.

"Say 'choose happy,'" Saffron said, snapping a photo of Natasha looking confused beside a beatific Demi. Then she handed back the phone and gestured to the fire, indicating that it was time to move along.

But Natasha wasn't giving up so easily. "Demi, there's something else… I have this book idea and I'm really interested in trying to get it published."

There was a momentary lapse in Demi's tranquil smile, the smallest slip in her blissful demeanor. A moment later, all was right again. "That's amazing, sweetie. Have you been following the manifesting process?"

"Yes, to a T. I created my vision board, I practice my affirmations every day, and I've opened my heart to receive the abundance."

"That's so perfect."

"Right." Natasha glanced nervously at the woman with the headset, then gestured toward the papers she was holding. "I was wondering, though, if you'd be willing to take a look at the proposal, just to let me know what you think."

Her eyes fell to the printed pages. With a laugh, she said, "I can't manifest your dreams, sweetie. Only you can."

"Yes, but since you're such a successful author, I was simply hoping you might—"

"Did you attend our publishing workshop earlier today?"

"I did. And I have to say, it was a little disappointing. They didn't talk about any of the practical steps you need to take to get from proposal to publication."

"Aha!" Demi's blue eyes widened, and she pointed a finger in Natasha's face. "That's the problem. You're too hung up on practicalities. Forget the practical, focus on the magical. Pretend your book is already published, and the universe will make it so."

"Well, I've written it in my manifesting journal and I've visualized it a million times. But it's not like a book deal is going to descend from the heavens, right? I need to actually do something to make it happen. So, I'm asking you, what did you do?"

"I wanted it. And that's what you need to do, too. You don't need to worry about the 'how.' You just need to want it more than you've wanted anything you've ever wanted in your whole life."

"I do want it." There was a tinge of annoyance to Natasha's voice. The pages of her book proposal trembled in her hands.

Demi shrugged, resigned, tired of this conversation. "I don't think you want it enough, sweetie. Because if you wanted it—*truly* wanted it, *truly* believed you deserved it—the universe would provide. Try my Prosperity Oil & Crystal Package, we're selling them at the marketplace this weekend. They'll help to anchor your energy and raise your vibrations so the universe can hear your desires more clearly."

With that, she cast a meaningful glance toward the woman with the headset, who approached Natasha with a, "Let's be respectful of our other Tribe members and allow them each to have their moment with Demi."

Before Natasha could lift her feet off the ground, the woman hustled her off to the side, crowding her out of the space so abruptly that her papers went flying out of her arms. The seconds slowed down as they went airborne, suspended against the night sky. And then, just as quickly, time sped back up, and the desert breeze swept them directly into the ceremonial fire.

Let's get real: this was by no means a tragedy. After all, these pages were merely printouts of documents Natasha had stored safely on her hard drive back at home. (Also, backed up in the cloud because she organized not only her physical spaces, but her virtual ones, too.) Still, it was hard to ignore the symbolism here. Her words, her sketches, her hard work, her original ideas. All of it instantaneously reduced to ash because she'd been strong-armed by one of Demi DiPalma's hired goons.

There was no question Natasha wanted to achieve her dreams, and in my eyes, there was no one who deserved it more. She was smart and determined. She tried, she strived, she hustled. And she always stayed positive and productive in the face of adversity. So if something she wanted was out of her reach, it wasn't because she lacked drive or desire or the right combination of crystals and oils. It was simply because we can't always get what we want, when we want it.

Sometimes, the cards just don't line up in our favor. Sometimes, we get dealt a shitty hand. Sometimes, luck never happens because there are no opportunities to prepare for. And choosing happy isn't always an option.

But for me, from that moment on, making a choice—any choice—was a necessity. Even if I wound up making the wrong choice, even if it didn't lead me on the path toward happy, it was better than giving up and allowing someone else to make my choices for me.

The woman in the headset motioned for me to step up, her

arms flailing impatiently, while Demi's face remained serene, smooth, expressionless. As I moved forward, I reached into my purse and pulled out my copy of *The Aspirational Action Plan*.

"We're not doing book signings right now, sweetie." Demi gazed at the book in my hands, contempt burning through those Botox-frozen eyebrows.

"I don't want it signed," I said. "I just have a quick question because *The Aspirational Action Plan* was such an inspiration to me."

That was the truth. The book *had* been inspirational. It made me aspire to goals I'd never dreamed possible. It made me believe in magic, at least temporarily.

She nodded, an invitation to proceed which I quickly accepted. "You say no dream is too big for any one person, and that the greatest obstacle to realizing that dream is your own negative energy. That if you want something enough, it'll be yours. Is that right?"

"Absolutely." Her voice was stiff and cold. "It's all laid out in the four-step manifesting process."

"Well, I was wondering, how can we harness this power to help people who really need it?"

She shook her head. "I don't understand the question."

"There are a lot of people who can't afford to come to a retreat like this who could really benefit from this sort of magical thinking. For example, there's a homeless couple in my neighborhood. Would you be willing to donate a Prosperity Package so they can manifest themselves an apartment?"

Through a tight smile, she said, "I'll speak to my merchandise coordinator to see what we can do."

"Great! And my best friend, she coordinates donations to a safe house for women escaping abusive relationships. A lot of them live there with their kids and it's a situation with a lot of negative energy all around. I was wondering, what kind of sacred cleansing ritual would you recommend for the shelter? You know, to help the women and children choose happy."

Suddenly, her smile disappeared.

I held *The Aspirational Action Plan* aloft. "There's surprisingly little action in this plan of yours. It's mostly empty promises."

Her eyes were icy slits. "I'm inspiring people to live their dreams."

"You're inspiring people to give you piles of money for products that don't do anything to actually help them." I turned to the line of women behind me. "How many of you struck it rich after investing in one of Demi DiPalma's Prosperity Packages?"

Not a single woman raised her hand. Some were scowling, while others had their phones out. A few seemed totally bewildered, like they couldn't believe I had the audacity to disrupt this faux spiritual event by running my big mouth.

Then Headset Lady started bearing down on me, and I knew my time was up. As she hustled me off to the side with her canned "Let's be respectful" line, I caught Natasha's eye. She was standing next to the fire, flames dancing in her pupils, corners of her mouth turned up triumphantly. It almost felt like she was proud of me. Either that, or she was plotting my death.

When I reached her side, I said, "Hi," worried that it might just be the latter.

Until she said, "Bree, that was extraordinary."

My whole heart surged with gratitude. For Natasha and her unyielding support. For Mari, who helped me to see the truth about others. For Trey, who helped me see the truth about myself. For my mistakes, for my failures, for the opportunities I'd had and the ones I'd yet to encounter. Mostly, I was grateful for the freedom to choose.

With a flick of my wrist, I tossed *The Aspirational Action Plan* into the fire, where it exploded in a flash of sparks.

Goodbye, negative energy.

"Let's get the hell out of here," I said.

"Good idea."

Natasha took my hand and led me toward our tent, where we packed our bags before leaving the desert behind.

CHAPTER 27

Nine thirty at night was late to get started on the road back to San Diego, but we certainly weren't going to hang around in our tent-yurt any longer than we had to. Something told me breakfast the next morning would've been supremely awkward had we stayed.

Fortunately, there was a twenty-four-hour Starbucks right next to the highway on-ramp, so we loaded up on venti flat whites with extra espresso shots. Then we tuned Natasha's XM radio to the Pop2K channel—the music of our childhood—and launched into our own little version of Carpool Karaoke. It was hard to stay sleepy while singing along to Outkast and Avril Lavigne at the top of our lungs. And when Natasha whipped out a pace-perfect rendition of "Thong Song," I nearly peed my pants.

Finally! The sisterly bonding experience we'd hoped for. Too bad it only got started on the ride home.

Of course, there was a restlessness beneath all that laughter. Neither of us had forgotten the words that had been spoken the night before, and as much as I wanted to, we weren't going to be able to ignore it forever. Eventually, we'd have to talk things through. For now, though, we would sing in our seats as we flew down the desert highway, enjoying this precious time alone together.

By the time we arrived back at Natasha's, it was after midnight. With Al and Izzy still away on their camping trip, her four-bedroom house was empty—the perfect setting for a private, gut-wrenching conversation. But our voices were hoarse from all those sing-alongs, and we were beyond emotionally drained from the events of the past forty-eight hours.

"Bed?" I asked.

"Bed," she replied.

Then she led the way upstairs. With a hug and a kiss, we parted ways on the landing, where Natasha went off to the master suite and I went off to the guest room.

Sleep came easy in that comfy bed without a bunch of people chanting fifty feet away from my pillow. I stretched out on the diagonal and drifted off, luxuriating in the silence and the space. It was a deep, relaxing slumber, and I probably would've slept a whole lot longer if the guest room didn't have an east-facing window.

In the morning, sunlight streamed in through the cracks in the blinds, brightening the room beyond my closed lids. All things considered, it wasn't a bad way to wake up. Certainly better than the thunderous boom of a garage door grinding open beneath me. This felt warm, like a snuggle.

Or maybe that warm, snuggly feeling was Natasha, who had crawled into bed with me at some point during the night. She was asleep now, her soft, even breathing the only sound in the room.

Yawning, I pushed myself up onto my elbows, and her eyes fluttered open. With tousled hair and a makeup-free face, she looked almost exactly the same as she did eleven years earlier, when it was just the two of us in a home much smaller than this. She gazed up at me. My big sister, my rock, my role model.

"I'm sorry," she said.

"I know. You said that already. It's okay."

"It's not okay." Natasha sat up and leaned back against the headboard. "It was uncalled-for and cruel and untrue."

I wasn't sure which part she was referring to—when she said I was terminally indecisive or when she told me I'd ruined her life. Whichever one it was, we both knew it wasn't necessarily untrue.

"You were stressed-out about the book proposal and meeting with Demi," I said.

"That's not an excuse." She hugged her legs to her chest. "The whole thing was a huge waste of time, anyway."

"I'm sorry the retreat wasn't what you expected it to be. But there are a lot of other ways to get your book out there in the world. You know, I read that self-publishing an ebook can bring in thousands of dollars in passive income."

"No, I don't just mean the retreat was a waste of time. I mean everything—the book proposal, the Instagram account. Demi was actually right when she said I didn't want it enough."

"What?" I grabbed her by the shoulders, trying to shake

some sense into her. "After everything that happened this weekend, you are not going to allow this scamming cow to destroy your dream."

She took my hands and placed them gently in her lap, covering them with her warm palms. "That's the thing. It wasn't really my dream. I wanted it because it was something I could point to for clout, not real fulfillment. I didn't want a book, I wanted bragging rights. A way to prove to people that I'm worth something. That I'm smart."

"But you're the smartest person I know." How could she not see that?

"Maybe you feel that way, but it's hard to believe it when…" Her voice caught. She dropped my hands, scrubbed her palm down the side of her face, and started again. "You didn't ruin things for me, okay? I don't ever want you to think that, and I'm sorry those words came out of my mouth. I have never regretted quitting school to take care of you. Not for one second. What I regret is never going back."

"So why didn't you?"

She answered by gesturing to the walls around us. "I started a family. And trust me, I don't regret that, either. Al and Izzy are the reasons I breathe. They're a stabilizing force in my life. But for a while there, I felt like I existed only as a member of the DeAngelis family, and not as my own self-actualized person. That's when I found *The Aspirational Action Plan*, and the way Demi DiPalma wrote those words, it felt like she was talking directly to me. Like she understood me."

"Right." That's exactly how I'd felt when I'd read it for the first time.

"Look, I know Demi DiPalma is a scam artist," she said, "but I do feel like this book was helpful. It was exactly what

I needed at the time. It encouraged me to wish big and to think deeply, and without it, I honestly never would've started my business, because I never would've dreamed up the idea.

"It was only the catalyst, though. Like you said, it takes more than dreams and thoughts and wishes to change your life. To make a difference, you actually need to take action. Which is something you did all weekend, calling people out on their horrible behavior. I'm proud of you." She snorted. "God, the faces of those women when you threw the book into the fire. I wish I'd taken a picture."

"Plenty of people had their cameras out," I said. "I'm sure if you search Instagram for the #synergysummit hashtag you'll find some."

"Please. I'm ready to delete my Instagram at this point."

"Me, too. Especially now that I'm done fulfilling all my collab obligations. Despite what you think, I *was* taking it seriously. I just realized it wasn't what I wanted to do with my life. Though it's not like I have any better ideas."

She took a deep breath, clearly searching for a diplomatic way to ask the question I knew she'd always wanted the answer to. "Do you ever plan on going back to college?"

"No," I said instantly, and it felt right. "I don't feel like I need a college degree to have a purpose in life. I guess I might change my mind in the future, but I'm already drowning in student loan debt, and I have no interest in adding to that. Plus, I still don't know what I'd study, and I don't wanna get a degree just to say I have one. That's why I went to college the first time and look where it got me."

Natasha nodded, a pained expression on her face.

"I know that sucks for you to hear," I continued, "and it sucks for me to say it to you. Especially considering I squandered my chance at an education, while you were forced to sacrifice yours."

"No," she said. "No one forced me to do anything. I chose to do it. And I'd do it again. Taking care of you was my number one priority, Bree. I promised Mom I would always take care of you."

Tears slid down her dewy, pink cheeks. She looked nineteen again, so strong and so vulnerable at the same time.

"You did more for me than you ever had to," I said. "Mom would've been proud."

"I miss her." Her voice was barely above a whisper.

"So do I. It's been so long, though, I feel like I'm forgetting her."

I'm not sure if it was Natasha's tear-streaked face, or the warmth of her body next to mine on the mattress, or the fact that we'd finally aired all our mildewed grievances and asked the unspoken questions that had been building up for years and years. Whatever the reason, I suddenly felt inspired to confess the secret I'd been hiding from her ever since she cleaned out Mom's old closet.

"There's this box under my bed. It has some of Mom's stuff in it—a T-shirt, a book, things like that. Whenever I have a hard time remembering her, when I feel like I'm forgetting her face or her voice or whatever, I take out the box and I go through it. Sometimes just touching the things that she touched makes me feel close to her again."

The words came out shaky. As I spoke, Natasha searched my face. "Where'd you get it from? The stuff in the box, I mean."

"I snuck them out of a garbage bag on the day you emptied her room. I never told you because I know how you feel about sentimental clutter. And you were right, we had to get rid of everything so we could start to heal, but… I couldn't let it all go. I needed something of hers to hold on to."

Natasha's mouth hung open. "I'm so sorry. I had no idea you felt that way."

"You were going through a hard time, too. We both were."

"I thought it was the right thing to do. I had read a self-help book on how to cope with grief and it said to sort through all your loved one's belongings as soon as possible so you can concentrate on moving forward. Don't look back, it said, because that's not where you're going. I knew there were things in her room we should've kept, important things, but I didn't have the strength to do it on my own and I didn't wanna burden you with it, either. I just needed it all out of my sight, as quickly as possible."

"Right, I understand. Getting rid of everything was the fastest way to move on."

She gnawed on her lower lip. "I didn't exactly get rid of everything."

It was hard to make sense of what Natasha was saying. I had seen her fill those garbage bags, seen her stuff them into the trunk of her car, then watched as she drove away, presumably to the Goodwill donation truck permanently parked on the side of the I-5.

Then it hit me. "The box. The seashell box in Izzy's room. It's Mom's, isn't it?"

"Yes." She took a deep breath, let it out. "But there's more. Come with me."

I followed Natasha along the hallway and down the stairs, my mind racing with possibility. I'd seen every square inch of this house, and I knew how Natasha worked. There was no hidden clutter lurking behind any closet or cabinet door.

Unless one of those neatly organized bookcases in the living room opened to reveal a hidden chamber, I couldn't see where she'd have stashed any of Mom's old stuff.

Until she opened her junk drawer—yes, even professional organizers had junk drawers—and pulled out a bright orange key tag.

"StoreSmart." This was unreal. "We were just there."

"We went to the one in Mission Valley. My storage unit is in Carlsbad."

She handed me the key and I turned it over in my palm. Unit #429. "How much of her stuff did you keep?"

"All of it. For the past eleven years, it's been sitting in a five-by-five climate-controlled room on the side of the freeway."

"But, the BUGS acronym. Sentimental clutter. You always say to throw it away."

"Clearly, I don't practice what I preach." She threw up her hands. "Guess I'm a big faker."

We didn't bother to change out of our pajamas. We simply threw on our flip-flops and hopped in the Audi. Fifteen minutes later, Natasha pulled into the StoreSmart parking lot, in the shadow of a massive orange warehouse that held all of my mother's worldly belongings.

I couldn't run to unit 429 fast enough.

The key was still firmly gripped in my sweaty hand. I shoved it in the lock and turned, but before I could raise the gate, Natasha stopped me. "Are you sure you're ready?"

Was I sure? No. Everything I'd thought had been lost forever was on the other side of this thin metal barrier. I had no idea what it was going to be like to see all those physical reminders of my mother in one room. Was everything still in garbage bags? Would her once-treasured possessions now be musty and deteriorating? And if so, would that make me feel worse than if I'd never seen them at all?

But in the moment, none of that mattered. I wanted in, now. "I'm ready."

The gate rumbled up. Cool, dry air whooshed in my face. Natasha flicked on the light.

Of course this is what it looked like. My sister would not have dumped a bunch of garbage bags into a cement room and called it a day. Not at all.

This was possibly the neatest, tidiest, most pristine storage unit in history. One wall was lined with rolling clothes racks, the items hanging from them organized by style and color. There were heavy-duty shelves set against the other two walls, each of them laden with clearly labeled boxes and drawers.

The whole space smelled of cedar. "It keeps the fabrics fresh and protects them from household pests," Natasha said. Of course she knew that. She knew everything.

I walked the perimeter in silence, cataloging the contents of the room with my eyes, remembering things I had forgotten long ago. The dress Mom had worn to Natasha's high school graduation. The Luther Vandross CD she always played while she cooked Sunday dinner. And the books. So many books, so many nights spent next to her on the couch. I touched their well-worn spines, felt a connection to the love I'd lost, the love of words and stories. I shouldn't have stopped reading when she died.

Natasha had even stored Mom's old makeup. By now, that must've been rancid, but I still enjoyed cracking open the eyeshadow palette, seeing how worn down the purple was compared to the other colors. Mom liked purple eyeshadow. I was learning new things about her, even now.

I just had one question for Natasha. "Why?"

"I told you, I had to get it out of my sight, but I knew I couldn't throw it away."

"But it's been eleven years. Why have you kept it all for so long? And why didn't you ever tell me about it?"

She grasped the edge of a steel shelving unit, like she was using it for support. "I meant to tell you about it, I honestly did. I knew you needed to go through it—you had a *right* to go through it. At first, I wanted to wait until you were a bit older, until you'd had a chance to heal a little. But the more time that passed, the harder it got for me to say anything about it. I never wanted to rip off the Band-Aid and open your old wound. Though it seems ridiculous now, as I say it.

"Anyway, I wanted to keep everything organized and prevent it from getting damaged, so I set it up like this. That way when the time came, you wouldn't have to wade through some disheveled mess."

I fingered a strand of faux pearls, set inside a clear container labeled Costume Jewelry. Mom had worn these the night we saw *The Nutcracker* in Balboa Park. "How often do you come here?"

"Once every six months or so. Just to check up on things, make sure the temperature's okay, replace the cedar blocks." She watched me pull the pearls from the box and put them around my neck. "Are you mad at me?"

I walked the two steps over to her and squeezed her hands in mine. "Not at all. I'm grateful for you, Natasha. I can't believe you went through this alone."

"I wanted to protect you. I did the best I could." Fresh tears fell down her face. I wiped them away with the pad of my thumb.

"You did amazing." With a meaningful glance around the room, I added, "We can't keep all of this forever, though."

She nodded. "I know."

"So let's go through it. Together."

"I can't do it now, it's getting late. Izzy and Al will be back soon. I have to meal plan and do their laundry and all the other stuff I usually do on Sundays."

"Then we'll do it later this week. Little by little, every day, until it's done."

Before we left, I took one last walk around the room, stopping when I got to Mom's bookshelf. I removed one at random, a historical romance with a watercolor cover, an image of a woman staring down at what looked like pink peonies, a man in the distance, visible just over her bare shoulder. *Lord of Scoundrels.*

It was time to start reading again.

CHAPTER 28

The next morning, Natasha drove me to the debt lawyer's office, which was essentially the front parlor of Nazanin Ansary's Encinitas home. Before we arrived, I was terrified, expecting to be scolded and shamed for the duration of our meeting. But the experience was almost pleasant. Ms. Ansary was kind and helpful, walking me through the complicated process of filing legal paperwork to unfreeze my accounts, then showing me how to develop a step-by-step strategy for negotiating a debt settlement and, eventually, a repayment plan. She also stressed the importance of creating a budget, a task which Natasha was more than thrilled to help me with.

If the courts processed everything correctly, Ms. Ansary said my accounts would likely be unfrozen by the end of the week. After that, I could apply to become a HandyMinion again.

When the meeting was over, Natasha hustled off to clear

out a client's messy closet, and sent me back to PB in a Lyft. The whole ride home, I felt a growing sense of optimism about the future.

I was going to claw my way out of debt, one HandyMinion assignment at a time.

I was going to start volunteering at a worthy charity, to help make the world a slightly less unfair place.

I was going to read books. Lots of them.

And I was going to clean my apartment—*really* clean it, this time—and set up my space in a way that was both comfortable and functional. Or as functional as possible for a place where the toaster and hairdryer couldn't be plugged in at the same time. The point is, I'd make it a home I could be proud of, so I wouldn't find myself constantly daydreaming about living somewhere else.

Though I did hope to spend plenty of time in the blue bungalow—that is, if Trey would have me. We hadn't spoken since I'd rushed him off the phone in the middle of the Passion Powwow. Would things be awkward when I saw him again? Thinking about it made my head hurt.

The throbbing intensified when the Lyft pulled up at the curb in front of the triplex, and I was faced with the possibility that my apartment may not have been empty. I'd instructed Rob to leave by Monday morning. Now it was Monday afternoon. He said he'd be gone by the time I got home, but he wasn't exactly a man of his word.

Sure enough, as I headed toward the back of the building, the distinct odor of marijuana wafted from my open windows.

Goddammit.

Naturally, he hadn't locked the door, so I didn't have to

take out my keys. I just pushed it open and screamed, "Why are you still here?"

It took him a second to register my presence; with Rob, there was always a momentary delay before his brain caught up to his surroundings. In that silent span of time, I took in the scene. He'd made himself right at home. And apparently, he'd been to Best Buy.

All the electronics I'd sold on Craigslist had been replaced. Actually, scratch that: they'd been upgraded. Rob had even installed a gaming chair in the center of my living room, which he sat in, headset strapped to his ears. First-person shooter graphics filled the TV screen, which I realized now was also new.

"You bought a new TV?" My screeching could not be contained. "I thought your parents cut you off!"

He slipped off the headset and paused his game. "Well, they kinda did. I mean, they kicked me outta their house, but I still have the Amex. I just told you that because I thought you'd feel bad for me and take me back."

"I will never take you back! What you and I had was a joke. The only reason you liked being with me is because I let you do whatever you want and never complained. Well, I'm done. No more lying around my apartment smoking weed and playing video games. This all goes, and so do you."

With a haughty flourish, I pressed the power button on the TV. Except it wasn't the power button, it was the input button, and the screen went all blue. So I pressed another button, but that brought up the settings menu. So much for a dramatic gesture.

As I continued smashing buttons, Rob casually stood up from his gaming chair and crossed the room to the kitchenette, where he pulled a packet of frosted blueberry Pop-Tarts from a box. "What are you doing?" I yelled. "I told you to leave."

"Yeah, I heard you," he said, completely unruffled. "But I'm hungry. Lemme make myself something to eat real quick."

The balls on this guy.

I watched in disbelief as he tore open the foil packaging and slipped a pastry in each toaster slot. The moment he pressed his finger to the handle, though, I realized he was making a terrible mistake.

"Don't!" I screamed, but it was too late. Between the giant TV and the gaming chair and who knows whatever else Rob had plugged in at the time, the shady old electrical system couldn't handle the extra load of warming a couple of Pop-Tarts. The outlet sparked, then sizzled, then a wisp of smoke curled out from the opening in the wall.

"Oh, shit." That was Rob's helpful contribution.

Meanwhile, I dove forward to unplug the toaster and felt a jolt from my fingertips to my elbow. The smoke increased, from a thin plume to a billowing cloud and that's when I really started to panic. Instantly, I reached for the box under my bed. Because if this place was going up in flames, my memories of Mom were the one thing I wanted to save.

Racing down the steps, I dialed 911, then set my box down next to the curb, where I waited to flag down the fire department. Rob paced beside me, vaping up a storm.

"Why did you have all that stuff plugged in at once?" I asked, even though I already knew the answer. "You know how easy it is to overload that circuit. You lived here for three years."

He took a hit from his vape pen and shrugged. "I forgot."

Of course he did.

Minutes later, a fire truck turned onto Beryl Street, and we pointed our brave heroes toward my apartment in the back. There didn't appear to be any smoke or flames coming from the windows, which meant the fire had probably not escalated, but they told us to hang back at the curb until they gave the all clear, anyway.

The thing about a fire truck is that it attracts a lot of attention from the neighbors. People I'd never seen before were suddenly sticking their heads out of open doors and hovering around at a respectful distance. Close enough to gawk, but far enough to avoid serious injury should the apartment spontaneously explode. I sent a wish out into the universe: *Please, don't let Trey be home.*

Predictably, my request was ignored.

He came striding out of his front door in board shorts and bare feet, then rushed down the pathway and through the picket fence. His eyes went to the fire truck, the firefighters running back and forth behind the triplex, and finally, they settled on me. My pulse quickened a bit, not simply because he was gorgeous and the very sight of him affected me on a visceral level, but also because I was trapped.

This was not how I wanted our reunion to go down. At the very least, I had wanted to shower first. But I very much did not want Rob to be here, an awkward third wheel with bloodshot eyes. How was I supposed to explain his presence, or the fact that he'd just set my apartment on fire?

It seemed I didn't have to do much explaining, though. As soon as Trey approached, Rob lifted his fist for a bump. "Yo, yo, my man."

My man?

The worst part was that Trey bumped him back. "What's

going on with the fire truck?" He directed his question toward Rob, not me.

This was bad.

"Not sure, man," Rob replied. "Outlet started smoking for no reason."

"It wasn't for no reason," I said. "There were too many things plugged in at once."

"Sounds like shady electrical." Trey gazed at me with something like disappointment in his eyes. "Might wanna talk to your landlord about bringing things up to code."

"Definitely, definitely," Rob said. When he saw the way Trey was looking at me, he said, "Oh, sorry, man. Remember I was telling you about my girlfriend? This is Bree."

"I'm not your girlfriend," I said. "And Trey and I already know each other. I didn't realize you two had met, though."

"Yeah, he got my poke bowl," Rob said, then broke out in hysterics.

Trey seemed to find the whole situation less hilarious. "His GrubGetter order was delivered to my house by mistake. Apparently, your apartment doesn't have an official address number, so it was hard for the delivery person to find. So I helped her out." He clenched his jaw, eyes blazing. "It took a second for me to figure out where she meant, though, since you told me you were away for the weekend. I hadn't realized Rob moved back in."

"He didn't move back in," I said, glaring at Rob who was still laughing like a hyena. "He showed up on my doorstep Thursday night and told me he had nowhere to go. I let him stay here while I was in Palm Desert, but he was supposed to be gone by now."

"Palm Desert." There was a teasing lilt to Trey's words. "I

thought you said you were going to Encinitas, that your sister needed you at the last minute or something."

Shit.

"I meant that I went to Encinitas on Thursday night. She drove us to the desert the next morning."

"Cool. What were you doing out there?"

This felt uncomfortably like an inquisition, though he wasn't asking anything unreasonable. His tone wasn't particularly hostile, either. Then again, it wasn't particularly warm.

"I was at a wellness retreat. Kind of. Actually, I'm not really sure what it was supposed to be."

"From your Instagram, it looked like some sort of influencer conference."

"My Instagram?"

"Yeah, Rob showed me. Bree by the Sea, right?"

I was going to murder Rob.

Though it was my own fault for leaving those incriminating padded envelopes around my apartment instead of throwing away my garbage like a civilized human.

"Right," I said. "But I'm not really keeping up with that anymore."

"Really? 'Cause you posted some great shots from the weekend. Like the one of you blowing glitter around. That one got a lot of likes, if I remember correctly."

What was he talking about? The only photos I'd posted this weekend were the obligatory collaborations. I'd never bothered to upload the one he was referring to, the one Natasha took of me during the Passion Powwow.

Unless that's what she was doing poking around in my phone while I watched the glitter float away into the desert.

I was going to murder her, too.

But frankly, I didn't like the way this conversation was going. I felt attacked, ambushed, like he was trying to corner me into admitting something scandalous, or make me feel like an even bigger fool than I already did, standing here on the sidewalk next to my baked ex-boyfriend while an electrical fire ravaged my home.

"If you have something to say to me, say it. Because it feels like you're dancing around your point, instead of getting straight to it."

He let out a sarcastic laugh. "You've been lying to me since the moment we met, and suddenly *now* you care about being straightforward?"

"I haven't been lying to you. If it's about my Instagram, I can explain—"

"Were you planning this all along?"

"Planning what?"

He pointed to me, then back at himself. "This. Us."

I shook my head, confused. "I have no idea what you're talking about."

With an irritated sigh, he jammed his hand in the pocket of his board shorts and pulled out his phone. "You know, I reinstalled the app just to see this because I couldn't believe it." His thumb tapped around his screen and I struggled to understand the problem. Was he really so upset that I'd posted a few poorly filtered photos of myself wearing ugly lip gloss and even uglier shoes?

"Here we go." Trey turned his phone around, showing a picture of his adorable blue bungalow, hashtagged #choose-happy and #noexcuses. I'd taken this photo on my walk to the beach, the day of the stingray attack, the day Trey had helped me to safety. At the time, it was simply a dream for my vision board, no more.

"I can explain."

Trey wasn't interested in explanations. "Your life is your life, and what you do is none of my business. But you know how important my privacy is to me. You know I don't want to be on social media."

"That could be anyone's house," I said, but then Trey scrolled down to a comment: **Trey Cantu lives here, I saw him waxing his board outside one day, omg are they dating?!?**

Shit.

"It's not what you think. I told you, you live in my dream home. I took this photo for my vision board, before anything ever happened between us."

"Wait, something happened between you two?" That was Rob, ever slow on the uptake.

Trey ignored him. "You know, I thought about that, because of the time stamp on the post. But then I saw the photo before it, and it got kinda creepy."

He swiped up, revealing the picture of the girl on the beach in the bright red bikini, the one fearlessly wading into the waves, her back turned to the camera. The inspiration for my ill-fated dip in the ocean.

"How do you explain this?" he asked.

"That's just some random photo I found on Instagram. It was part of my vision board, to inspire me to get over my fear of the water."

His eyes narrowed to suspicious slits. "Why did you put Shayla on your vision board?"

It took a second to work out what he was saying. "This

picture…that's Shayla in the water?" When he nodded, I said, "But you can't see her face. How can you tell?"

"I know it's her because I took this picture. Last year, when we were still dating." The screen went dark and Trey pocketed the phone. "You know it's her because she posted it on her Instagram account."

"No." I shook my head. Granted, I didn't remember which account I'd swiped this photo from. All I remembered was the #goodvibesonly hashtag. But it was a recent photo, not one from a year ago. Wasn't it?

Regardless, now I looked like some unhinged stalker who'd conspired to hook up with Trey—and had documented the whole wacko plan on the internet for the whole world to comment on.

Even worse, did he think I was trying to build an influencer career off his name, just like Shayla had?

"Okay." I took a deep breath. "I know this looks bad, but—"

Trey raised one hand to silence me. "I'm sure you have some perfectly plausible excuse," he said. "But you might as well save your breath. At this point, I don't believe a word you say."

A thousand different responses raced through my mind—I'm sorry! You've got it all wrong! I'll delete my Instagram and we can start over!—but I couldn't force my voice to form the words. Then someone tapped me on the shoulder, and I spun around to see a firefighter removing his heavy-duty gloves.

"Excuse me," he said, "are you the occupant of this residence?"

"Yes," I said, frantic. "Is everything okay? How bad is the damage?"

He met my panic with calm, rational explanation. "None

of your personal effects seem to have suffered harm, but that outlet in the kitchen is destroyed. The whole electrical system needs to be rewired, but to be frank, there are a number of safety concerns I have about that apartment. It's not up to code by any stretch of the imagination. I doubt it's even legal to be living there. I'm going to schedule an inspection with the city, but in the meantime, you'll have to find someplace else to stay."

Goddammit.

Just like that, I was evicted.

CHAPTER 29

Remember when I said my sister wasn't a safety net?

I was eating those words right about now.

With nowhere else to go, I sent Natasha a quick **Help!** text, to which she responded by sending a Lyft to pick me up and bring me back to her place.

"Jonathan, red Prius, seven minutes."

Before Jonathan arrived, I ran inside to pack the LeSportsac tote bag full of clean clothes. Meanwhile, Rob didn't glance my way as he unplugged his gaming chair and hoisted it over his shoulder. I guess finding out I'd moved on from our dysfunctional relationship with the hottie prosurfer next door was a blow to his ego. He tossed all his expensive electronics into the back of his brand-new Jeep and hightailed it outta there without so much as a goodbye. Where he was going, I didn't know or care. Truthfully, I hoped I'd never see him again.

I arrived at Natasha's doorstep just before dinner. She answered the door with a spatula in her hand, giving me a one-armed hug. "I made a keto lasagna bake. It's amazing, trust me."

It actually was pretty amazing. Sausage, ground beef, three kinds of cheese—what's not to like? I scooped a second helping while I sat at the dining room table, listening to Al discuss the perils of untreated overbites and Izzy talk about who was mean to whom on the school playground that day. I smiled and nodded and said things like, "Oh, how interesting!" But on the inside, I was crumbling to pieces.

There was no way my apartment would ever pass an inspection. With my horrible credit history (which was still very much in the present), I'd never qualify for anything better. And it's not like I could search Craigslist for illegal, unsanctioned hovels to live in.

Later that night, as I unpacked my clothes and put them in the guest room dresser, Natasha assured me, "Everything will be okay. You can stay here as long as you need to," before zipping off to draw Izzy a bath.

The way my life was going, I'd be living here forever. Not that sleeping in this heavenly bed was such a tragedy, but Natasha had saved my ass one time too many, and I wasn't going to take any more handouts. If I was going to stay here for an extended period of time, I'd insist on paying her rent.

As soon as my PayPal account was unfrozen.

Exhausted from the day's events, I crawled into bed not long after the sun went down, more than ready for the sweet release of sleep to sweep me away. The nature sounds app would help quiet my jittery brain, so I pulled out my phone and swiped through my home screens. But I stopped short when I saw the multicolored swirl of the Instagram icon.

Ugh. Instagram.

I'd been threatening to delete my account for the past few days, but never pulled the trigger. Maybe if I had, Trey would've still been speaking to me.

It still didn't make sense—how could a year-old photo of Shayla end up in my feed? With one angry finger, I tapped the Instagram icon and pulled up her profile to scroll through her recent posts. There she was, standing on a city street, her hands tangled seductively in her long hair. And in the next one, posing on the deck of a yacht, plucking plump strawberries from a goblet of fruit.

She was sickeningly beautiful. Though I wondered how much was real, and how much was filtered.

Then I saw it: the photo of her in the red bikini, the one I'd reposted to my vision board. The time stamp said May 3—the same day I'd seen it—but she'd hashtagged it #flashbackfriday.

Well, that explained that.

Swiping back to my profile, I took one final scroll through my feed, marveling at how quickly the whole thing had spiraled out of control. One moment I was faking my way through a vision board, the next I was a self-absorbed attention seeker, ravenous for whatever free junk people would send me. At the time, all those likes and follows and comments felt like validation. Now I realized it meant nothing at all.

With a few quick taps of my fingertip, I deleted Bree by the Sea.

The next morning, I bounced from bed with renewed energy, bounding down the stairs before the sun came up. Natasha was already at her Orangetheory class, but Al and Izzy were still fast asleep. In the silent, empty kitchen, I pulled up Alton Brown's French toast recipe on the screen of the smart fridge and prepared the whole family a surprise breakfast. It didn't turn out as perfectly as the batch Trey had cooked up for me, but no one seemed to mind.

"This is amazing," Natasha said. "Totally not keto, but amazing."

"You're staying forever, right, Auntie Bree?" Izzy spoke with her mouth full.

"Probably."

She laughed, but I wasn't joking.

While everyone else got showered and dressed, I cleaned up the kitchen, scrubbing pots and wiping countertops with Natasha-like precision. After dropping Izzy at school, my sister perused the daily schedule on the kitchen command center.

"Izzy's got ballet at 3:45," she said. "If we're gonna make any headway at the storage unit today, we'd better get moving."

Armed with a Costco-sized container of trash bags and a case of flattened boxes, we headed up the I-5 to StoreSmart, where we began the painstaking task of sorting through all of Mom's worldly possessions. No question, most of the stuff had to go, but there were some things we knew we'd want to hold on to. Plus, we wanted to say a proper goodbye to everything else, instead of tossing it away without a second thought.

At Natasha's suggestion, we approached it methodically, working our way around the room and evaluating each item one at a time. The BUGS acronym was completely useless to us, considering everything was sentimental. Instead, we asked ourselves meaningful questions: Does it bring back a great memory of Mom? Is there a space to keep it in our home—not jammed in the back of the closet or shoved in a box under the bed, but on display, where we can see it regularly and smile? Or would it be better to donate it, so someone else could benefit from its use?

Progress was slow. Each item had a story behind it, some long-forgotten history that we dredged up for the sake of remembering Mom. We laughed more than we cried, and we only got through half of what we'd initially aimed to accomplish on our first day. It wasn't particularly efficient, but as Natasha had recently taken to saying: *the only way out is through*.

So every day, after dropping Izzy at school, we trudged through another piece of our past.

By late Friday morning, all that remained in the storage unit were a couple of bare shelving units, the rolling clothes hangers, and over a dozen bags and boxes set aside for the donation bin.

"I can drop this off at the Goodwill truck tomorrow," Natasha said, surveying the stack in the corner of the nearly empty room. "Who knows if they'll even take it, though. Half the time, they're so full, they turn my clients' donations away."

"In that case, I know a place in PB that could really use donations. Let me get the address." I whipped out my phone and texted Mari.

> The place where you take the pastries, the one that gives stuff to women's shelters, what's the name of it again?

> Community Resource Center.
> Why?

> I've got a bunch of stuff to give away.

Clothes and books and jewelry.

All in good condition.

Think they could use it?

Definitely! They don't get many donations.

She sent me the address—not far from The Bean House, actually—so, on a whim, I added,

Do you think they might need volunteers?

YES!

They're super understaffed and

need all the help they can get.

Cool!

I'm gonna drop all this stuff off now.

I'll ask for a volunteer application

while I'm there.

Actually, would you mind swinging

by Bean House first?

You can bring them today's pastries

while you're at it.

👍

Also, I've got exciting news!

Wanna tell you in person.

I smiled, imagining what exciting tidbit she had to share with me. In the course of a week, Mari's life had turned upside down—in the very best way—all thanks to that video skewering Demi DiPalma. Her subscriber count was in the tens of thousands and her views were in the millions. And she didn't have to buy the following. She'd earned it.

"It's all settled," I said, turning to my sister. "Let's load up the car and drive down there now."

Natasha glanced at her phone. "I have to FaceTime with a client in a half hour. Would you mind dropping me home and going by yourself?"

"Of course not."

Twenty minutes later I was flying down the I-5 in Natasha's Audi to The Bean House, where Mari was waiting for me in the front garden. The tray of pastries sat beside her on a bistro table, looking perfectly delectable.

"What are you doing out here?" I asked, leaning in for a hug. "Don't you have angry customers to attend to?"

"It's slow right now. Besides, Logan needs to practice being in charge, since he's getting promoted to head barista."

"Good for him. So he'll be the boss on your days off?"

"No, he's taking over my shifts." Her face lit up with a wide, beautiful smile. "My last day's next Friday. I got a new job!"

"Oh my God!" I threw my arms around her again. "Congratulations! Doing what?"

"Turns out all it takes is one socially conscious viral video for Netflix to come knocking on your door. They recruited me as a staff writer for this sketch comedy show they're launching next year."

"Holy shit! That's incredible!"

"Yeah." Her smile faltered. "Except the job's in LA. I'm moving next weekend."

"Oh." I tried not to let the disappointment show on my face. After all, this was Mari's dream, and it was coming true.

But damn, I was gonna miss her.

"Don't worry," she said, sensing my sadness. "I'll come back to visit all the time. And Logan knows you get free coffee in perpetuity."

I laughed, despite myself. "Well, this is the greatest news ever. I get free coffee for life *and* you get your dream job."

Her smile was back in full force. "I still can't believe it's happening."

"I can. They'd be stupid not to hire you. Your last video was fire."

Two days earlier, she'd uploaded "I Thought I Told You to Fuck Off, Zach," a sequel to the classic "Fuck Off, Zach," in which she dissected an email he sent her in the wake of her newfound success. It was filled with backhanded compliments and condescending douchery, and at the end, he had the gall to ask her for a feature on her channel.

"When I say, 'fuck off,' I mean it," she said. "So, what's going on with your accounts? Are they still frozen?"

"No, thankfully. PayPal just released the hold today. I submitted my HandyMinion application as soon as they did."

"I can't believe HandyMinion is making you start all over again at level one. What a scam."

"It's not so much a scam as a total waste of resources, but I'm hoping the onboarding process goes fast so I can get back to work right away."

"And what about your apartment?"

I shook my head. "Haven't heard anything from the landlord yet, but I'm pretty sure I won't ever be able to move back in."

"So where are you gonna live?"

"Right now I'm with Natasha."

"In Encinitas?" She pulled a face. "You can't live there for-ever."

"It's not like I have any other choice. Not with my lousy credit score and nonexistent income. No landlord in their right mind would give me a legit lease. Hopefully, I'll stumble across another shady illegal situation at some point."

I crossed my fingers in a playful gesture to hide the misery I felt in my bones. Pacific Beach was my home, and I loved everything about it: the cute houses and the shady apartments; the bars on Garnet Street and the surf shops on the beach; the salty air and the brilliant sunsets. And the people, all of them.

Pacific Beach was my home, but I didn't live here anymore.

Then, Mari came through with a genius idea.

"Why don't you move into my place? My roommates are great, they keep to themselves, and I know they'd be thrilled to have my replacement be someone I personally recom-mended as opposed to some rando they found on Craigslist. You won't need a credit check, and the rent is cheap."

Now I was the one with the thousand-watt smile. "That's the best idea you've ever had."

"No, that self-help video was the best idea I've ever had. But this might be a close second." An older man strolled past us and entered the shop with two teacup Yorkies in tow. Mari followed them with her eyes and grimaced. "I should probably go. This guy's always a pain in the ass ordering puppuccinos for his dogs. I've gotta show Logan how to do it."

"Good luck." I picked up the tray of pastries and started down the stairs. "Let's get together this weekend, I wanna hear more details about your move."

"Sure. By the way, have you heard from Trey at all?"

Hearing Trey's name stopped me cold. I turned around and shook my head. "Of course not."

"Have you tried reaching out to him?"

"Why? He thinks I'm a stalker weirdo. And I lost all credibility when I lied to him about going to Palm Desert. Whatever we had together is done." *Not that we had much to begin with.*

"Are you sure? He came in here a couple of times, but he was kind of quiet. Once he didn't even order anything, he just poked his head around and left. I think he might've been looking for you."

"Maybe he wanted to chew me out again."

"He seemed sad," she said.

With a shrug, I turned around and walked away. There wasn't really much to say. Trey wasn't interested in my explanations or excuses, he'd made that much clear. Though I probably owed him a proper apology for involving him in my mess.

For now, I put thoughts of Trey behind me, and after securing the pastries on Natasha's front seat, I took off for the Community Resource Center. It was a nondescript building on Mission Bay Drive; I'd probably driven past here a thousand times but never noticed the tiny little CRC sign hanging over the narrow glass door. No wonder they didn't get many donations.

I parked out front and grabbed the pastries, eager to see what volunteer opportunities were available. If they were understaffed, it was probably hard to dedicate any resources toward fund-raising or marketing. Maybe I could put my newly honed Instagram skills to good use by building up their social media presence or something.

Feeling hopeful, I opened the door and stepped inside. The front office was tiny, no bigger than my now-condemned apartment. Shelves lined the walls, stocked with books and boxes and binders. To my left, there was a makeshift waiting room, consisting of two worn-out chairs, a community bulletin board, and a wire rack filled with brochures, their topics ranging from childhood nutrition to affordable housing to free transportation.

There were two desks in the center of the office, but only one was occupied. A woman sat there, one hand clutching a phone to her ear, the other frantically clicking a mouse as she stared wide-eyed at her computer screen, her voice stretched thin as she spoke into the phone.

"I can't load the inventory right now, I'm sorry. Our database appears to be frozen."

The person on the other line screamed so loudly I could hear it clear across the room.

"I said I was sorry." Her response was measured, but from the way she slammed the handset onto the receiver, she was clearly not feeling as calm as she sounded.

She looked up, suddenly aware of my presence. "Oh. I'm sorry. Can I help you?"

"I'm here from The Bean House." Raising the tray aloft, I said, "These are from Marisol Vega."

Her brow smoothed instantly and a warm smile spread across her face. "Wonderful, thank you so much. Would you mind—" The phone rang again and she groaned. "Sorry. Give me one minute, please."

As she answered, I stepped to the side and perused the flyers tacked up to the bulletin board. There were schedules for support groups, contact numbers for emergency shelters, and lists of public bathrooms—all of it available in Pacific Beach. This organization really did a lot for the community.

Behind me, the front door creaked open, and I turned to see a man walking in. From the looks of it, he was down on his luck—tattered clothes, unkempt beard, permanent wrinkles etched in his leathery forehead. I grinned at him, but he ignored me, charging straight in and yelling at the woman behind the desk.

"When's the meal service?"

Deep in her phone conversation, she held up one finger, the universal sign for "please wait a moment." Rather than take a seat in the waiting area, though, the man rounded on me.

"When's the meal service?"

"Uh, I don't work here."

He yelled even louder. "What are you talking about? Who the hell are you?"

His eyes narrowed to slits as he stared me down, and my hands gripped the tray tightly. If he tried any funny business, I could chuck these pastries at him and run like the wind.

Then I realized there was a better use for these pastries.

Removing the cover from the tray, I held it out toward him. "Would you care for a croissant or a muffin? I think there's a few scones in there, too."

His gaze dropped to the baked goods before him, and he grabbed two blueberry scones, biting into one instantly. In that moment, he reminded me a lot of Eddie Trammel, the day I arrived on his doorstep without the chipotle ranch dressing—just a hangry guy, demanding answers about his food.

Except this man actually said, "Thank you."

"You're welcome." Then I tilted my head in the direction

of the bulletin board. "Let's see if we can find information about the meal service over here."

We did, on a neatly printed schedule. He thanked me again, then grabbed a chocolate croissant for the road.

As soon as he left, the woman hung up the phone. "I'm so sorry about that."

"It was no problem."

"Well, thank you. You handled that perfectly. Sometimes our clients can get a bit aggressive."

"I have a lot of experience with aggressive clients." When her brow furrowed in a question, I said, "I was a GrubGetter for several years. People get really fired up about their food deliveries."

"I'll bet." She held her hands out for the pastries. "Here, let me take that from you." As she walked them over to the empty desk, she said, "You were a huge help. I've been drowning today."

"You guys are pretty understaffed here, huh?"

"Under normal circumstances, yes, but even more so now. My assistant quit on me last week. Said he wasn't getting paid enough to deal with 'these people'—he actually said 'these people'—and was going to start a new career as a SoundCloud rapper. As if he's going to become famous overnight on the internet. Can you even believe that?"

Sadly, I could.

"Well," I said, "I'd love to submit a volunteer application to help you out."

"That'd be great...but are you, by chance, looking for a job? Because I need to replace Mr. SoundCloud immediately."

It was like she saw right straight into my heart.

And it would've been perfect, if not for one tiny detail. "I don't have a college degree."

"You don't need a college degree to work here. You need people skills and common sense and compassion. From what I've seen so far, you seem to have all of those in spades." She plucked a business card from her desktop and handed it to me. "Here's my contact information. My name's Chandra. Email me your résumé and we can talk it over some more."

I stared at the card in my hands, barely able to speak. All I could manage was an astonished, "Thank you so much."

Even though I didn't believe in Demi DiPalma's four-step manifesting process, this sure seemed like a clear-cut, undeniable sign that the universe was listening.

CHAPTER 30

A week later, I had a job.

My first real job that wasn't a temporary, internet-based gig. There were no apps to install, no competition for tasks, no star ratings from total strangers. Instead, there was a set schedule and a steady paycheck and health benefits and a retirement account. There were even two full weeks of paid vacation. I'd struck the jackpot.

Best of all, it was with an organization that was doing great work, work that mattered to me—dare I say, work I was passionate about? And even though I was only an entry-level office assistant, I could see myself building this into a long-term career. Helping to make the world a little less unfair, one day at a time.

The weekend before I started my new position at the Community Resource Center, I helped Mari pack up a trailer with all her belongings. Then I waved goodbye as she drove off toward her future in LA. It was a bittersweet moment, but I didn't have time to brood about it. I had to pack up a trailer of my own.

Most of the stuff in my old apartment didn't come with me to my new room in Mari's old place. The ratty weed-smelling futon, the now totally dead aloe plant, the burned-out broken toaster—they all went in the trash. All I took with me were my clothes and my bed and my favorite pink coffee mug.

I also took one of those shelving units that Natasha had in storage. It fit perfectly in the corner next to my window, with plenty of room to display all the things that reminded me of Mom. Like photos I'd kept hidden away, and a necklace stand holding that strand of pearls she'd worn to *The Nutcracker*.

And, of course, all of her books.

After tearing through *Lord of Scoundrels* in one evening, I decided to keep Mom's entire library, at least until I'd read every last book she'd owned. It was an eclectic collection— everything from historical romance to graphic novels to *The Autobiography of Malcolm X*. In a way, it made me feel closer to her, devouring the same words her eyes had seen, touching the same pages her fingers had grazed. I'd get to know her in a way I never did when she was alive. Creating new memories to make up for the ones I had lost.

Natasha helped me set up the whole space, and this time, I gladly accepted her organizing advice. My new home was going to be clutter-free, from the get-go. She taught me the best way to fold my T-shirts, and how to make the most use of my vertical space, and even installed a miniature command center on the inside of my closet door, with a dry-erase calendar and a corkboard.

"It's easier to stay on top of your bills this way," she said, pointing to the calendar, where she'd written "LOAN PAYMENT DUE" on the fifteenth of the month in red block letters. "Do you like it?"

"I love it. Everything looks so amazing. Thank you."

"It's my job." Her chin trembled ever so slightly, and she whirled away, straightening the books on the shelves that were already neatly aligned. Her voice didn't waver when she said, "I haven't told you this yet, but I'm thinking of finishing my degree."

"Really?"

Natasha turned back around, all traces of sadness gone. "Locally, of course. I'm not gonna commute to LA every day. Right now, I'm trying to see if I can salvage any of my old college credits or if I'd need to start from scratch. One step at a time."

"One step at a time." My voice was a whisper. The idea of my sister finally achieving her long-abandoned dream was enough to take my breath away. "I'm so excited for you. Whatever you need, I'm here to support you however I can."

"Thanks. But you've got your hands full as it is." She gestured to the command center, to the books, to the whole room. "It looks like we're done, huh?"

"Yeah. I just have to run back to my old apartment and get my bike. It's under the outside stairs, I forgot all about it." And apparently, so had Rob.

"Let me drop you there on my way home."

"You know what? I wouldn't mind taking a walk."

We hugged goodbye in the driveway, and I set off on my way. My new place was on Missouri Street—about three blocks south and nine blocks east of my last place on Beryl. It meant I was a bit farther away from the beach now, but still within walking distance.

And most important, still in PB.

As I turned onto my old block, the blue bungalow came into view. This afternoon, I had no intention of stopping to daydream. That fantasy was part of my past. From now on, I wanted to focus on reality.

Unfortunately, today's reality involved Trey standing in his front yard wearing nothing but board shorts, hanging his wet suit from the eaves.

I'd been hoping to avoid him on this final trip back to Beryl Street. There were too many things I wanted to tell him—explanations, excuses, apologies—and I knew he didn't want to hear any of it. I knew we were done.

But as he propped his surfboard up against his front porch, I realized there was something else I wanted to tell him. Something he'd probably care about, that had nothing to do with us.

I rested my fingertips on the white picket fence and called, "Hey."

He didn't acknowledge me.

So I tried again. "I have something to tell you."

"Save your breath, I'm not interested." He didn't even look at me.

"This has nothing to do with what happened," I said. "It's about your nonprofit idea. I have a suggestion."

That got his attention. Slowly, he walked down the path until he reached the picket fence. He stood on the other side, jaw clenched, his eyes never quite meeting mine.

I swallowed hard. "There's this organization I started working with, the Community Resource Center. They help people in PB, connecting them with services they might need, like emergency housing or food distribution. Things like that. They also have a whole program specifically for children, especially those in shelters, providing mentors and activities and stuff.

"Anyway, it made me think of you and your idea for starting a surf school for kids who can't afford to pay. You might want to connect with them. They probably have kids who'd be interested."

He nodded, his bare chest rising and falling with each slow, deliberate breath. "Thanks. I will."

"Great, I'll text you the info."

"Are you volunteering there or something?"

"Actually, I'm working there full-time. My first day on the job is tomorrow. No more HandyMinion-ing for me!"

I forced a laugh.

He remained stone-faced.

Then finally, his eyes met mine. And even though I knew we were done, I couldn't help but feel a twinge of hope.

"I'm sorry."

His jaw muscles clenched when I spoke the words, but he didn't tell me to stop. So I kept going.

"I don't expect you to believe me, but I wasn't trying to use you to build some influencer career. I created that Instagram account as a vision board, and things spiraled out of control so fast. People started offering me free stuff and I couldn't say no, and then all those likes and comments made me feel special, for the first time in my life. And that picture of Shayla was just a truly horrible coincidence. When I posted it, I didn't even know who she was yet.

"And I'm sorry I lied about Palm Desert. I didn't want to go, but I'd made a promise to my sister, and I knew you'd think the whole thing was ridiculous. I didn't want you to think any less of me. Of course now I see how stupid that was."

Trey didn't respond. He just stood there, his hazel eyes burning into mine, his jaw muscles working overtime.

"Anyway," I said. "Thank you."

"For what?"

"For encouraging me to believe in myself. For helping me overcome my fear of the ocean. And for having confidence in me. My life has changed a lot these past few weeks, in a really positive way. I'm not sure that would've happened if we'd never met. So, thanks."

I didn't wait around to see what he would say or not say. I simply walked away, as quickly as I could, without looking back. When I ducked down the alleyway beside the triplex, my heart was racing. When I returned with my bike, Trey was gone.

My blood was pumping hard and fast, adrenaline coursing through my body. I couldn't go home now. I was too amped.

So I pedaled directly to my favorite place in San Diego: Law Street Beach. There were plenty of gorgeous beaches all over the county, but none of them had quite the same vibe as this one. It was the perfect mix of city and surf, laid-back and lively. Plus, it would always hold a special place in my heart because it was where I'd finally conquered my fear of the ocean.

The first time I'd tried to swim out on my own, a stingray took me down before I'd made it past the shallows. But when Trey had held my hand, I felt safe, even beyond the breaking waves.

There was no Trey now, though. There was only me.

And I was perfectly capable of doing this on my own.

The sun would be setting soon. I locked the bike up at the

lifeguard station and wandered down the ramp toward the sand. All I brought with me were the clothes on my back: shorts and T-shirt on top, bikini underneath. At the shoreline, I stripped off the top layer and waded slowly, carefully into the waves. Shuffling my feet, bracing my body.

Keep moving forward.

Trey said there was no need to fear the ocean. Merely to respect it, to understand it. To go with the flow.

One foot in front of the other, one step at a time. I was knee-deep, thigh-deep, waist-deep.

Keep moving forward.

The waves were at my breasts, at my shoulders. Then all at once, I was floating in the unknown. Nothing out here but me, the ocean, the endless sky.

But I wasn't afraid.

I stayed there for a while, treading water, my legs strong as they kicked out below me, my arms satisfyingly fatigued. Eye level with the horizon, I watched the sun slowly slip from sight.

Then I saw it. It was kind of like spotting a unicorn or a mermaid. A magical, mystical vision, indisputably real yet impossible to believe. Right before the sun disappeared, it momentarily changed color from bright yellow to deep green. For the first time in my life, I witnessed the green flash.

I didn't know if I believed in the concept of universal energy, and I was sure an expensive rock wouldn't solve all my problems. But I couldn't deny there were other, intangible forces at work on the beach that day. Because the moment I emerged from the ocean, salt water dripping from my skin, he was there.

Trey, looking every bit as gorgeous as the first time I'd laid eyes on him.

"You were great out there," he said, handing me a towel. Because, of course, I had forgotten one.

"Thanks." I wrapped the towel around my chest, feeling very exposed all of a sudden. "I'm sorry I bailed on our surf lesson. I really did want to get back in the water with you."

His gaze was like the thinnest drizzle of warm syrup: sweet, delicious, making me hungry for more. "I saw you now, though. You were so confident in those waves. You don't need my help. You could handle it all on your own."

"You're right, I probably could. I probably don't need you. But I want you."

I took a tentative step closer to him, wet sand sticking to my feet. He didn't make a move to meet me halfway.

"I really hope you believe me. I wasn't using you for clout." With a gesture to my flaw-ridden, not Instagram-model-worthy body, I added, "I'm obviously not Shayla."

Trey finally stepped forward and reached for my hand, then lifted it to his lips. His gentle kiss sent sparks up my arm, straight to my heart. "Obviously not."

"Does that mean you forgive me?"

He took a deep breath. "Look, I know things are rarely black-and-white. Situations aren't always what they appear to be, especially online, and the truth can get twisted pretty easily. Of all people, I should understand this. My reputation was ruined because of a tweet.

"But I also realized that I shouldn't be so hung up about what people say on the internet, anyway. Who cares if I'm tagged in an Instagram post? That's not the real world. The real world is right here. Right in front of me."

Another kiss to my hand, and my knees nearly buckled.

"I saw the green flash tonight," I said.

His eyes crinkled as he smiled. It felt like the sun had risen all over again. "See? It's real. We're not just fooling ourselves."

"Maybe we aren't. But if we are, I'm not sure I care."

I dropped my towel and leaned into Trey's body, feeling his skin against mine, his hands on my waist, the sand between my toes. His kiss was warm and slow, fulfilling my hunger. It was the abundance.

My life didn't look anything like an aspirational vision board, and chances are it never would. I was too messy, too flawed. I couldn't erase my mistakes with a swipe of a finger. I couldn't put a filter on reality.

But in that moment, on that beach, in the arms of a man who believed in me, my life seemed better than any vision board I could ever create.

It wasn't curated, and it certainly wasn't Instagram-worthy. But it was real.

And it was extraordinary.

★ ★ ★ ★ ★

ACKNOWLEDGMENTS

This book was hard to write. I thought by now it would get easier, but I was wrong. Maybe it never gets easier. Either way, I am beyond grateful for my editor, Brittany Lavery, who took my initial trash fire of a manuscript, saw right to the heart of the story and helped me shape it into something worth reading. Thank you for your insight, your guidance, and your kindness.

Everyone at Graydon House Books has always been delightful to work with. Thank you so much to the entire team, from the art department to the copy editors to publicity.

I'd be nowhere without my super-agent, Jessica Watterson, who is equal parts sweetheart and BAMF. Thank you for constantly talking me down off various ledges, and for being an all-around amazing advocate and business partner (and friend).

This story highlights some of the more horrifying aspects

of Instagram, but there are some wonderful parts, too—like the fabulous #bookstagram community. Thank you to all the bookstagrammers who fill my feed with gorgeous photos of my favorite things—books!—and a special shout-out to those of you who've championed my work. Your support means the world to me.

Thank you to my sisters, Christine and Jennifer, and to my almost-sisters, Marci and Jessica, for your unconditional love and enthusiastic cheerleading.

Thank you to Diffy, my rescue dog, who keeps me company during my writing marathons, and forces me to get up out of my chair for our daily afternoon walks.

Finally, thank you to Emilio and Andrew, for being you, and for loving me.